"My eldest daughter, Lord Austerfield."

The Viscount had his back to Carenza, but she did not miss the slight ————————————————————tive of surprise. So, ————————————————————nother unmarried dau————————————————————her at all as he enter————————————————— or relation, not w—————————————

He was gazing ————————————— ——— said now, a trifle uncertainly, "Miss, er, Bettridge?"

Carenza felt no sympathy for the Viscount's embarrassment. If he could not bestir himself to learn something of his hosts before descending upon them, then he deserved none.

"That's it, my lord," her father said.

Carenza quickly schooled her face into an expression of polite welcome, but as the Viscount turned toward her, the smile froze on her lips.

In contrast to the right side of his face, the left was disfigured by a web of scars that stretched from the temple to his jawline and beyond.

"Miss Bettridge, I am delighted to meet you."

He bowed, apparently indifferent to his appearance, but when he straightened, Carenza noticed that his eyes were wary. Her animosity disappeared and she wanted only to put him at ease. She gave him her friendliest smile, but before she could utter a word, Lady Bettridge came bustling up.

"Carenza, go and tell Hutton to bring in the wine."

Color flared in her cheeks. She was accustomed to the peremptory tone, but she had seen the Viscount's look of surprise, the haughty lift of his brows.

Author Note

Who doesn't like a Cinderella story? It was my favorite fairy tale when I was growing up, and my favorite pantomime. I think seeing the principal boy and Cinderella in their stylized eighteenth-century costumes helped toward my love of that period!

Carenza's story is not exactly rags to riches, but she is living with her stepmother and half sisters, who treat her like a servant and do everything they can to undermine her self-confidence. Like Cinderella, she is given the chance to escape from her life of drudgery.

But Ross is no Prince Charming. He is an ex-soldier and very troubled. Today we would say he has PTSD. In 1817 there was no name for it and little in the way of medical treatment. Thankfully, Ross has good people about him who understand, but will he allow Carenza to get close enough, so that she, too, can help him? I hope you will like the outcome.

SARAH MALLORY

———

Cinderella and the Scarred Viscount

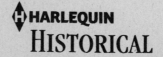

HARLEQUIN®
HISTORICAL™

PLEASE RECYCLE
THIS PRODUCT IS RECYCLABLE

Recycling programs
for this product may
not exist in your area.

ISBN-13: 978-1-335-40750-4

Cinderella and the Scarred Viscount

Copyright © 2021 by Sarah Mallory

This edition published by arrangement with Harlequin Books S.A.

For questions and comments about the quality of this book,
please contact us at CustomerService@Harlequin.com.

Harlequin Enterprises ULC
22 Adelaide St. West, 41st Floor
Toronto, Ontario M5H 4E3, Canada
www.Harlequin.com

Printed in U.S.A.

Sarah Mallory grew up in the West Country, England, telling stories. She moved to Yorkshire with her young family, but after nearly thirty years living in a farmhouse on the Pennines, she has now moved to live by the sea in Scotland. Sarah is an award-winning novelist with more than twenty books published by Harlequin Historical. She loves to hear from readers; you can reach her via her website at sarahmallory.com.

Books by Sarah Mallory

Harlequin Historical

The Scarlet Gown
Never Trust a Rebel
The Duke's Secret Heir
Pursued for the Viscount's Vengeance
His Countess for a Week
The Mysterious Miss Fairchild
Cinderella and the Scarred Viscount

Lairds of Ardvarrick

Forbidden to the Highland Laird
Rescued by Her Highland Soldier

Saved from Disgrace

The Ton's Most Notorious Rake
Beauty and the Brooding Lord

Visit the Author Profile page
at Harlequin.com for more titles.

For Willow,
my lovely canine writing companion
for the past ten years. RIP.

Chapter One

June 1817

London society was buzzing with the news: Lord Austerfield, hero of Waterloo, was in town and looking for a wife. Major James Rossington, Fourth Viscount Austerfield, felt his lips thinning as he read the report of his latest appearance at Almack's.

The newspaper described him as the most eligible bachelor in London. Perhaps that was true, in terms of wealth and rank, but there was no disguising the injuries he had suffered throughout his army career. Injuries that had people staring at him in the street, and made acquaintances so uncomfortable it was as much as they could do to look at him. Muttering, Ross folded the newspaper and threw it aside. He had had enough. He would go back to Auster as soon as he could arrange it. He didn't *want* a wife and he was damned if he would spend another minute looking for one.

The family wouldn't like it, of course; they were desperate for him to find a suitable bride. Dido, his widowed older sister, and his aunt Beatrix, Countess of Malham, had begun their offensive in the spring, persuading him that he should go to London for the season. He had bowed to the pressure, which was easier than withstanding the onslaught of those two formidable ladies, but he had spent six miserable weeks in town and now he wanted nothing more than to return to the peace and solitude of Auster.

The crowded streets were bad enough, but it was as much as he could do to enter Almack's. It wasn't just the stares—or worse, the way some acquaintances avoided looking at him—it was the memories it evoked. The last ball he had attended had been the Duchess of Richmond's, on the eve of Quatre Bras, and the loud chatter and hot, overcrowded rooms in King Street brought the horrors of what followed rushing back.

Somehow, he had got through that first visit to the Marriage Mart and managed to attend twice more. On each occasion he had gone to bed exhausted, yet his sleep had been shattered by terrifying nightmares full of noise and pain and loss.

His glance fell to the papers scattered over his desk: bills, letters, invitations. It would all need to be dealt with before he could leave London. Why the devil had he allowed himself to be persuaded to come here?

He knew the answer, of course. Guilt. He had not wanted to become viscount, and when he had heard of his brother's death, he had railed against it, angry that his brother had not married and produced an heir, so that he, Ross, might continue with his career as a soldier. But Sebastian had seen no reason to rush into marriage; he had been enjoying himself too much.

Ross remembered his bitter resentment when he had read that last letter. It had reached him on the eve of Waterloo when his mind was fixed upon the forthcoming struggle against Bonaparte. Seb wrote of his success at the York races and the charms of his latest mistress, whom he had taken with him to Comers. Only later did Ross learn that even as he was reading that letter, his brother was already dead, having broken his neck in a riding accident.

A quiet cough interrupted his reverie.

'Lady Malham and the Honourable Mrs Burnley to see you, my lord. I have shown them into the drawing room.'

Ross looked up at the butler, his face inscrutable.

'Thank you, Tyler. See that they have refreshments, will you? I will be with them directly.'

He pulled all the papers into one pile, wishing he might have put off this meeting but knowing it was impossible. He was a soldier; he could deal with recalcitrant lower ranks, argue his case with fellow officers and even hold his own with brigadiers and colonels. But women, and specifically the women of his family, were another matter altogether.

Girding his loins for the coming fight, he pushed himself out of his chair and prepared for battle.

The two ladies waiting for him in the drawing room looked harmless enough. Both matrons of middling years, they were elegantly attired in the latest summer fashions and were sitting at their ease in two of the armchairs, while a small table before them held an array of tiny cakes and two glasses of the Viscount's finest Madeira for their delectation.

But looks, as Ross knew, could be deceptive. After initial greetings had been exchanged, his aunt Beatrix went directly to the attack.

'I thought to see you at Lady Fretwood's ball last night, my lord. Where were you?'

'I did not wish to go.' Ross poured a glass of wine for himself and sat down. 'I shall be leaving London shortly.'

'Leaving!' Beatrix sat up in her chair. 'But you have not been here five minutes.'

'On the contrary, I have been here several weeks.'

Dido said hopefully, 'Perhaps my brother has found a lady to his liking and has been invited out of town for the summer. Is that it, Ross?'

'No, it is not. I have decided to end this foolish charade.'

'There is nothing foolish about it,' retorted Lady Malham. 'You must take a wife.'

Dido's hand came up and his aunt, recognising this as a warning, drew a breath before continuing in a milder tone, 'It has been two years since Sebastian died. A good eighteen months since you left the army. There can be no excuse for further delay, James. At five-and-thirty it is time for you to choose a bride.'

James! No one had called him that for years. He had always been Ross to his family, except when they were seriously displeased with him.

Dido noticed his frown and said quickly, 'Indeed, it is your duty to do so, Brother. We really do not want that wretch Amos Paston inheriting the title.'

'But why not?' Ross raised his brows. 'I know he doesn't bear the Rossington name, but the ancient patent is very clear: as the son of Father's eldest sister, he is my legitimate heir.'

'But the man is a toad,' Beatrix declared. 'His nose was very much put out of joint when he learned you had survived Waterloo.'

'Really? Since I returned to England he has gone out of his way to help me recover.'

Beatrix gave an unladylike snort. 'His father was a money-grubbing little man. My father would never have agreed to the marriage if they had not eloped and it became necessary to hush it up. He always maintained Fred Paston had no breeding. His son is of the same ilk.'

'At least he doesn't press me to take a wife!' Ross retorted, his patience beginning to wear thin. 'In fact, when I mentioned the idea, he advised me not to rush into anything.'

'Of course he doesn't want you to marry, he is your heir!' Beatrix retorted. 'But we digress. It is *your* marriage that concerns us, Austerfield. You know what is required, a well-mannered woman of impeccable breeding.'

Dido added her mite. 'There are any number of women in town who fit that description. Some of them are exceedingly handsome, too.' She clasped her hands together and regarded him with a hint of desperation in her eyes. 'All you need do is choose one.'

'And make sure she has good teeth,' Beatrix advised him.

Ross's flare of anger had died down and now his lips twitched. 'My dear aunt, I am not buying a horse.'

'Same principal,' she replied crisply. 'She will be the mother of your heir. She needs to be sound in wind and limb. A modicum of intelligence would be quite useful, too. And of course, she must have all the usual accomplishments.'

'Perhaps I should allow you to choose for me,' he muttered, his irritation growing again.

Dido regarded him with a look of mild disdain. 'This is no laughing matter, James! The succession is in your hands.'

He was very tempted to reply that, surely, they meant

it was in his loins. It would almost certainly see both ladies flounce out of the house in high dudgeon, but his good manners surfaced and he kept quiet.

'Actually, Austerfield has a point,' remarked Beatrix, sipping thoughtfully at her wine. 'It might well be best if we select an eligible bride. After all, we know exactly what is required—'

Suddenly Ross saw the situation slipping out of his control.

'Absolutely no need for that,' he said tersely. 'I have already seen a suitable young lady. Two, in fact.'

Dido clapped her hands together. 'Oh, Ross, do tell!'

'I met them at Almack's the other night. Danced with them both.' Not that there was any avoiding it, after their mother had almost thrust them under his nose. 'They are sisters. The Misses Bettridge.'

'Well, well!' said Dido, her eyes brightening. 'I am not *personally* acquainted with the family, but I have seen them about town. Two very pretty young ladies, excellent manners and good figures—what they call willowy, I believe. Do you know the family, Aunt?'

'Not well, but they are perfectly respectable. Lord Bettridge suffers from poor health and hasn't been seen in town for years, so it falls to his wife to try to find husbands for the gels.' The Countess pursed her lips. 'Having two daughters myself, I cannot blame the woman if she is a little, er, *eager* in putting them forward. Which of them do you prefer, Austerfield?'

'I really could not say.' In truth, Ross was hard-pressed to tell them apart. 'I need to, er, improve my acquaintance with them.'

'Then you have not given up the idea of marriage,' exclaimed Dido. 'What a tease you are, Brother! We came here thinking you did not have anyone in mind as your prospective bride, when in fact there are two.'

'Which is very good news.' Lady Malham rose and shook out her skirts. 'We will leave you to pursue your interest with one or other of these young ladies, James. But Dido and I will put our heads together and decide upon a few more suitable gels, in case the Misses Bettridge should prove unsatisfactory.'

When his visitors had gone, Ross walked across to the side table to pour himself more wine, then he stared at the empty wall. A large mirror had been fixed there, until he had had it removed when he came to town. He did not need a looking glass to remind him of his hideous scars. He raised his glass in a mocking salute.

'Well, my lord, it appears you will have to go at least one more step in this damned farce, after all.'

Morwood Manor was basking in the late June sun, soaking up the heat in the creamy stone walls. Windows and doors had been thrown open to allow what little breeze there was to waft through the building and even Lord Bettridge had been coaxed out of doors to sit in a shady spot on the terrace with a shawl about his thin shoulders and a rug wrapped around his knees. It was here that Carenza found him.

'Papa, there is an express come from Tavistock Square!'

He looked tired but his face brightened when he saw her hurrying towards him. She held out the letter but he waved it away.

'I pray you will read it, my love. Your sharp eyes are so much better than mine.' He watched anxiously as she broke the seal and read the note. 'What is it, Carenza,

have the girls been taken ill? Or perhaps some accident
has befallen your mama!'

She is not *my mama!*

No matter how many times Papa used the term she
could not help herself silently, stubbornly, correcting
him. She had been but five years old when Papa had
brought home his new bride, little more than a year after
the death of the first Lady Bettridge. Carenza had tried
to be a dutiful daughter but she could not love her stepmama and she knew the feeling was mutual.

'No one is ill,' she assured him, after reading the
first few lines.

'Then you may precis it for me, if you would, my
love,' he murmured as Carenza sat down on the bench
beside him. 'I am sure it is full of details about their
stay in town, but it tires me too much to hear of all their
gadding about.'

'Yes, of course, sir. However, this letter is mercifully short.'

No more than Papa did Carenza enjoy her stepmama's boastful and exhaustive accounts of all the new
gowns they had ordered, every ball and party they had
attended and how many times dear Letitia and Adelaide
had been asked to dance. Surprisingly, there was nothing of that nature in this short missive.

Carenza gave a tiny gasp. 'They are on their way
home, Papa! Lady Bettridge says they are cutting short
their stay in town because Viscount Austerfield has
shown a *particular interest*.' She looked up, her eyes
wide. 'She has invited him to Morwood!'

'A viscount.' Her father chuckled. 'Gertrude must be
in raptures. I suppose it is Letty who has captured his
fancy—she is the older of the two.'

'It does not say.' Carenza looked at the letter again,

in case she had missed something, but no. 'How strange. All she says is that we are to set the house in readiness. She expects to be home with Letty and Adelaide on Wednesday. The Viscount is to follow a day or so later. Good heavens, we have less than a week to prepare!'

'Your mama will wish to impress our guest.' Her father's thin fingers plucked anxiously at the rug across his knees. 'It must be the best guest chamber, naturally. And he will have a carriage, servants. His valet, of course…'

'None of this need concern you, Papa.' Carenza put her hand over his and squeezed it. 'I will have a word with Mrs Trudby, who will see to everything indoors, and I will ask Fewston to make room in the stables for His Lordship's horses. May I tell them to hire extra help from the village, if they need it?'

'Why, yes, my love. You have no need to ask me about such matters, I trust your judgement on anything to do with the household.'

'Thank you, Papa.'

She sat with him for another half an hour, until Evans appeared, but even after the valet had helped her father away to his room to rest before dinner, she remained sitting on the bench, her mind going over all the preparations for the Viscount's visit. Between them, she and Mrs Trudby, the housekeeper, would arrange everything satisfactorily. However, Lady Bettridge would want everything just so, and if any detail fell below her exacting standards, Carenza knew the blame would land squarely upon *her* shoulders.

Ross swung the curricle towards the open gates of Morwood Manor and drove through without checking, a manoeuvre that caused the one-armed man sitting beside him to mutter a curse and an exhortation to his master not to be so damned reckless. Ross merely laughed.

'Losing your nerve, Sam?'

'Not I, Major,' retorted his groom. 'But I ain't lost the will to live, neither!'

'I have not overturned you yet, and I don't intend to start now.'

'No, and I don't suppose you means to injure those greys you've paid a fortune for, either. But you will, Major, you mark my words, if you carries on driving in that neck or nothing fashion.'

Many masters would consider such blunt speech to be gross insubordination, but Ross had known his groom a long time. They had fought together in the Peninsula, in the days when Ross had been a young, inexperienced officer and Sam a corporal. He had valued the man's opinion then and he still did. In his heart he knew Sam was right and now slowed the pace to a gentle trot.

'I beg your pardon,' he said ruefully. 'Since being injured, my temper has become far more hasty. I have been venting my anger on my horses.'

'What beats me is why you agreed to break your journey here, when Basingstoke has a perfectly good posting inn.'

His mood somewhat mellowed, Ross shrugged. 'I was bounced into it, but having allowed myself to be invited, I cannot cry off now. However, I do not intend to stay more than a day or two. Ah, here we are.'

The house was in sight, a fine stone building of the last century set within a small park.

'Remember,' he barked, guiding the curricle around

the final sweeping curve of the drive, 'we will not be here long, so do not make yourself too comfortable in your quarters!'

'So, my dear. We have been summoned,' declared Lord Bettridge as he descended the stairs to join his daughter in the hall.

'Yes, Papa. I believe Lord Austerfield is expected shortly.'

Carenza waited patiently while Evans helped her father down the final few steps.

'And we will be gathered in state to greet him.'

Lord Bettridge thanked his man and beckoned Carenza to take his free arm; then, leaning heavily on his ebony stick, they walked slowly across the hall to the drawing room.

'I understand your sisters have been at their dressing tables all morning, prettifying themselves.'

'Yes, they have.' Carenza laughed. 'Adelaide told me she was awake half the night with excitement and Letty changed her gown at least three times this morning before returning to her original choice!'

'And you, Carenza? What have you done to prettify yourself for our visitor?'

'Me? I have changed my gown, but I have no expectations that the Viscount will notice me.'

He had come to see Letty and Adelaide, so what did it matter that the pale blue muslin with its excessive adornment of lace and ribbons did not suit her? She had chosen it because it was the newest and most recent of her dresses, all of them made-over gowns that had been rejected as outmoded or unwanted by her half-sisters. Letitia and Adelaide were taller than Carenza, but they were both on the thin side: modishly slender, accord-

ing to their mother. Two rashers of wind was how Mrs
Trudby had described them, in an unguarded moment.

It was easy enough to shorten the skirts but it took
some ingenuity upon the part of Carenza and Mrs
Trudby to alter the gowns to fit Carenza's more generous curves, but the result was generally satisfactory. She
could have ordered a new gown from the seamstress
in the village, even at such short notice, but it would
have meant asking Papa for more money, and explaining to him that she received not a penny of the generous dress allowance he made to Lady Bettridge. That
would only cause an argument, and with Papa's heart
being so weak, Carenza did everything she could to
spare him any upset.

'The Viscount might well notice you, if you did not
wear that lace cap,' he said now, with uncharacteristic
severity. 'It makes you look like an old maid.'

'At five-and-twenty I *am* an old maid,' she reminded
him, laughing and in no wise offended. They paused
while she opened the drawing room door. 'Naturally, I
am anxious his visit should go off well, but it can make
little difference to me.'

'Please do not keep your father at the door, Carenza!'
Lady Bettridge's shrill voice was like a shower of cold
rain. 'You know he cannot stand for too long!'

No longer having any desire to smile, Carenza escorted her father to his chair and made sure he was comfortable. She arranged the cushion at his back, rested
his ebony cane against the wall and moved a small table
closer, in readiness for the refreshments, when they
were offered. Her half-sisters were slumped on either
end of a sofa, looking bored, but Carenza did not suggest they help her with any of this. They made a show
of filial obedience and fawned over Papa whenever they

wanted new gowns or extra dancing lessons, but otherwise they paid little heed to his comfort.

'And why did *you* have to bring in your papa?' Lady Bettridge continued, her tone sharp. 'Evans could have done it just as well and you would have been free to make sure everything is in readiness for Lord Austerfield's visit.'

'I have already done that, ma'am,' Carenza replied. 'The servants will have the Viscount's valet and his bags sent up to the Blue Bedchamber when they arrive. You informed me His Lordship will be driving himself in his curricle, with his manservant following in the chaise. I have instructed space to be cleared for the carriages and the extra horses. I have just come in from talking to Fewston about it.'

'Good heavens, girl, do you not know better than to visit the stables in a clean gown?' Lady Bettridge's eyes snapped angrily. 'I have a good mind to send you to your room!'

'Viscount Austerfield, my lady!'

The footman's sonorous pronouncement worked like magic upon the company. Lady Bettridge's angry speech ended abruptly; Letitia and Adelaide jerked upright, straightening their shoulders and composing their features into smiles, while Carenza sat down quickly, curious to catch her first glimpse of their visitor. Her stepmama and half-sisters had offered very little information about Viscount Austerfield and she had received the impression that he was old and ill-favoured, although presumably these disadvantages were as nothing when weighed against his title and his fortune. Thus, when the Viscount walked in, she suffered a severe shock.

Carenza had been sorely misled. To begin with, Lord

Austerfield was not old. She guessed he could not be much over thirty, and as for being ill-favoured, it was nothing of the sort. He was above average height and powerfully built with broad shoulders and a deep chest. He moved confidently and had the straight back and upright bearing of a soldier. From her chair in the corner, she could see nothing amiss in the Viscount's profile. It was a strong face with lean cheeks and a straight nose, but from the light brown hair brushed back from his brow to the sculpted lips and firm jaw, Carenza thought him handsome. She felt a slight fluttering deep inside. Very handsome, in fact.

She watched as Lady Bettridge flew up from her chair to welcome the Viscount, fawning about him, solicitously suggesting he should sit down and even pressing him to take a glass of wine before she realised he was waiting to be presented to his host. The introduction was hastily made and the two men exchanged a few words.

The Viscount's voice was deep and well-modulated. As attractive as his profile, thought Carenza. She would have been happy to listen to him speak for much longer but the conversation was cut short by Lady Bettridge.

'Such a journey you have had, Lord Austerfield, you must be fatigued. I pray you will sit down and take your ease.'

'My dear,' Lord Bettridge interrupted her, his tone perfectly pleasant but resolute, 'I fear there has been an omission. You have not presented His Lordship to Carenza.' He turned back to their guest. 'My eldest daughter, Lord Austerfield.'

The Viscount had his back to Carenza but she did not miss the way his head went up and the slight straightening of his body, indicative of surprise. So, he had not been told there was another unmarried daughter at home. Worse, he had not been interested enough in the family to find out. If he had noticed her at all as he entered, he probably thought her a poor relation, not worthy of attention.

He was gazing at his host and he said now, a trifle uncertainly, 'Miss, er, Bettridge?'

Carenza felt no sympathy for the Viscount's embarrassment. If he could not bestir himself to learn something of his hosts before descending upon them, then he deserved none.

'That's it, my lord.' Papa gave him an encouraging nod.

Carenza quickly schooled her face into an expression of polite welcome, but as the Viscount turned towards her, the smile froze on her lips.

In contrast to the right side of his face, which she had seen when he entered, the left was disfigured by a web of scars that stretched from temple to jawline and beyond, disappearing beneath the collar of his fine linen shirt.

'Miss Bettridge, I am delighted to meet you.'

He made her a very elegant bow, apparently indifferent to his appearance, but when he straightened Carenza noticed that his grey-green eyes were wary. Her animosity disappeared and she wanted only to put him at his ease. She gave him her friendliest smile, but before she could utter a word, Lady Bettridge came bustling up.

'Carenza, go and tell Hutton to bring in the wine. And on your return, fetch up the little cakes from the kitchens.'

Colour flared in her cheeks. She was accustomed to the peremptory tone but she had seen the Viscount's look of surprise, the haughty lift of his brows, and she was embarrassed for Lady Bettridge. She thought, as she hurried away, that all her stepmama's plans would come to naught if such behaviour gave the Viscount a disgust of the family.

Chapter Two

By the time Ross made his way upstairs to change for dinner, he was heartily regretting that he had agreed to visit Morwood. He went into his room and shut the door, standing for a moment with his back against the wooden panels and his eyes closed.

'Is anything wrong, Major?'

Dan Brisco, his valet and manservant, had emerged from the dressing room and was regarding him anxiously.

'Nothing, save that I would rather be anywhere than here. Tell me why in heaven's name I allowed this to happen.'

His fears alleviated, Brisco grinned. 'You were being nagged to death by your family.'

'Aye, but my cowardice has rebounded. If I had stood firm, I could have saved myself this purgatory.'

'Surely it ain't as bad as all that!'

'Oh, ain't it?' He rubbed a hand over his eyes and sighed at his own folly. 'I shall have to make it plain I have no intention of offering for either of the daughters. Or rather,' he amended, 'for any of 'em. There's a third one.'

'Oh?' Brisco chuckled at the gloomy announcement. 'Not yet out, is she?'

'Very much out and on the shelf! She must be the product of His Lordship's first marriage. Nothing like her sisters. Strange little dab of a thing. I thought at first she was a companion or some such.' He frowned. 'She is treated like one, too.'

The valet nodded sagely. 'I understand that is what happens to single ladies when they are beyond marriageable age.'

'Aye, it is, unless they have funds of their own.' Ross grimaced. 'Ah well, that is not my concern. My object now is to extricate myself from this place with all possible speed and continue my journey to Auster.'

Brisco waved a hand towards the clothes laid out over the bed.

'I have selected your evening coat, together with the black breeches of Florentine silk, but perhaps, my lord, if you are not wishful to impress, you might prefer to wear the smoke stone trousers?'

'No, I have no wish to offend my host. He appears to be a very gentlemanly sort and I suspect he will be wearing full evening dress at dinner. Besides, I doubt anything I do will give his wife and daughters a disgust of me. They have shown from the start that my wealth and rank outweigh all other considerations.' He caught sight of himself in the looking glass and his lip curled with self-loathing. 'They can even endure my repulsive face with only the occasional shudder!'

Silence followed his words. Like Sam Rigby, Brisco was an ex-soldier. He had been a sergeant in Ross's regiment but was wounded at Quatre Bras and spared the horrors of Waterloo. Brisco knew his master too well to offer him Spanish coin so he would make no attempt to deny that his master was hideously scarred. Ross swung away from the mirror and shrugged off his coat.

'Pour my hot water, Dan, there's a good fellow. I must prepare to return to the fray!'

Carenza chose her most sober gown to wear for dinner. Her stepmother, unable to upbraid Papa for bringing his eldest daughter to the Viscount's notice, had turned her wrath upon Carenza and accused her of putting herself forward in a most unbecoming fashion. It was unfair and unwarranted, but Carenza listened in silence, head bowed, knowing that any attempt to defend herself would only result in more spiteful retribution, and since unpleasantness within the family always had an adverse effect upon Papa's health, she closed her lips against any retort.

Having put up her hair and pinned a fresh lace cap over it, Carenza took a last, critical look in the glass before leaving her room. Her nose wrinkled. She looked like a governess.

The grey silk had no more than a thin edging of white lace to relieve its severity and had been passed on to her without ever being worn. Lady Bettridge had bought it when the demise of a distant cousin had obliged her to go into mourning, but she preferred the contrast of deep black against her fair curls and, since her daughters considered the gown far too dull and plain for their taste, it had been given to the housekeeper for disposal. But Mrs Trudby had other ideas. She had been at Morwood since before Carenza was born and was more of a trusted friend than a servant. She had immediately taken the gown to Carenza.

For once she had a gown that was too big for her frame, rather than too small. She and the housekeeper worked hard to make it as modish as possible, tailoring the bodice to fit smoothly into the high waistline and coaxing the skirts to fall in soft folds to her ankles. Upon seeing her attired for the first time in the finished gown, Mrs Trudby had declared:

'The colour might not suit you, but there's no denying it shows off your figure.'

Regarding herself now, Carenza thought that was small comfort. All the fashion plates bore illustrations of tall, slender females, very like her half-sisters. She knew they were regarded as very handsome young ladies, while she was too short and her figure too full to look well in the current fashions. She could not remember receiving a compliment in her life, except from Mrs Trudby or Papa, who were both far too fond of her to tell the truth.

Shaking out the silk skirts, she thought that she should be free from censure tonight, for there could be nothing in her dowdy appearance to attract any man's attention, let alone a rich viscount.

As an ex-military man, Ross wasted little time changing his dress and he was ready with plenty of time to spare. Lord Bettridge had invited him to make free use of his library and, rather than skulk in his room, Ross decided to do just that. From the little he knew of the Misses Bettridge, he guessed that reading was not one of their pastimes.

He found the library easily enough. It was a large room, elegantly appointed with bookcases lining three walls and also built between the long, south-facing windows of the fourth. He had almost reached the centre of the room before he realised he was not alone. The eldest Miss Bettridge was sitting in one of the wing chairs.

She had an open book on her lap but she appeared to be fast asleep.

No wonder he had not seen her, for she was too small for her head to show above the high back of the chair and she was wearing a grey gown that blended into the shadows of the room. Ross was about to withdraw when her eyes fluttered open.

'Oh!' She jumped to her feet, making a belated clutch at the book, which evaded her grasp and fell with a thud to the ground.

'I beg your pardon.' Ross stepped forward to retrieve the book. 'I did not mean to startle you. Lord Bettridge said I might like to use this room.' He glanced down at the rather worn volume he had picked up and was surprised to find it was not a novel, as he expected.

'Thank you, my lord. I must have fallen asleep.'

'I am not surprised.' He smiled and handed her the book. 'I think *The Experienced English Housekeeper* would make tedious reading material.'

'Oh, no, in general I find Mrs Raffald's book most interesting and informative.'

She gave him a shy glance and, clutching the book before her, took a few hasty steps to the door.

He said quickly, 'Oh, please, do not leave! I shall think I have frightened you away. I am not an ogre, you know, despite appearances.'

Silently he berated himself for those last words. They sounded odiously self-pitying.

She stopped and turned back towards him. 'I am not at all frightened, but I *am* embarrassed that you should find me napping.'

'Pray think no more of it. Will you not return to your chair and continue with your book? I shall withdraw again, once I have found something to read.'

'Thank you.' But she remained on the spot, standing halfway between him and the door. 'I am very familiar with the books here, my lord. If you are looking for something in particular, I might be able to help you?'

'I wondered if your father had a copy of *The Gentleman's Magazine*, perhaps, or if not, a book to pass the time.'

She waved towards one of the bookcases. 'The novels are over there, on that side of the window. Poetry you will find on the other side and any periodicals will be on the table, in between. Or Papa has the newspaper sent from London, but that will be in his room.'

'And he will be resting before dinner, so I would not have him disturbed,' he said. 'I am sure I can find something of interest. The novels are over here?' He walked across and pulled one off the shelf. 'Waverley. That will do, although I am already familiar with it. Have you read it, Miss Bettridge?'

He saw that she was shifting awkwardly from one foot to the other and glancing towards the door. It was clear she was repelled by his appearance and could not wait to get away. Angrily he pushed the novel back onto the shelf.

'No, it had better be a magazine, since I shall be leaving in the morning!'

'So soon? But you are to remain at least four nights!'

Now she was staring at him in dismay and his temper flared even more.

'An arrangement I have been regretting ever since I agreed to it!'

'No, no, you cannot leave,' she cried, coming closer. 'Please, my lord, please reconsider!'

'Impossible.' His jaw tightened, pulling at the scars on his face. He said coldly, 'I am grateful to you, Miss

Bettridge, for doing me a service. You have provided the perfect reason to cut short my visit, since my presence clearly upsets you.'

'No, no! It is not *your* presence here, sir, but mine,' she replied, glancing anxiously around the room.

'Hah, you cannot even *look* at me!'

That caught her attention. Her head came up and she fixed him with her dark, serious eyes.

'That, my lord, is nonsense.'

Ross found himself being scrutinised, every blemish, every scar. His lip curled. 'If you think this frank appraisal will convince me I am wrong about you, madam, you are mistaken. Your unease in my presence is only too obvious.'

'I *am* uneasy, but you are not the reason for it,' she said earnestly. 'I admit I was shocked when I first saw you, but I had not been warned. Believe me, my lord, it is not your damaged face that makes me nervous, but the wrath of Lady Bettridge! When she learns I am the reason you are leaving she will be so angry with me. She has such high hopes of you marrying Letty or Adelaide.'

'I have no intention of offering for anyone, so the sooner I quit Morwood Manor the better!'

He went to step around her but she moved across, blocking his way.

'Oh, please, my lord, please think again. Not about offering for Letty or Adelaide—that, of course, is entirely your decision. But if I have offended you, then I am very sorry for it, and shall avoid your company while you are here, but *pray* do not leave so precipitately!'

Her dark eyes were clouded with anxiety and Ross

found his anger melting away but he was not going to capitulate.

'No, I am sorry, Miss Bettridge. I could not ask you to shut yourself away on my behalf.'

'Oh, but I should not object to that! In fact, I should *prefer* to stay out of everyone's way.'

That sounded so disingenuous that he was tempted to laugh, but there was no guile in her countenance, only genuine distress. Confound it, he could not hold out against the entreaty in those deep brown eyes!

'There will be no need for such drastic measures, *if* I remain here,' he said at last. 'I will think about it and leave the final decision until the morning.'

'Oh, *thank* you, my lord!'

Her relief was so evident that it surprised a laugh from him. 'Is it so important, then, my staying?'

'To Lady Bettridge it is, yes. She puts great store by such things, you see. However, for my part I am more pleased for Papa. He does not leave the house now, and has very few visitors, so he is very much looking forward to having some company other than his family.'

Ross could believe that, remembering how warmly Lord Bettridge had welcomed him and the look of pleasure in the old man's face when Ross had told him he was partial to a game of chess.

'And if you can bring yourself to remain,' she concluded, 'I shall keep out of sight as much as I can for the duration of your stay.'

'That you will not!'

'But I assure you, it would not be a penance to do so while you are here.' Her hands flew to her mouth. 'Oh, dear, that did not come out as it should!'

'I hope it did not,' he retorted, amused.

The thick black lashes swept down over her eyes, but not before he had seen the answering gleam in them.

'What I *mean* is that my stepmother is anxious you should become better acquainted with Letty and Adelaide,' she said seriously. 'She will not want anyone getting in the way.'

Remembering how Lady Bettridge had thrust her daughters under his nose, Ross could easily believe it.

'Is that why you did not accompany them to London?'

'I was needed here, to look after Papa.' An engaging dimple appeared in her cheek. 'Not that I had any wish to go. I am much happier here at Morwood.' A clock somewhere chimed and she jumped. 'Oh, dear, is that the time? Everyone will be gathering now in the drawing room.'

She looked at him uncertainly and he waved her away.

'Go along, then. I will stay here for another ten minutes, to make sure no one guesses we have been alone together.'

'Thank you, my lord. I am sorry to be so troublesome. '

'You should be.'

'And…you will consider staying for a few days? I promise I can easily find excuses to keep out of the way.'

His eyes narrowed. 'If I do decide to remain at Morwood, Miss Bettridge, then the very least I expect is that you will be one of the party!'

She looked surprised, but gave a little nod and hurried away, leaving Ross to wonder what the devil he was doing. He had as good as agreed to stay. It would mean three full days to while away. Ah well, his host appeared to be an educated man. He would seek him out and spend most of the time in his company.

One thing was for sure, he thought, picking up a magazine at random and carrying it over to the chair Miss Bettridge had so recently vacated. He would have to make it plain from the outset that he had changed his mind about marrying anyone. Ever.

Chapter Three

Carenza slipped out of the library and across to the drawing room, where the rest of the family were already gathered. Her father held out his hand to her and she went to join him on one of the sofas. He was not a great talker, content to listen while the others chattered away, and since no one bothered to include Carenza in the conversation she was free to let her thoughts wander.

She was not completely reassured by her conversation with the Viscount, because when Lady Bettridge discovered he had no plans to offer for either of her daughters she would be looking for someone to blame. Carenza did not want to give her stepmama any reason to believe the fault was hers and she must therefore be careful to avoid Lord Austerfield's company as much as possible.

Which was disappointing, because she was pleasantly surprised in His Lordship. Far from being cold and aloof he'd been quite friendly, once they had established that she was not embarrassed in his company. And indeed, she was not. In fact, she had completely forgotten about his scarred face when they were talking. He had a sense of humour, too. What a pity that he had decided against offering for either of her half-sisters, because she thought he would make an ideal husband, kind and considerate.

This pleasant reverie was interrupted when she suddenly heard her name. She turned to Lady Bettridge.

'I beg your pardon, ma'am, did you speak to me?'

'I was saying how convenient it is that you, as eldest daughter, will be sitting to the right of your father at dinner.'

Carenza looked puzzled and Adelaide gave a little huff of exasperation.

'We shall put Lord Austerfield on *your* right,' she explained, as if to a child. She gave a little shudder and whispered, 'Next to his *scars*.'

'Not that there will be the least need for you to look at him,' put in her stepmother. 'We shall all be working to keep him entertained, but I just wanted to give you a little notice, that you may prepare yourself to ignore his disfigurement.'

'I do not need to prepare myself.'

'It is a pity about his face, to be sure,' remarked Adelaide, 'but I suppose his wife will learn to live with it.'

'Lord, yes, I can scarce bring myself to look at him,' giggled Letitia.

'How can you both be so unfeeling?' cried Carenza, unable to keep silent. 'You may be sure His Lordship will have noticed!'

Letty tossed her head. 'Why should we worry about that? With such grotesque scars, Lord Austerfield must be grateful to receive *any* invitations!'

Lord Bettridge said, in a tone of mild reproof, 'He is our guest, Letitia, you will remember that, if you please.'

'Yes, girls, enough of this now,' put in his wife. 'Let us think what we are to do this evening.'

They began to discuss various plans for the Viscount's entertainment and it was left to Carenza to blush for her family's bad manners, her discomfiture noticed only by Papa, who took her hand and squeezed it.

Lord Austerfield came in soon after, followed almost immediately by Hutton to announce dinner. In the ensuing bustle it was an easy matter for Carenza to slip into her seat beside the Viscount. During the meal they exchanged barely a dozen words, because her stepmother kept up a constant flow of small talk, ably assisted by Letty and Adelaide. They bombarded their guest with questions and Carenza felt a little sorry for him, but she reminded herself of how he had ripped up at her for her supposed embarrassment in his presence. He could not complain that his hostess or her daughters showed any similar awkwardness, for they were positively fawning over him!

Carenza struggled through her dinner and, when the ladies retired to the drawing room, she was relieved to hear Lady Bettridge declare that the evening was going very well.

'But which one of us do you think he prefers, Mama?' asked Letitia. 'It should be me, because I am the eldest, but he seemed to spend just as long talking to Adelaide!'

'That is because I complimented him upon the matched pair pulling his curricle,' replied her sister, unable to keep a note of triumph out of her voice. 'It is clear he would much rather be talking about horses than London.'

'Well, you will look no-how when he discovers you are morbidly afraid of them,' retorted Letty.

'And what of it? You will not ride anything at more than a snail's pace and that is hardly likely to impress him!'

'Enough!' cried their mother, throwing up her hands. 'It really does not matter which of you takes his fancy. It is enough that he marries one of you.'

It was not to be expected that such a declaration would be received well, and both her daughters protested loudly until she shushed them again.

'Do you not see?' she explained, with barely controlled impatience. 'Whoever becomes Lady Austerfield will move in the very smartest circles and be able arrange a good match for her sister.'

'Then as the oldest, Letty should have him,' declared Adelaide, a sly smile lighting her face. 'Then I may find a husband who does not look like a monster!'

'Shame on you, that is a disgraceful thing to say!'

The words were out before Carenza could stop them and immediately she prepared herself for a sharp rebuke. To her surprise, Lady Bettridge turned instead upon Adelaide, berating her in an angry whisper.

'You thoughtless girl, have you forgotten what we agreed in town? The Viscount's appearance must never be mentioned, remember that! We must not give the slightest hint that his countenance disgusts us. He would only need to hear one ill-advised word and our hopes are at an end. We must keep up the pretence until we have him safe.'

Carenza turned away, feeling slightly sick. That explained why they had said nothing to her about his injuries. It was not that they were being kind, quite the opposite. It was a cold calculated ploy to snare the Viscount into marriage.

'And that applies to you as well, miss high and mighty!'

Her stepmama's strident hiss carried across the room to Carenza like a slap. She turned back, her chin lifting a little.

'I hope I would never be so unfeeling, ma'am. To anyone.'

'Neither will you go putting yourself forward,' added Letitia. 'Even though, at your age, you must be quite desperate for a husband.'

'I assure you I am not!'

Adelaide tittered. 'Just as well, for who could be interested in such a dark, foreign-looking little creature?'

Carenza was accustomed to her sisters' jibes and she merely looked at them, saying coldly, 'I have no interest at all in Lord Austerfield. In fact, I mean to keep very much out of the way during his visit.'

'Now that is a very good scheme,' replied Lady Bettridge, nodding in approval. 'It would be an excellent thing if you kept to your room while he is here. However, your father would never allow that, so you must do your best to be invisible!' She threw up her head, listening. 'Hush now. I hear voices—they are coming!

The door opened and the gentlemen came in. Carenza was pleased to see that they were both smiling, and appeared to be getting on well together.

'Ah, so here you are at last,' exclaimed Lady Bettridge. 'I hope you enjoyed your dinner, Lord Austerfield?'

'It was most satisfactory, ma'am, thank you.'

She beamed at him. 'We employ an excellent cook, but I have always maintained that the lady of the house must have the last word in what comes to the table. It

is something I have been at pains to teach Letitia and
Adelaide.'

Carenza's eyes widened slightly, trying to remember
the last time her half-sisters had shown any interest in
culinary matters.

'I believe there are some excellent books upon the
subject,' replied the Viscount. 'They must be indispens-
able in any household.'

His words were met with blank stares from Lady
Bettridge and her daughters while Carenza held her
breath, afraid he would mention seeing her in the library.

'My mother was herself a great admirer of Mrs Raffald,' he continued. 'She kept a copy of *The Experienced
Housekeeper* in every establishment.'

There was a heartbeat's silence, then Lady Bettridge
gave a little trill of laughter. 'How you do joke with us,
my lord! I am sure a viscountess would have house-
keepers, cooks and I do not know how many servants
to take care of these things. But whatever the case may
be, I can assure Your Lordship that *both* of my daughters are more than capable of keeping a household, no
matter what size the establishment.'

'I do not doubt it.' With another little bow he moved
away and Carenza, unable to resist peeping up at him as
he passed her chair, was obliged to fight down a giggle
when he winked at her.

She was immensely cheered by the gesture and
hoped it signalled that the Viscount did not intend to
leave in the morning. Certainly, no mention was made
of it and she was able to go to bed that night with her
heart a little lighter that she had not ruined her stepmother's plans.

* * *

Much as Carenza would have liked to follow Lady Bettridge's wishes and be invisible, it was just not possible, as she quickly realised the next morning. First, she had to meet with the housekeeper to discuss the menus, then a second meeting was required after Lady Bettridge, at breakfast, changed her mind and declared they must have lamb on the dinner table rather than beef. This required no little amount of diplomacy, since Mrs Trudby had already passed on the menu instructions to the temperamental artist who ruled the kitchens. After a bruising encounter, in which Carenza was informed that the kitchen staff had more than enough to do providing meals fit for a viscount without having everything turned on its head at the last moment, Carenza emerged to discover she was required to intercede in an argument between Grimshaw, Lady Bettridge's dresser, and the housekeeper, after one of the maids was accused of breaking an ornament in my lady's bedchamber.

Having succeeded in pacifying the warring parties, Carenza would have liked to retreat to the library with her book for an hour, but she thought it quite likely that the Viscount might be taking refuge there. Neither could she slip into the gardens, for the same reason. She decided to repair her credit with Cook by offering to collect the lamb from Home Farm, thus leaving the overworked kitchen staff free to carry on with their duties.

The weather was fine and Carenza wondered if she should persuade Papa to come with her for the drive but then she remembered that it was Mr Crossley's day to visit. He and Papa had been at Oxford together. Mr Crossley had subsequently gone into the church but six months ago he had given up his living and now resided in Morwood village, from where he walked to the manor once a week. Carenza knew how much Papa enjoyed his company, so she sallied forth alone to Home Farm.

She returned two hours later, much refreshed. After delivering the lamb to the kitchens she made her way to her father's apartments in the east wing.

'Papa? Is Mr Crossley gone?'

'Ah, come in, my love. Yes, he has left now.'

'May I sit with you for a while?' she asked, walking over to him. 'Or perhaps you are too tired.'

'On the contrary, Hubert's visits always cheer me up.' He held out his hand to her. 'Come and sit down and tell me what you have been doing today.'

She made herself comfortable on a little footstool beside his chair, saying, 'I am sorry I could not come to see you earlier, Papa, but before driving to Home Farm I was obliged to negotiate peace terms…'

She went on to give her father a lively account of her morning, making him laugh with her description of Mrs Trudby bristling like a terrier in defence of her housemaid, while Her Ladyship's dresser was demanding the girl be turned off at once.

'It was all a storm in a teacup, of course. The poor maid had not even been into the bedchamber. Then I discovered paw marks on the dressing table, just where the ornament had been standing, and we eventually surmised that the kitchen cat had come in, Mrs Grimshaw having left the window open.'

'Oh, dear, I cannot imagine Grimshaw would like admitting it was her fault.'

Carenza laughed. 'No, she did not, but we had a sort

of grudging apology and I persuaded Mrs Trudby to accept it. The main thing is, poor little Hetty did not lose her place.'

'You have achieved a miracle, my dear, and then to go to the farm, too! But you should not be having to do all this. You should be enjoying yourself with your sisters.'

'I did enjoy myself, driving out in the gig.' Carenza carried on, keeping her smile in place with an effort. 'Adelaide and Letty do not really want my company, Papa, and I am much happier being useful.'

'You should not have to be *useful* in your own home!'

She was a little shocked at the unwonted ferocity of her father's reply and she looked anxiously at him.

He sighed. 'Forgive me, my love, I should not have said that. But I so want you to be happy.'

She twisted around on the stool and took his thin hands in her own.

'But I *am* happy, Papa,' she said. 'I want nothing more than to be here with you, for ever.'

He looked at her for a long moment, his faded blue eyes full of something she did not understand, then he smiled.

'You are too good to me, my love, too kind. But let us forget that now. How much longer can you stay—do we have time for a game of backgammon?'

There was barely enough time to change for dinner when Carenza left the east wing. She scrambled into a clean gown and adjusted her cap over her dark hair before hurrying down the stairs to join the family. The butler was crossing the hall and he stopped when he saw her.

'Oh, dear, Hutton, is everyone else in the drawing room?'

'They are, Miss Bettridge. Would you like me to hold dinner for half an hour?' He gave her a fatherly smile. 'I am sure we could find some reason to do so.'

'Ah, that is very kind but no, thank you. I would not have everyone else inconvenienced. I am sure they are all ready to sit down to dinner.'

'Very well, ma'am.' With a nod he opened the door for her, and she went in.

Her father, sitting in his usual chair, raised his hand in silent greeting, but Lady Bettridge, Letitia and Adelaide disregarded her entrance and continued to talk to the Viscount. He, however, rose from his seat and moved across to welcome her.

Carenza's heart sank. There was no mistaking her half-sisters' indignation, nor the angry gleam in Lady Bettridge's eyes, but she could not avoid the Viscount, who bowed to her.

'Allow me to escort you to a chair, Miss Bettridge.'

'Thank you.'

Where was Hutton? She had thought he would follow her in and announce dinner, but he had retreated. Carenza realised he was giving her time to enjoy a little conversation, but in truth she was too on edge to derive any pleasure from it. The Viscount guided her to a seat close to his own and tried several times to include her in the conversation but she could only answer in monosyllables, feeling ever more uncomfortable. He must think her a veritable pea-goose, a simpleton with no social graces or intelligence.

Carenza could only be thankful when at last dinner was announced but even then her ordeal was not over, because she was once more sitting next to the Viscount.

She did not know whether to be most relieved or disheartened when he barely spoke to her during the meal. On the one hand, her stepmama and sisters could not accuse her of trying to gain favour with the Viscount, but it was very depressing to know he thought her quite unworthy of his attention.

Chapter Four

Ross was finding it increasingly difficult to be polite to the younger Misses Bettridge and their mother. He had not intended to single out Carenza, but their behaviour in ignoring her had grated with him. However, he soon realised that he had only made the situation worse. The looks directed at Miss Bettridge by the other ladies were positively deadly, and when they sat down to dinner, he thought the wisest course of action was to ignore her as much as possible.

With this end in mind, he engaged his host in conversation, although they were often interrupted by Lady Bettridge, who constantly tried to bring his attention back to her daughters. It was like taking part in a Drury Lane farce. In time Ross thought he would be able to laugh at the situation, but at present he felt only irritation and anger that he had allowed himself to be put in this position. Well, he had had quite enough. In the morning he would make his excuses and leave.

Matters improved considerably once the ladies had withdrawn and he could enjoy an uninterrupted conversation with Lord Bettridge. His host was a scholarly man and it did not take long for Ross to conclude that a gentle nature and ill health had caused him to re-treat from the world, leaving his second wife to rule the roost. What was harder to understand was why he had allowed his eldest daughter to become little more than an unpaid help. Had she suffered a disappointment in her youth? Not that she was old. Why, she must be at least ten years his junior, and at five-and-twenty a lady was still young enough for matrimony. Or perhaps not, if the lady in question had little conversation, wore a cap, dressed herself in dowdy clothes and was treated by her family as a drudge.

The Viscount's opinion of the eldest Miss Bettridge was confirmed when he accompanied his host across the hall to rejoin the ladies. She was just leaving the drawing room with her stepmother's strident tones fol-lowing her out into the hall, adjuring her to fetch the sheet music from the morning room and to be quick about it.

'Ah,' murmured Lord Bettridge, 'my daughters are going to entertain us. Do you enjoy music, my lord?'

'Why, yes, I do,' said Ross. 'In the army there was not as much time for music as I would have liked, but now I am trying to make up for that. I enjoyed several concerts when I was in town.'

His host nodded. 'Hmm. Pity.'

Ross wondered if he had misheard, but they were entering the drawing room and the moment was lost as Lady Bettridge bustled up.

'Ah, Lord Austerfield. We thought we would have a little recital tonight. Letitia and Adelaide have been practising for you. Do come and sit down, sir.'

There had clearly been a flurry of activity. Chairs and sofas had been arranged to face the pianoforte, where the young ladies were now moving the candles to best advantage.

'We are ready, Mama,' declared Adelaide, taking her seat at the instrument. 'All we need now is the music.'

'Yes, where is that foolish girl?'

Carenza hurried in with a sheaf of papers. 'I am here, ma'am.'

The three young ladies made a charming picture, gathered around the pianoforte, and Ross thought that, although she was not as tall as her half-sisters, there was something much more striking about the eldest Miss Bettridge. Or there would be, he decided, if she were properly attired.

Her dark hair and eyes and that golden skin contrasted strongly with her angelically fair half-sisters, but the pale blue gown did not suit her. It was too tight, her figure being much more voluptuous than the others'. Had she outgrown it, or was it one of her sisters' cast-offs? He folded his arms, frowning. Lady Bettridge wanted her own daughters to shine, but allowing her stepdaughter to appear like a poverty stricken relative did not reflect at all well upon the family.

Carenza moved to the back of the room, out of his sight, and her sisters began their recital, taking turns to perform a series of songs and sonatas that seemed to Ross to drag on much longer than the half an hour recorded by the clock. Their playing was accomplished, in as much as their technique was good, but it left Ross unmoved. Their singing, however, performed in thin, reedy voices with a tendency to screech, moved him with a strong desire to leave the room.

He joined in the applause, but nothing would induce him to beg for an encore, and it was with relief that he heard his host suggest they should retire to his private sitting room for a game of chess. Ross accepted with alacrity, beyond caring if he offended the ladies. Not for the world would he stay in that room a moment longer than necessary.

Lord Bettridge's apartments were situated in the east wing, and the sitting room was furnished for comfort rather than elegance. Two bookcases and a small desk stood at one end, while at the other, two armchairs flanked the fireplace. Although it was high summer, a small fire burned in the hearth. In the middle of the room stood a small table with a chair at either side.

'I hoped you would come,' remarked his host, waving a hand towards the table. 'I had Evans set out the board in readiness. I hope you will forgive the presumption.'

'Gladly, sir. It means we can commence even sooner.'

Ross noticed a man was already in the room. The valet, he surmised, looking at the man's plain black coat, and by the way he hovered solicitously about Lord Bettridge, a devoted retainer.

They took their seats, glasses of wine were placed on small tables beside them and they settled down to play. The first two games were over quickly, both men gauging their opponent rather than playing to win. The third threatened to stretch on for a considerable time. Ross had no objection, but he was very aware of his host's indifferent health, and when Evans came in to refresh their glasses, he took advantage of the break in play to ask if Lord Bettridge would like to postpone the game until the morning. The old man shook his head.

'No, no, I am never fatigued playing a good opponent, and I would put you in that category,' he said, removing one of Ross's knights from the board. 'We will continue, if you are happy to do so.' The old man's eyes twinkled. 'Unless you would prefer to return to the drawing room?'

'No, I thank you!'

Lord Bettridge gave a soft laugh and threw him a look of understanding. 'Your move, Viscount.'

Ross did not immediately return to the game but fixed his eyes upon his host.

He said, choosing his words with care, 'I think you may be labouring under a misapprehension, my lord. I must make it plain to you that I am not looking for a bride.'

'Really?' Lord Bettridge raised his brows. 'I was led to believe you gave a very different impression in town.'

'That is true.' Ross picked up his glass and studied the rich ruby liquid. 'I was persuaded that it was my duty to take a wife and I went to London fully prepared to oblige my family. But it was a mistake, sir. I realised that even before I arrived at Morwood. I have decided it is better if I do not take a wife and can only apologise if I have misled Lady Bettridge.'

The old man was watching him expectantly. Ross felt obliged to continue.

'There is already a perfectly satisfactory heir. I know there are those who think I should marry and have a son of my own, but I consider it unnecessary.'

Lord Bettridge nodded and regarded him with a kindly eye.

'That, of course, is for you to decide, Lord Austerfield,' he said gently. 'Shall we continue our game?'

Ross looked at the chessboard. Having unburdened himself thus far, he found he now wanted to continue.

'If I may speak frankly, my lord, it is damned tiresome to be constantly under siege,' he said bitterly. 'I cannot go anywhere without having prospective brides paraded in front of me.'

'But that will continue for as long as you remain a bachelor,' the old man pointed out.

Ross moved a pawn and sat back, sighing. 'I am aware of that, and I know I must learn to put up with it. However, I have come to the conclusion that it is best that I never marry.' He put a hand up to his scarred face. 'No woman could love this abhorrent countenance. I would not inflict it upon a wife. Not even to produce an heir.'

'Many would overlook it.'

'Aye, in order to secure a title and my fortune! Is it arrogant of me to say I do not want that? However, neither do I wish to be pursued by matchmakers for the rest of my days!'

They played a little more in silence, then Lord Bettridge spoke again.

'Perhaps there is a way out of your dilemma.'

Ross gave a snort of derision. 'If there is, I wish you will tell me!'

His Lordship selected his queen and took Ross's bishop.

'Find yourself a sensible woman for your bride. One who understands what you want of her and who has no expectations that you will swear undying love. A lady who wants no more than a secure future and a comfortable home, somewhere she can be happy.'

Ross looked at him through narrowed eyes. 'You have a candidate in mind, sir?'

The old man sat back and steepled his fingers, hesitating as though choosing his next words with care.

'My eldest daughter, Carenza. Her life here is not what it should be. I am aware that her stepmother dislikes her, that her sisters despise her.' His countenance was suddenly transformed by overwhelming sadness. 'Perhaps, if I had been stronger at the outset, I might have made a difference. But there, I can do nothing about that now.'

'Lord Bettridge—'

'All I would ask is that you spend a little time getting to know Carenza, my lord. She is a diamond, but she does not shine when she is with her stepmama. Or with her sisters. She is worth a dozen of either of them, but she cannot be brought to realise it.

'If it were possible, I would give her the means to set up her own establishment, but such a venture would take more money than I can afford.' He shrugged. 'And it might not answer if I *could* do it. A single woman living alone often becomes the subject of much gossip and speculation, even ridicule. I would like to see Carenza comfortably established and in a situation where she is respected.'

'But Miss Bettridge is already comfortably settled here at Morwood,' said Ross. He moved his knight away from a potential trap, then added, remembering their conversation in the library, 'She told me herself that she is very content with her life.'

'But *I* am not content with it! My health is not good. I do not expect to survive many more years and then what will become of Carenza? She will receive little support from my wife or her half-sisters and there is no other family she can call upon. If she wishes to be independent, she will be obliged to find employment, and without references, how is she expected to find a good position?' The old man's voice cracked a little and he paused to take a sip of wine. 'I have done very wrong by my daughter and have no way to make reparation.

The thought has been troubling me for some time now, but here I see a solution that might suit both of you.'

Ross felt his fingers tighten around his wineglass as he listened and he was obliged to stifle his irritation. He liked Lord Bettridge and had no wish to quarrel with him, but the idea was preposterous. It was too outrageous to be contemplated! He gave his attention to what was happening on the chessboard, but other thoughts intruded and he broke the silence again.

He said carefully, 'I believe you are being too pessimistic, my lord. Your daughter will not find herself without a home. Her stepmother would hardly cast her out.'

Ross watched a shadow flit across the old man's face. The clock on the mantel ticked several times more before Lord Bettridge gave a little shake of his head and smiled.

'No, no, you are quite right, my lord. I am being very foolish and indulging in megrims that are as absurd as they are unnecessary. I beg your pardon.'

They continued with their game and Ross tried to concentrate but his mind kept wandering. Carenza Bettridge's situation was not a happy one, he could see that, but would she be any happier married to him, with his scarred body and his mercurial temper? He was not fit to be a husband. There were times when he felt almost too wretched to live. His trusted servants understood, but he did not want a wife. If she cared for him at all she would fuss around him and her sympathy would be unbearable, like the prodding of an open wound. The alternative was to allow her to live her own life. He knew many such marriages, but that idea did not appeal to Ross at all.

'It would not work,' he said aloud. 'If I took a wife,

I could not allow her the freedom to go her own way. It is very selfish of me, I know, but I do not think I could share my wife with any man. And if she did not love me, then she would be doomed to be unhappy. How can that be sensible?'

'My dear sir, I think you underestimate our ability to be rational beings and to make the most of a situation.'

'But when emotions become involved, then rational thought is too often vanquished. I cannot, I will not, take that risk, sir. It is better that I never marry.' Distracted, he moved another pawn, almost at random. 'That is my final word upon the subject.'

Lord Bettridge studied the board, his thin hand hovering over the pieces. He said, without looking up, 'Never is a very long time, Lord Austerfield. You might find by the morning my suggestion appeals a little more.'

'I think that is highly unlikely.'

'We shall see.' The old man's fingers swept down to move his knight and then he looked up, smiling. 'Checkmate, I believe.'

Chapter Five

Bright sunshine was streaming into Carenza's room when she woke the next morning. She jumped out of bed and ran to the window, looking out at the unbroken blue sky. It was going to be a glorious day and for a moment her spirits lifted, but soon the reality of her current situation closed in on her again.

The memory of last night's musical evening caused her to shudder. No one could blame Lord Austerfield for going off to play chess with Papa after the less than perfect performances from her sisters. She had no doubt he was even now rehearsing the excuses he would make to Lady Bettridge to cut short his visit, and if he left without making an offer to either Letty or Adelaide, life would become very uncomfortable at Morwood.

There was a peremptory knock at the door and she turned to see her stepmother's dresser entering the room, carrying a tray.

'Her Ladyship says you are to break your fast in your room today.'

'Oh. Thank you for fetching it up for me, Mrs Grimshaw.'

The dresser put the tray down none-too-gently on the table and turned to fix Carenza with her basilisk stare.

'She also wishes it understood that you are not required to join the family downstairs until dinner time. Things have reached a very delicate stage with Lord Austerfield.'

'Oh, is he leaving?'

Mrs Grimshaw blinked. 'Leaving? No, of course not.'

'Oh, I thought, after last night…'

She hesitated, not wishing to put into words how bad the recital had been. Mrs Grimshaw folded her arms across her skinny bosom, a hint of triumphant satisfaction in the thin smile she gave Carenza.

'Her Ladyship considers that *An Offer* is imminent.'

'Good heavens,' exclaimed Carenza, considerably surprised. 'Then I shall certainly stay out of the way.'

'As to that, Her Ladyship has written down the things she wants you to do, since Miss Letitia and Miss Adelaide will not have time for them today.'

She handed over a sheet of paper and went off, leaving Carenza to study the list. There was nothing particularly onerous. Her half-sisters contributed very little towards the smooth running of the house and she decided she would be able to complete most of the tasks that morning, after her daily visit to Papa.

It was mid-afternoon and Carenza had one task left on her list, to go to the rose garden and pick the very best blooms for display. Her instructions were to leave them in the morning room, together with a suitable vase.

All must be in readiness no less than an hour before dinner.

These last words caused a little flutter in Carenza's breast when she read them. Her stepmother was confident the Viscount was about to make an offer and he would be given every encouragement to do so. She had no difficulty imagining the situation Lady Bettridge had in mind: His Lordship would be directed to the morning room, where he would find the bride of his choice charmingly engaged arranging the flowers.

Carenza had no idea whether he had chosen Letitia or Adelaide, but she knew neither of them enjoyed collecting roses, because of the thorns that pricked their fingers. They also disliked being too long in the sun, which spoiled their milk-white complexion. Fortunately, Carenza had no such qualms about her skin, which only became a deeper gold, never red and blotchy with the heat. Having spoken to Hetty about a vase, she went off to collect the flower basket and scissors before slipping out of the house through one of the back doors.

The rose garden was situated on the south side of the house and enclosed by a sheltering hedge of clipped yew trees. Lady Bettridge and her daughters rarely walked there, partly because they claimed the heavy scent made them sneeze, but mainly because they feared for their fine muslin skirts and trailing scarves becoming snagged upon the bushes. Carenza, however, had dressed most practically for the task in hand. She wore an old twill pelisse over her gown and had no light-as-gossamer scarves to float on the breeze.

She revelled in the peace and seclusion of the rose garden and found it soothing to breathe in the perfumed air. It always lifted her spirits, making her realise how fortunate she was. She had a comfortable home and a loving father. Her stepmother and half-sisters might be unkind, but she was hopeful that for the next few years at least, they would be spending a great deal of time husband-hunting and away from Morwood.

She had not been long engaged in collecting her flowers when a movement at the gate caught her eye and she looked up to see Lord Austerfield walking down the path towards her.

'Good morning, Miss Bettridge. Am I disturbing you?'

Carenza's serenity was put to rout. How should she answer? She had been ordered to avoid the Viscount but here they were, alone together in a garden screened from prying eyes. Short of picking up her skirts and running away, there was no escape.

He was waiting for an answer, but all her befuddled brain could do was notice the grace and power of his movements, the way his broad shoulders filled his blue coat and how the wide brimmed hat he wore shaded his face, making the scars much less conspicuous. Indeed, as his mouth and left ear had escaped injury, one might not notice them at all, especially if one was beguiled by those green-grey eyes...

'You are collecting flowers, I see.'

His gentle prompting brought her wandering mind back with a jolt.

'Y-yes.' She waved at her basket. 'We need fresh flowers for the morning room.'

'Then allow me to help you.'

'Oh, no, you cannot! I mean, thank you, but it is not necessary.'

'Oh, but it is, ma'am,' he said earnestly. 'I am presently avoiding your sisters, who are determined I should drive them around the countryside, while *I* am equally determined I shall not! What is to be done but to hide?'

'You cannot hide here,' she told him, looking around

and feeling very much like a hunted animal. 'If Lady Bettridge should find you…'

'That is unlikely. When I saw Her Ladyship, she was declaring she would retire to her boudoir to read, leaving me to the tender mercies of your sisters.' He caught the stem of a particularly perfect bloom and held it steady for her to cut. 'I was hoping to engage your father in a game of backgammon, or chess, but I am informed that he is resting. Miss Letty and Miss Adelaide, however, are only too willing to entertain me. Which is why I, er, escaped.'

He was smiling down at her and she could not help but respond, but she was mortified, too. It was clear the Viscount had no illusions about the intentions of Lady Bettridge and her daughters.

'I am very sorry,' she whispered.

'It is not your fault but entirely my own, for agreeing to come here.' His smile faded. 'My plan was crass and ill-conceived and I am heartily ashamed of myself. I believe now it would be a monumental mistake for me to marry anyone. I have been trying to give Lady Bettridge the hint, but she does not take it.'

'She does not wish to take it,' replied Carenza frankly. She cut a few more roses and laid them carefully in her basket. 'One cannot really blame her. You would be a very eligible catch, my lord.'

'And I can never forget it!'

She heard the bitter note in his voice and a spurt of sympathy overrode her shyness.

'One might ask how a grown man could be cajoled into this situation.'

'One might indeed. You must understand that the ladies of my family are quite formidable. They are convinced I should marry and for a while I thought I could go through with it.' He put a hand up to his cheek. 'It did not take me long to realise it was impossible.'

She stopped and looked up at him, her head on one side. 'I think you dwell too much upon your appearance, my lord.'

'The devil I do!'

He stared at the path, his brow furrowed. Carenza knew he wanted to say more and she waited patiently.

'It is not just my face. My body, too, is heavily scarred and unsightly.'

'You were badly wounded at Waterloo, I believe.' She began to walk again, thinking it would be easier to talk if they were moving.

'Artillery shell. Oh, I know I should not complain. It would have been a lot worse, even fatal, if there had not been several other fellows standing beside me. They took the main force of the explosion.'

'Oh, good heavens, how truly appalling! And were they…did they…?'

'Yes.' His head was up, but she knew his thoughts were miles away and he saw nothing of the beautiful garden. He said curtly, 'They died. Every one of them.'

'I am so sorry.'

There really was nothing else she could say. They had reached the next rose bed and she sought for something to divert him.

'The gardener has allowed these bushes to get out of hand. Which is a pity because there are some particularly fine flowers here, but they are beyond my reach.'

'Then allow me.'

He stopped and pulled a branch down so that she could snip off three delicate blooms. He reached out for another and they moved on slowly, searching for the finest specimens and arguing over which colours would look best together. The Viscount's mood lightened and Carenza quite forgot she was not supposed to be in his company. In an effort to keep his thoughts away from the past she chattered quite freely, asking him about the gardens of his various properties, until at length he stopped her, laughing.

'I am afraid I know very little about these things, Miss Bettridge. I never expected to inherit, you see, so I have taken little interest in them.'

'Very well, which house will be your main residence?' she countered. 'I heard one of my sisters say that Comers, in Yorkshire, is your principal seat.'

'Aye, but it is my least favourite. My brother died there.'

'Oh, I beg your pardon. I did not know.'

'No, how should you? He broke his neck in a riding accident while I was in Belgium. I did not learn of it until I returned to England.'

Impulsively she touched his arm. 'How wretched that must have been for you.'

Beneath the fine woollen sleeve, the muscles were knotted hard. Carenza realised she was standing far too close but for some inexplicable reason it was impossible to withdraw her hand. She suddenly felt giddy, aware of the heady scent of roses in the air and very conscious of the man towering over her, his eyes cold and bleak as a grey December sky. Her heart went out to him. She wanted more than anything to put her arms around him and ease the desperate sadness she could feel emanating from his rigid body.

Her reaction shocked her to the core. It would not do! Why, they were almost strangers. But she must find some way to relieve his gloom. She stepped away from him and forced herself to speak cheerfully.

'So, my lord, which house do you think of as your home now?'

He gave his head a little shake, as if to throw off the sombre mood, and followed her lead.

'It is undoubtedly Auster, which is where I am bound when I leave here. It is not the largest nor the grandest of my properties. Indeed, it is a hotchpotch of styles dating back centuries, but it is a comfortable house and I spent many happy years there as a boy.'

'And are the gardens a hotchpotch too?' she asked him, wanting to encourage these sunnier thoughts.

'The grounds are quite small, but there are some flower beds, surrounded by sheltering walls. The house is situated on the Devon coast,' he explained. 'It is high on a cliff and less than a half mile from the sea. Fierce winds blow in from the Atlantic, scouring the exposed land. I am afraid Auster has been neglected somewhat. My father spent his last years in Bath and my brother, Sebastian, divided his time between Comers and London. However, having sold out of the army I intend to make Auster my principal residence. That is another reason for not taking a wife,' he added, his tone mocking. 'It is too far from London to suit any lady who wants to cut a dash in town or to be forever gadding about the country.'

'Not all women want that, my lord.'

'Your sisters do.'

'But they are very young and have as yet seen very little of the world.'

'And you have?'

'Well, no, most of my knowledge of the world comes from reading,' she confessed. 'But I would never want to leave Morwood. I have everything I want here: a pleasant garden, my books, music—'

'Music? You did not play for us last night.'

'No. I play only on the pianoforte in Papa's room.' She did not add that any performance in front of Lady Bettridge or her half-sisters only elicited criticism. 'So you see, my lord, I am very content to stay here and look after Papa.'

How dull her life must sound to a soldier, she thought. How dreary, to someone accustomed to excitement and adventure. Embarrassed, Carenza busied herself cutting a few more roses to add to her basket.

'Thank you, my lord. With your help I have amassed a beautiful array of flowers. Now I had best get them back to the house.'

'Just one moment.' He plucked a white rosebud from a nearby bush. 'A final flower for your collection.'

He held out the rose and Carenza reached for it, aware that her heart was pounding quite erratically. Suddenly she wished she wasn't dressed in such ill-fitting clothes and a matronly cap. She wished she was wearing a beautiful flowing gown with diamonds glittering at her throat and a diamond aigrette nestled into her hair.

She wished she was beautiful.

'Carenza!'

Lady Bettridge's screech of outrage startled her and she dropped the rosebud.

'Are you still out here, you foolish girl? Those flowers should have been in the morning room an hour since. You know full well that Letitia wants to arrange them before dinner!'

'I b-beg your pardon, ma'am.'

Carenza jumped, her voice shaking with nerves. Lady Bettridge had not struck her for years, but the memories were still there, and the fear. Now she almost quailed as her stepmother surged closer. She was clearly in a towering rage, although she moderated her tone and her manner slightly, for the Viscount's benefit.

'Well, well, what a dreamer you are! Take them in this minute, and no more of your dawdling. What must His Lordship think of you?'

His Lordship was thinking rapidly how best to save Carenza from any further scolding. Lady Bettridge was smiling but her gaze was flinty, promising retribution. Carenza, deathly pale, stuttered something incoherent and fled.

'It is entirely my fault, ma'am,' he said, stooping to pick up the rose. 'I came upon Miss Bettridge quite by chance and we have been talking. I believe we both quite forgot the time.'

He saw immediately that he had made a mistake. The lady's smile widened, but there was no softening of her features. If anything, she looked even more furious. He held up the rosebud.

'This is the reason I ventured forth into the garden, ma'am. I wanted to find a perfect bloom to pin to my coat this evening. However, 'pon reflection, I think it would look better upon a lady's gown and, therefore, I beg you will accept it.'

He presented the rose to Lady Bettridge with a flourishing bow and she took it, simpering like a schoolroom miss. Fervently hoping he had retrieved the situation, Ross offered her his arm.

'May I escort you back to the house, ma'am?'

When they reached the hall, he excused himself, saying there was a letter he needed to write. He ignored Lady Bettridge's offer of refreshment and her thinly veiled hints that Miss Letitia would be arranging the roses in the morning room just before dinner, and *Quite Alone*. He ran quickly up the stairs, wishing he had left this damned house directly after breakfast as he had originally planned.

It had been his intention from the moment he woke up that morning, but it promised to be such a hot day that he knew his groom would prefer him not to drive the matched greys too far in the heat. Then Brisco had prophesied there would be thunder later and that had decided him. He would not risk the high-spirited pair coming to harm just because he was not enjoying his visit to Morwood.

And it was not all bad here. He liked Lord Bettridge, a very knowledgeable gentleman who had been laid low by ill health. If Ross could have spent more time with him he would have been content, but his host rarely left his rooms until dinner time and now, after a most uncomfortable day, Ross found himself wishing he had risked the thunder and quit Morwood that morning. He might have taken the journey to Devon in easy stages, rested his team regularly. Surely that would have been better than being hounded by the younger Misses Bettridge. He had avoided the trap today but he had no doubt their mother would find another opportunity tomorrow!

'And so it will go on,' he told himself bitterly. 'Until I am married. Or dead.'

Scowling, he strode along the corridor that led to his guest chamber. He noticed that the door to the backstairs had been propped open to allow what breeze there was to drift through the upper floors. Voices could be heard from the stairwell, engaged in a furious whispered tirade. Intrigued, Ross stepped through the door and glanced over the rail to see the housekeeper at the bottom of the stairs. She was talking with a man clad in funereal black. Lord Bettridge's valet. Ross knew he should retreat, but the barely contained rage in the housekeeper's speech held him there, listening.

'I tell you, Mr Evans, I was never more shocked in my life than when Her Ladyship said she was sending Grimshaw up to poor Miss Carenza this morning. Sent up her orders, too! As if the poor mite doesn't work hard enough, but she is to do the work of those two lazy besoms today.'

'It's to keep her out of the Viscount's way, Mrs Trudby, you mark my words.' The valet's tone was low and disapproving.

'Aye, she is determined one of her daughters will snare the Viscount. I believe she would have locked Miss Carenza's door and kept her in her room all day if she could have done so, but she knows the master would never stand for that.'

'And I would have made sure he learned of it,' replied Evans. 'Apart from Grimshaw, there is not a servant in this house who approves of the way that poor young lady is treated...'

A door opened somewhere below and the valet broke off. Guiltily, Ross moved away. A gentleman did not listen to tittle tattle, but he could not deny feeling angered by Carenza's plight. Yet she was happy enough at Morwood Manor. She had said so yesterday and told him so again today in the rose garden, had she not? It was no concern of his what became of her. However, he decided he would fulfil his obligation to remain at Morwood for the next couple of days. Then he could drive to Auster with a clear conscience.

Chapter Six

Carenza ran back to the house with the roses, but even then she was not free of her tormentors. Letitia and Adelaide were waiting in the hall.

'Here she is, the sly little cat!' hissed Letty. 'Where have you been?'

'Completing your work as well as my own,' Carenza retorted with spirit.

'How dare you sneak away with the Viscount!'

'I did not sneak away with him, Adelaide. I was already in the garden when Lord Austerfield arrived.'

She walked off and they followed her, Letty saying as they went into the morning room, 'If you thought to impress him, then you will be disappointed.'

'That was not my intention, so there is nothing to disappoint me.'

'Hush!' Adelaide muttered, standing by the door. 'Mama is coming in with the Viscount!'

They fell silent and Adelaide pushed the door until it was only open a few inches, but the voices in the marble hall carried alarmingly well. Carenza heard her stepmother's tinkling laugh.

'My dear Lord Austerfield, are you sure I cannot

tempt you to join me in the drawing room for some refreshment? It is so hot…'

'Alas, ma'am, it is precisely *because* it is so hot that
I'd as lief take my time changing for dinner, once my
letter is written,' replied His Lordship. 'I should not
wish to shock my valet and disgrace myself by appearing with wilted shirt-points.'

They heard his brisk footsteps crossing the floor,
then the unmistakeable sound of him climbing the
stairs. Adelaide closed the door.

'He has gone up to change,' she said, unnecessarily.

'Ooh…confound it!' Letitia stamped her foot, her
fingers curling with rage and frustration. 'Was ever
anything so unfortunate!'

'Never mind, Letty,' said Adelaide, 'there is always
tomorrow.'

'But the roses will not wait,' said Carenza, putting
her basket down on the table. 'They need to be put into
the vase of water as soon as possible. I suggest you decide which of you is going to arrange them.'

Letitia picked up a handful of the roses and looked
at them contemptuously.

'There is no point in it now. You should have delivered them here a good half hour since.'

Carenza was unable to resist answering, 'So that the
Viscount could come upon you arranging them artisti-
cally? How romantic.'

'It might have been, if you had not been so late!'

'And if the Viscount had not run away from you,'
she murmured.

'He did *not* run away!' Angry spots of colour flooded
Letty's cheeks. 'Mama was looking for him and one of
the servants said she had seen him strolling off to the
rose garden.'

'Where *you* were lying in wait!' added Adelaide.

'Where I had been instructed to go,' Carenza retorted. 'Now I suggest one of you deals with these flowers before they wilt.'

'How *dare* you tell us what to do!' shrieked Letty. 'You arrange them!'

Carenza was looking at the basket and did not notice Letty lift her arm. The roses were still in her hand and the long stems whipped Carenza's face, the sharp thorns digging into her skin. She cried out and put her hand up to her cheek, staring in horror at her half-sister.

'I am not sorry,' declared Letitia defiantly, dropping the hapless flowers. 'You served us a horrid trick today, you harpy. It is all your fault and so I shall tell Mama. Come along, Adelaide!'

She caught her sister's arm and they flounced out, slamming the door behind them.

Carenza's cheek was stinging and there was blood on her fingers. She drew out her handkerchief and wiped her hand as she walked over to the mirror to inspect her face. There were lots of little scratches, but a couple of the deeper ones were oozing blood. She cleaned herself up as best she could, then turned back and looked around the room. The roses Letitia had dropped lay on the carpet, their petals scattered far and wide. That must all be cleared away, but first, the basket was still overflowing with colourful blooms and Carenza could not bear to let them go to waste.

She set to work.

Ross took his time changing into his evening dress and kept to his room until the last possible minute. With luck, his entrance would be swiftly followed by the butler coming in to announce dinner and, afterwards, he would suggest to his host that they should play chess. That would take care of his third night at Morwood. Only one more day to avoid the clutches of Lady Bettridge and her daughters and he could shake the dust of this place from his feet. For ever.

He eventually left his room and found the corridors were mercifully empty of servants. However, when he reached the half-landing he heard someone else approaching. Flying down the stairs from the family's quarters was Miss Carenza Bettridge.

She was wearing another of her unflattering gowns, a pale pink creation decorated around the hem with an overabundance of white frills. At the sight of him she stopped suddenly and the frills bobbed and frothed like waves around her ankles.

'Miss Bettridge. I thought I would be the last. Shall we go down together?'

She looked as if she would like to refuse; there was reluctance in every line of her body as she descended the last few steps to join him on the half-landing.

He frowned. 'What have you done to your face?'

When she did not reply he put his fingers under her chin and gently tilted her head up. Blushing, she pulled away, but not before he had seen the scratches on the left side of her face.

'What is this?'

Her hand fluttered. 'Collecting the roses...'

'Nonsense,' he retorted. 'I was with you in the rose garden. I know it did not happen there!'

'Oh, please, do not ask me about it,' she implored him. 'It was an accident.'

She was so upset that his suspicions were aroused.

'Did someone strike you?'

'No, no. I—' She glanced up and, seeing his expression, broke off from whatever lie she had been about to tell him. She clasped her hands together and looked around to make sure there was no one to overhear, then she took a deep breath. 'Lord Austerfield, I pray you will not question me further. My father is bound to notice and ask me how this occurred. I shall say I received these scratches when I was collecting the roses today. Anything else would upset him greatly.'

His mouth thinned. He'd wager Lady Bettridge had inflicted this on her. Or those damned daughters of hers. How, he did not know. *Why* it had happened, he could well guess. He felt something stir, deep inside, a desire to comfort and protect.

Damnation, man, leave this. She is not your concern!

Carenza was looking at him, her near-black eyes beseeching. 'Please, my lord. Please do not be angry that I cannot tell you more!'

'Angry, with you?' He shook his head. 'I am not angry with you at all, Miss Bettridge.' He took her writhing hands between his own and held them. 'I think we should go on to the drawing room before we are disgracefully late.'

He tried to draw one of her hands within his arm but she resisted.

'Not together!'

'You are shaking so much there is every danger you will fall down the stairs if you do not let me help you,' he told her, holding her fingers firmly on his sleeve as they set off down the stairs. 'Never fear, I shall release you before we go in.'

Descending the half-flight of stairs and walking across the marble hall beside Lord Austerfield seemed to take for ever. Carenza was painfully aware of her hand on his sleeve. She tried not to think of the muscled arm beneath, or the tall, powerful body of the man at her side. She considered pulling free, but he had been correct to say she was shaking. There was a very real possibility that her knees would buckle beneath her at any moment. However, when they did at last reach the drawing room door, she wished the journey had been longer.

She hung back, saying in a hasty whisper, 'We cannot go in together!'

His lips twitched. 'No, you said the same thing on my first night here, did you not? This is becoming a habit, Miss Bettridge.' He put one hand on her back and gave her a little push towards the door. 'Off you go. I will take a turn around the hall and follow shortly.'

Carenza drew in a long, steadying breath and opened the door. All eyes turned towards her and she forced herself to be calm.

'I beg your pardon, am I late?'

'No, no, Lord Austerfield has not come down yet.' Her father held out his hand to her. 'Come and sit beside me, my dear. I wanted to thank you for the roses you sent to my room earlier. Their scent is exquisite.'

'We needed some for the morning room, Papa, and it was no trouble to pick a few extra for you.'

'It was my suggestion they should be collected.' Lady Bettridge gave a little laugh. 'It has been so sultry, I was convinced there was a storm on the way, and you know how that can quite destroy the roses.'

'Yes indeed, my dear,' he replied absently, his eyes fixed upon Carenza's face. 'Is that how you received those marks on your cheek, my dear? You were scrambling amongst the rose bushes, I suppose.'

Carenza knew Letitia was watching her and she did not answer immediately. She had no intention of laying the blame upon her half-sister, but she was happy for Letty to worry about the possibility, just for a few moments.

'Yes, Papa,' she said at last. 'It was the thorns.'

He cupped her cheek and regarded her anxiously for a moment.

'Silly girl, you might have injured an eye, you know. I wish you would take more care of yourself.'

Her heart swelled at the affection in his tone and silently she raised her hand to cover his. At that moment the door opened and the way the other ladies sprang to life told her Lord Austerfield had arrived. He came into the room, murmuring an apology which was quickly brushed aside by Lady Bettridge.

'No need for that, my lord, we do not stand upon ceremony here, you know.' A little giggle followed. 'And you will see that I am wearing your flower, sir.' She placed a hand upon her corsage as she turned to her husband to explain. 'The Viscount was good enough to present me with this rosebud, my lord. Was that not gallant of him?'

'Indeed, it was, my dear. So, you have seen my rose garden, my lord?'

Ross inclined his head.

'I went out there for a stroll this afternoon and was most impressed. You have a truly magnificent selection of roses, Lord Bettridge.'

'I am sure they looked better before Carenza hacked at them,' put in my lady, sending a cold glance towards her stepdaughter.

'I noticed no lack,' Ross said quickly. 'Miss Bettridge was most careful in her choice.'

He said this with a slight bow in Carenza's direction, an attention that was not well received by her stepmother, who gave another ill-tempered tut.

'Yes, yes, but there really was no need for her to take quite so long over the task. Dear Letitia should have had the arranging of them. She has such an eye for colour, you know, but Carenza has thrown them together without any care at all.'

Carenza clasped her hands tightly in her lap and kept her eyes lowered. She was accustomed to her stepmother's strictures but it was mortifying that she should criticise her so openly before their guest. Not that it mattered what he thought of her. The Viscount would be at Morwood for only one more day and she was very sure he would not wish to see her, or any of her family, ever again!

When Hutton came in to announce dinner, Carenza ignored the general bustle in the room and went to help her father out of his chair. She was about to take his arm when Lady Bettridge stepped up.

'I have asked Lord Austerfield to escort the girls into dinner tonight, Carenza. I shall go in with your father.'

Lord Bettridge looked nonplussed. 'But he cannot escort all three of them, my dear.'

My lady waved her hand. 'Carenza is quite capable of walking on her own.'

Her father was looking troubled and she said quickly, 'It is perfectly true, Papa. I am very happy to follow on.'

She fell in behind the Viscount, who was flanked by her half-sisters, and as the little party crossed the hall, Letty and Adelaide both turned to look back at her. There was no mistaking the triumph in their eyes.

Ross remained calmly polite during the dinner, but he was acutely uncomfortable. He had been outflanked by Lady Bettridge, but if she thought closer acquaintance with her daughters would endear them to him, she was quite wrong. He found their inane chatter irritating and their compliments facile. However, he could have tolerated their silliness with equanimity if it had not been for the ill-treatment of their elder sister. It was far too blatant to be ignored. Every word, every action, they directed towards Carenza was designed to wound. The slights and disparaging remarks were passed off as funning, but Ross could see no humour in it. He had witnessed such bullying in the army and knew how it could wear a man down and ruin him. He had done his best to stamp it out, where possible.

Carenza was once more sitting to his left but he addressed only a few unexceptional remarks to her. They were being jealously watched by the other ladies and he did not wish to make her situation any worse. Yet he was painfully aware of her beside him—her dainty movements, the little hand reaching for her glass, the summer scent she wore that occasionally assailed him. The fact that her thigh was but inches from his own…

His appetite deserted him. Confound it, what was it about the lady that made it so difficult to ignore her? It must be pity, he decided. Sympathy for her situation. Having resolved that point, Ross gave his full attention to his dinner but he enjoyed very little of it, and was relieved when the ladies finally withdrew.

It had been agreed earlier that the gentlemen would remove to the east wing directly after dinner to play a game of chess. However, it was clear to Ross that his host was very tired, and before they quit the dining table, he suggested they postpone their game.

'We could play tomorrow, if you wish,' he offered. 'In the morning, perhaps, when you are rested.'

Lord Bettridge's lined face lit up with a smile. 'You are very kind, my lord, but it promises to be another fine day tomorrow. Surely you would wish to be doing something other than humouring an old man when the sun is shining.'

Ross smiled. 'I believe you know I would feel safer playing chess or backgammon with you!' There was an answering twinkle in the old man's eyes and Ross was emboldened to go further. 'If you will forgive my plain speaking, my lord, I believe my presence here is causing some rivalry within your family, and Miss Bettridge is its innocent victim.'

His host appeared to shrink a little in his chair.

'Alas, I fear you are right.' He sighed. 'You wonder that I do not stop it, but the truth is I do not know how. If I defend Carenza, then they wait until I am absent to take their petty revenge and that only makes life more uncomfortable for my darling girl.'

'But it will not be for ever,' said Ross, trying to find some comfort for the old man. 'Lady Bettridge is fixed upon finding husbands for her daughters. Once they are wed and have households of their own, many of the problems will disappear.'

'Yes, there is that.' The old man toyed with his glass. 'Carenza is secure, while I live, but I could wish…' He broke off and glanced at Ross, 'You have not changed your mind about the little matter we discussed last night?

'I have not. I am sorry if that disappoints you, but

I am convinced it would not be right. To take a wife merely to avoid being constantly pestered by matchmakers would be a most cowardly thing to do. Consider, sir: I would be tying your daughter into a loveless marriage. A life sentence, even if the cage is a gilded one.'

Lord Bettridge regarded him for a moment, then nodded.

'I understand, my lord, and I commend your honesty. I beg your pardon for burdening you with my concerns. My estate is entailed, you see, and my successor a man whom I have never met. You will understand that I am anxious as to what will happen to my family. But we will say no more on the subject.' He struggled to his feet. 'We will postpone our game, then, if you do not object, Lord Austerfield, but I wonder if I might trouble you to give me your arm to my room?

Chapter Seven

Ross delivered his host into the tender care of Evans, his manservant, then returned to the drawing room, having promised to give His Lordship's apologies to the ladies. As he descended the stairs a movement in the marble hall caught his eye. He heard the faintest pad of kid-soled slippers and, bending a little, he was in time to see someone disappear into the morning room in a flurry of white-frilled skirts.

If that had been all, Ross would have thought nothing of it and gone on his way, but he caught the unmistakeable sound of a sob, just before the door was fully closed. Telling himself it really was no business of his, he continued to the drawing room, but as he was about to enter, the girlish giggles he heard within checked him. Confound it, what were they about, to be laughing while their sister was in distress? Turning on his heel, he strode back across the hall.

Ross gave a brief knock and went in. A single candle flickered on the mantel, and in its dim light he could see Carenza standing beside the table. She had her back to him but he could tell that she was hastily wiping her eyes.

'What the devil are you doing in here in the near darkness?' The words came out more roughly than he had intended and he tried again, softer this time. 'Is there anything I can do, Miss Bettridge?'

'No, no. It is nothing.' She was folding and refolding her handkerchief, trying to find a dry patch. Ross pulled his own freshly laundered handkerchief from his pocket.

'Here, have mine.'

She took it gratefully, but remained half turned away from him. He could only see her profile with its straight little nose and dainty chin, and three dark lines on her cheek, where the rose thorns had drawn blood. Ross cursed silently. The hour or so spent in the rose garden with Carenza was one of the happiest memories of his stay at Morwood, surprisingly, but it was spoiled by seeing what had come of it.

'Has this anything to do with your sisters?' he asked gently as she wiped her eyes. 'Forgive me, one cannot help but notice how they pick at you. Your stepmama, too.' He frowned. 'Why do you not defend yourself?'

'Because that only makes the situation worse. They ensure our disagreements come to Papa's attention, which makes him unhappy, and that has an adverse effect upon his health. Discord in the household upsets him, you see. The doctor has advised that he should be kept as tranquil as possible.'

She blew her nose and straightened her shoulders.

'I beg your pardon, my lord, I am indulging in a fit of the megrims and there really is no need. I am only sorry that you have caught me behaving like a watering-pot. That is most uncomfortable for you.'

'It is uncomfortable watching your sisters torment you!'

She tried to smile. 'The situation is not so very bad.

In general, we rub along together well enough. I have plenty to occupy me, looking after Papa and helping Mrs Trudby to run the house. It is only...' She broke off, pulling the handkerchief through her fingers several times before continuing. 'My stepmother does not like me to...to put myself forward, when we have guests.'

'You do not put yourself forward,' he retorted. 'I daresay, if they did not constantly carp and criticise, no one would notice you.'

She winced at that, but answered him calmly enough. 'You are perfectly right. Everything will settle down again once you have left Morwood.' She summoned up a smile. 'So, you see, my lord, we have only to get through tomorrow and breakfast the following day, and after that we can both be easy.' She went to return his handkerchief, glanced down at the damp, crumpled linen and changed her mind.

'I will have this washed and pressed before you leave, sir.'

He wanted to tell her there was no need, but the words dried on his tongue. She was standing before him, eyes lowered, and his hand itched to cup her cheek, to run his thumb over her full lips and tease a smile back onto her mouth. The pretty ormolu clock on the mantel chimed, interrupting his thoughts.

His head came up. 'I should go. I promised to inform Lady Bettridge that His Lordship has gone to bed. Will you come to the drawing room now?'

'No, if Papa is not there, then I shall retire, too.'

He nodded and walked across to open the door for her. As she went to pass him, she paused.

'Goodnight, Lord Austerfield. I pray you will not re-fine too much upon finding me like this. It is nothing,

I assure you, and I should be obliged if you will put it from your mind.'

He inclined his head. 'Goodnight, Miss Bettridge. Sleep well.'

She smiled, but he could see it was an effort. Ross watched her hurry across the hall and up the stairs before making his way to the drawing room. Thank heaven he had stifled a sudden impulse to take her in his arms and comfort her. He was no chivalrous knight in armour who could ride to her rescue. He couldn't even save himself!

Having delivered his host's message, Ross remained in the drawing room until the tea tray was brought in, but he drank no more than one cup before making his excuses. He found Brisco waiting for him in his bedchamber.

'Well, Major, do we leave in the morning?'

'Are you so eager to quit this place, then?' Ross asked, unbuttoning his waistcoat.

'Makes no odds to me, but I thought you would be. You don't enjoy being toad-eaten.'

'Oh, Lord, is it that obvious?'

Brisco grinned. 'It's common knowledge below stairs that Her Ladyship is trying to leg-shackle you to one or t'other of her daughters. Miss Letitia or Miss Adelaide, that is.'

'And what do they say downstairs about that? I am sure they must have an opinion!'

'Aye, they do. Most says the sooner those two young ladies are wed the better it will be for Morwood. It seems they plague the life out of Miss Carenza Bettridge, who is little more than an unpaid servant for them all. According to Evans, His Lordship's man, it's

Miss Bettridge who keeps this house running. And a very good job she would do of it, too, if her stepmama wasn't forever contradicting her.'

'But how will marrying off the younger girls help Carenza?' asked Ross.

'Jealous of her, they are, because she is her father's favourite. Not that you'd think it to look at her. Perhaps you've noticed that Lady Bettridge loses no opportunity to give the poor young lady a set down. However, Grimshaw, Her Ladyship's dresser—who, by the bye, is universally disliked below stairs—holds that once the younger girls are established, Her Ladyship will be off to stay with them, or even to live in town, leaving Miss Bettridge to look after her father.'

Ross nodded. 'That seems an ideal solution, if they really do not get on.'

'Aye, although it seems a shame that such a pretty behaved young lady as Miss Bettridge should be hidden away, caring for her papa, when she could be at parties and the like.'

'Perhaps she does not enjoy parties,' argued Ross.

'Well, she will never know, will she, if she is stuck here looking after an invalid? But it does seem a waste. Evans says as how she sings, plays and dances like an angel, but with only her father to see.' Brisco picked up his master's shoes. 'What is it to be, Major, can I pack these away in the trunk now?'

'I am afraid not, Dan. I shall need them again tomorrow night.'

Brisco straightened and stood for a moment, staring at his master.

'Well, that has fair flummoxed me, and no mistake! I thought you'd have been keen to cut your stick with all haste.'

'Damn you, it's not that I *want* to stay! But having said I would remain for four days, I am committed. There is a real possibility too that Miss Bettridge will be held to blame if I, er, cut my stick a day early.'

Shaking his head, the valet went off and Ross climbed into bed. He blew out the candle and settled down, but sleep eluded him. It was hot in the room, and after an hour of tossing and turning he padded across to the window, where he pushed back the curtains and threw up the sash. A gibbous moon sailed high above, casting its silver blue light over the landscape. It was silent, peaceful and quite beautiful.

No wonder Carenza loved Morwood so much. The frown gathered on his brow again. Once old Lord Bettridge died it was not to be supposed that his successor, a distant relation, would want an unmarried spinster remaining at the manor, unless it was in the role of housekeeper. The alternative, as described by his host, was that she would have to live with her stepmother. Having witnessed the animosity between them, Ross did not think that would be very comfortable for her.

'Bah, what of it?' he muttered, returning to his bed. 'Miss Carenza Bettridge is not my responsibility!'

Opening the window had cooled the room sufficiently for Ross to fall asleep but it was not long before his rest was disturbed by dreams. That was not unusual, but this time it was not bloody scenes of violent combat. It was the peaceful woods near Auster. Carenza appeared before him, her eyes dark and anxious. He knew she needed his help but he turned away from her, pushing his way through the dense undergrowth. Only it wasn't bushes that snagged his clothes and tugged at his sleeves, it was hands. Small, female hands.

Letitia Bettridge and her sister were grabbing at his

coat-tails. There were other women, too, all clawing and clutching at him, holding him back, dragging him down. Then he was no longer in the wood but a ball-room, surrounded by grasping, predatory women trying to tear him apart. Looking over their heads he could see Carenza, silently watching him, reaching out to him, but growing ever further away.

Ross awoke in a cold sweat. Morning sunshine was already filling the room, but it could not dispel the lin-gering menace, or the familiar sense of despair, that made him feel physically sick. Even the entrance of Dan Brisco with his usual cheerful greeting failed to restore his spirits. With a groan Ross rolled over and buried his head in the pillow.

'Heavy night, my lord?' Brisco put the jug of hot water on the washstand and arranged the fresh towels over the rail. 'I didn't think you was in your cups when you came upstairs to bed. A bad bottle, perhaps. That and the heat. It has been oppressive all night. We're in for a storm later, if I'm not mistaken.'

'Well, it didn't happen yesterday, so you may well be wrong again!'

Ross passed a hand over his eyes. As the nightmare faded, so did the nausea, but he could not shake off the heavy cloud of depression that was wrapped about him. He watched Brisco drop something on the dress-ing table.

'What is that?'

'One of your handkerchiefs, my lord. It was lying on the floor outside your door when I came up just now. Freshly laundered and still warm from the iron.'

Ross remembered giving it to Carenza to wipe her cheeks. She had been crying and tried to pass it off as nothing, but there had been the same downward droop to her mouth and trouble darkening her eyes that he had seen in his dreams. By heaven, how he hated to see such unhappiness!

Do you, though? Lord Bettridge has suggested a way to help her, and yourself.

No! That was impossible. Wasn't it?

'I said, did you lose one yesterday, Major?'

'Hmm? Oh, yes, the handkerchief. I suppose I must have dropped it.'

Brisco accepted this without a murmur and turned to more pressing matters. He said, 'Shall I bring your coffee, my lord, or would you prefer small beer, it being so warm?'

'Nothing yet, thank you.' Ross threw back the covers. 'I am going for a walk. I need some fresh air.'

He needed to think.

Lord Austerfield did not appear at the breakfast table and Lady Bettridge reported to her daughters that he had been seen earlier, striding across the lawns in the direction of the Home Wood.

'And goodness knows how long he will be,' she ended, a note of dissatisfaction in her voice. 'This is your fault, miss!'

'Me?' Carenza looked up, startled.

'You ruined Letty's chances of receiving a proposal from His Lordship yesterday!'

'She's a minx,' hissed Letty. 'She was too busy flirting with him herself, in the garden!'

'If he is so easily distracted, then I wonder you should want to marry him,' said Carenza, goaded into a response.

'Carenza thinks she has a chance,' sneered Adelaide.

'That is why she is not wearing a cap today. As if hair as thick and black as a crow could ever be considered beautiful!'

'Conceited, arrogant girl,' exclaimed Lady Bettridge angrily.

Carenza kept her eyes on her plate as her stepmother gave vent to her frustration by ringing a peal over her. It was nothing she hadn't heard before—her lack of breeding, her ingratitude for all Lady Bettridge had done for her and the prophesy that she would come to a *Bad End*.

'When your father is no longer here do not look to me to support you,' she finished, waving her knife at Carenza. 'You will have your fifty pounds a year and not a penny more! To think I should have nurtured a viper in my bosom all these years,' she continued, buttering her toast with quick, angry movements. 'It is a pity the fever did not carry you off, along with your mother!'

Such callousness shocked Carenza but it also enraged her. She could feel the red mist descending. Letty and Adelaide waited, open-mouthed and eager for her to enter into battle royal with her stepmother. Fortunately, their obvious glee added to her resolve to fight down her anger.

She was not concerned about the retribution that might come her way from crossing swords with Lady Bettridge. It had happened on numerous occasions when she was younger, but now she realised how much it distressed Papa and she was determined not to inflame the situation. With a dignity she was far from feeling, Carenza rose from the table and walked silently out of the room.

Carefully closing the door behind her, she stood for a moment, one hand over her mouth, the other pressing on the door frame. She must steady her breathing and prevent the little seed of panic inside her taking root. Lady Bettridge had made it very clear to her that once Papa was gone, she would be obliged to fend for herself. Carenza had guessed for years that it would be the case, but to hear her stepmother declare it so openly and with Papa growing ever more frail, this morning's outburst had brought home to her just how precarious her position was at Morwood.

She glanced about her. She could not go to her father. He would see immediately that she was not herself and press her for an explanation. She remembered there were menus to plan for the coming week with Mrs Trudby. Afterwards they could spend a quiet hour drinking tea and discussing household matters. That would do the trick, she decided. After that she would be calm enough to face the world again.

Carenza had just emerged from the housekeeper's room when she saw her father's manservant coming in from a side door. It was so unusual to see him in this part of the house that she felt a sudden burst of alarm.

'Is anything amiss, Mr Evans, is my father not well?'

'On the contrary, Miss Carenza,' returned the valet, beaming at her. 'He is in fine fettle. He partook of a substantial luncheon, too, ma'am, and is currently resting, but he asked me to come down to the stables with a message to be carried to Mr Crossley. His Lordship wishes to see him this afternoon, and you know His Lordship rarely invites anyone to call!'

'Yes, yes, that is a very good sign,' she replied, relieved. 'I was about to slip upstairs to see him myself, but if he is resting, I shall wait until Mr Crossley has gone. Instead, I shall…'

Her words trailed away and Evans gave a little cough.

'If I might suggest a walk in the shrubbery, Miss Carenza?' He added, in a voice devoid of all emotion, 'I understand Lady Bettridge has retired to her room with the headache, and the other young ladies are engaged with their watercolours in the morning room. There may not be another opportunity to step out of doors again today,' he advised her. 'Fewston tells me his rheumatics is playing up, which invariably means there's a storm brewing.'

Her eyes twinkled. 'The shrubbery it shall be, then! Thank you, Evans.'

It was so warm she did not bother wasting time fetching a shawl but left the house by the same door Evans had just used, making her way through the kitchen gardens and into the formal grounds.

It did not take her long to reach the shrubbery. It was one of the original features of the garden and slightly neglected now, the serpentine walks bordered by encroaching branches of honeysuckle and sweet briars, laburnum and syringas. Its sheltered nature made it a pleasant walk at any time of the year but on warm days such as this it was particularly enjoyable with the scent from the flowers hanging heavy in the sultry air.

'A storm brewing,' she thought, taking a deep breath as she strolled along the grassy path. 'Yes, indeed there is. I must make the most of these quiet moments.'

Lady Bettridge would be furious when Lord Austerfield left Morwood tomorrow without making an offer for either Letty or Adelaide. She would be sure to find fault with everything and, with the exception of Grimshaw, every member of staff could expect to suffer her wrath.

It would not only be the servants. Carenza was well

aware that Her Ladyship's ire would also be directed towards herself. She would bear it, as she had done so many times before, and she would work with Evans, Hutton and Mrs Trudby to make sure Papa did not suffer. Indeed, most of the servants could be relied upon to rally round her father.

She drew in a long and impatient breath. 'Oh, how much better it would be if the Viscount had never come here!'

But even as the words left her mouth she knew she did not mean that. Papa had been much brighter since Lord Austerfield had arrived, and despite the trouble his presence had caused for her, Carenza would not have missed his visit for the world. He had been a breath of fresh air at Morwood. She had not realised how tedious life had become.

Lord Austerfield had shown her more kindness in the few days he had been here than she had received from anyone save Papa for many years. He had even loaned her a handkerchief to dry her tears! She had insisted on ironing it herself and indulged in a pleasant daydream while she did so, remembering his kind words, his gentle voice. She felt a little sorry that he was determined to remain a bachelor, but extremely glad he would not be marrying either of her half-sisters. They did not deserve such a man.

She was so caught up in her thoughts that she gave a violent start when she heard his familiar, deep voice behind her.

'I was told I should find you here.'

'Lord Austerfield!' Had she conjured the Viscount, merely by thinking of him? She swung around, her heart thudding like a hammer against her ribs. 'Oh, pray, go away, I c-cannot be seen with you!'

'But you will not be seen with me,' he reasoned. 'This garden is quite secluded.'

'That is the point! If Lady Bettridge learns of it I shall be in *such* trouble!'

She looked about her, half expecting to see her stepmother even now bearing down upon them. She was not, of course, but the Viscount was looking amused and Carenza said, crossly, 'You may find the situation comical, my lord, but I assure you it is not!'

He held up his hands. 'Calm yourself, I am here at your father's behest.'

'My father?' She looked up, momentarily arrested.

'Yes, he sent me to talk to you.' He gestured to the path. 'Shall we walk?'

Carenza assented with a slight nod and turned to walk beside him. He was on her left, so she could not see the scars, but he looked so serious that she felt another flutter of alarm, this time on his behalf.

'Is something wrong, my lord?'

'No. I hope not.'

He fell silent and they strolled on along the winding path. She noted that he was absently playing with his heavy signet ring, turning it round and round on his finger. As if he was nervous, which was clearly preposterous. He drew a breath.

'You are aware, Miss Bettridge, of my intention never to take a wife.'

'Not from Morwood Manor, certainly,' she said drily.

'Not from anywhere! After Waterloo, I made up my mind to remain a bachelor and saw no reason to change that decision when I became viscount. It is not as if the succession is in any danger. My cousin, Amos Paston, is my heir and he is already the father of two healthy sons.'

Carenza clasped her own hands together. Why was he telling her this?

She said, 'Do you not *want* a wife, my lord?'

There was a heartbeat's pause.

'My injuries, the disfigurement to my face and body, must be abhorrent to any lady of sensibility.'

'Not if she cared for you.'

'I think you are being naïve, Miss Bettridge. My face is bad enough, but the injuries to my body are worse. Much worse.'

'Oh,' she exclaimed, coming to a halt. 'Does that mean that you cannot have—' She broke off in confusion, her cheeks very red. 'I beg your pardon. I did not mean to pry!'

'I am still a man, and perfectly capable of fathering an heir,' he ground out, 'if that is what you wish to know, madam!'

She blushed even more fierily and put her hands over her face. 'Oh, dear, I should never—that is—it is none of my concern!'

'Pray do not distress yourself. It is something that must be addressed at some point, I suppose. Come let us continue to walk.'

Bewildered, Carenza fell into step again and after a moment he continued.

'Allow me to speak frankly, Miss Bettridge. I am well aware that many women are prepared to overlook my abhorrent defects in exchange for the advantages of becoming Lady Austerfield. Your half-sisters, for instance. Their play acting is very good, only occasionally do they allow the mask to slip and I see the shadow of distaste, of *revulsion*, behind the smiles.' His mouth twisted. 'I do not believe they would be able to keep up the pretence, especially in more…intimate moments.'

The idea of being *intimate* with the man walking beside her turned Carenza's insides to water. She closed her eyes as an unexpected frisson of pure pleasure ran through her body.

The Viscount cleared his throat.

'In the bedroom, for example,' he went on. 'That would be embarrassing for both parties.'

She was blushing, but not from any maidenly confusion that he should talk to her so openly. She was shocked by the quite scandalous thoughts that were buzzing around in her head. They were making it very difficult to concentrate.

'This is frank indeed,' she managed to say at last. 'But why are you telling me this, my lord?'

'I have only known you for a short time, but we get on well together, I think. You are a practical woman, and one of superior sense, too. I want you to understand the nature of the arrangement I am about to propose to you.'

'An arrangement!' She took a deep breath, trying to cool the heated imaginings running riot in her mind. She needed a clear head if she was to understand just what the Viscount was offering her. 'You said Papa sent you to talk to me. Does that mean he *knows* of this?

'Of course. I discussed the whole with him this morning. He has been fretting over what will happen to you, when he is no longer here to protect you. He thinks this arrangement would be the answer.'

'He…he does?' She breathed slowly, but it did little to daunt the sudden and unexpected seedling of hope growing inside. 'Are…are you offering me the post of *housekeeper*, my lord?'

He laughed. 'Good heavens, no! Your father would never countenance you becoming a mere servant! No,

Lord Bettridge knows what I am proposing is not ideal and a little unusual, but he is very concerned for your future, Carenza, and also conscious that your relationship with Lady Bettridge is not a happy one. He would like to make you independent but he does not have the means to set you up with a decent pension for life. I *do* have the means, however, and—'

She interrupted him.

'I pray you will say no more!' Her cheeks were hot again, but this time with indignation. 'Papa must have misunderstood you. I do not believe he would ever condone such a plan as you have in mind!' She drew in a deep breath and continued, in outraged accents. 'I may be on the edge of desperation, Lord Austerfield, but whatever plans I make for my future will not include becoming any man's mistress!'

He stared at her for a moment, then to her astonishment, he threw back his head and roared with laughter.

'Carenza, you ninny, that is not at all what I am suggesting!' He saw her shocked face and smiled at her. 'My sweet chucklehead, I want to *marry* you. To make you my viscountess!'

Chapter Eight

It was not the way Ross had intended to make his proposal. In fact, it was so far from perfect that he deserved the lady should slap his face. He quickly reached out and took her hands.

'I beg your pardon. I have been quite cow-handed with this, have I not?

'P-positively brutish,' she stuttered, still shaken off balance. 'I th-thought, when you said…'

'I know very well what you thought and can only apologise for not explaining properly.' They had reached the centre of the shrubbery, where an iron seat had been placed beneath a small arbour. 'You are trembling. Pray sit down and allow me to explain. Or at least, to try!'

Ross drew her gently towards the bench and they sat down, one at each end and leaving as much space as possible between them.

'What I was trying to tell you is that I have changed my mind about marriage,' he began, watching her carefully. 'You see, I am constantly hounded by matchmakers, even members of my own family. One can never relax for a moment. It was your father who pointed out it would not change, as long as I remained unmarried.

He thinks it not impossible for me to find a sensible lady who would agree to be my wife in name only. Someone who needs a home and the protection of my name and fortune. I can offer all that. And friendship, too, is not out of the question, I believe. I wondered, I very much hoped, Miss Bettridge, that *you* might consider such an offer?'

Carenza kept her head bowed. The indignant flush had died from her cheeks, leaving them very pale, but he had no idea what she was thinking. He pressed on.

'I spoke to your father this morning, to ask his permission to pay my addresses to you. He gave it readily, not only because he *wants* to see you comfortably settled, but he truly believes it would work. As Lady Austerfield you would be respected, you would have security for life and be mistress of your own house. Of several houses, in fact.'

'And what do you ask of me in return?' she enquired, not looking up.

'Loyalty, ma'am, and honesty. We shall neither of us give nor receive false protestations of undying love. It is to be a marriage of convenience, for our mutual benefit. There will be occasions when I shall need you to accompany me, but they will be infrequent. You know I have no intention of leading a very public life. It would be best if we both live at Auster, at least at the start, until any gossip about our marriage has died down. The house and grounds are large enough that we need not live in each other's pockets. I think we might rub along quite well together, but if you prefer to set up in one of the other properties, then I will not object. You shall have a generous allowance—your father's lawyers would ensure the settlements are favourable towards you. For the most part you would live your life very much as you please, within reason.'

She was studying her hands, which were clasped tightly in her lap.

'And what would you consider *un*reasonable, my lord?'

'Causing a scandal. Dragging my family name into disrepute by flaunting your love affairs in public.'

She said, in a low voice, 'You mean we might both do as we please, as long as we are discreet?'

'Why, yes. After a great deal of thought I have decided it is the only solution in a marriage such as I am proposing.' He suppressed any hint of disapproval in his tone. 'I have no intention of taking a mistress, but the world would not condemn me for doing so. It would hardly be reasonable for me to deny you the same freedom.'

Carenza kept her eyes lowered and thought hollowly that they might as easily have been discussing her employment as a housekeeper. She could not deny she had sometimes dreamed of finding a husband, but in her dreams the offer and acceptance were accompanied by joyful tears and declarations of eternal devotion. At five-and-twenty, she was well aware that her chances of finding such a suitor had dwindled almost to nothing, but she was not sure she was ready to accept such a sterile business arrangement as this.

Would she have been more tempted by his offer if Ross had pretended to be in love with her? She thought not. She respected him for his honesty. It was a sound basis for any future arrangement between them and what he was proposing would indeed solve the problem of what was to become of her. However, she could not ignore the tiny voice of caution in her head, warning that if she married the Viscount, she might be exchanging one form of unhappiness for another.

She said now, 'Thank you, my lord. I am very flattered by the honour that you do me, but I should like a little time to consider before I give you my answer.'

'Of course. I will not hurry you to make a decision. Is there more you would like to discuss now, or shall we return to the house?'

'I think I should like to talk to my father before we say anything further.'

The Viscount rose and held out his hand to her, smiling. 'Come along, then.'

The sky was still a clear blue as they walked back to the house, but it had become very close and a faint, ominous rumble of thunder stirred the air.

In her room, Carenza threw open the window but it made little difference. The oppressive heat had given her a headache. At least, she told herself it was the weather, and not the thoughts racing constantly around her mind. The Viscount's offer had been a shock and she was desperate to talk it over with her father, but Mr Crossley was still with Papa and she must wait until he had left Morwood.

She lay down on her bed and tried to consider her situation in a cool, logical manner. There was no doubt that marriage to Lord Austerfield would secure her future, but balanced against it was concern over her father. How would he go on without her? Even if Papa pressed her to accept the Viscount's offer, she would not even contemplate the idea until that question had been answered.

* * *

'Papa?' She peeped into his private sitting room. 'Evans said you were free to see me now. Are you too tired to talk, after Mr Crossley's visit?'

'No indeed, I am wonderfully restored by it.' He beckoned her to come in and she hurried across to take her place on the little stool beside his chair.

'Now,' he said, caressing her cheek and twinkling down at her. 'I believe you have some news for me?'

'Yes, I do, Papa.' She bit her lip. 'Lord Austerfield has made me an offer but I do not know what to do.'

'Now, why should that be?' he asked her gently. 'You are generally such a sensible little puss.'

Her smile was perfunctory. 'Well, for one thing, it is not a love match, Papa. How could it be, after such a short acquaintance?'

'It is rare, but not impossible, my love, I promise you. I fell head over heels in love with your mama the moment I saw her.' He sighed. 'It was at Truro. She was standing on the wagon along with all the others seeking work, but there was something different about her. She was so dignified and serene. I gazed into her beautiful dark eyes, so much like your own, and I knew she was the only one for me. At four-and-thirty I had not thought I should ever fall in love, but it only took one glance!'

There was a faraway look in his eyes as he related the familiar story. Carenza knew he was back in a time before she was born and she waited patiently until his gaze was focused upon her once more before she continued.

'I understand the Viscount's reasons for wishing to marry me, sir. He has explained it all very clearly to me and told me *exactly* what to expect.' She flushed slightly. 'He intends that…that we should never be more than friends.'

'And does the prospect disturb you, my love?'

She shook her head but looked away from him. It did disturb her, although not in any way that she could explain to her father. She liked Lord Austerfield, very much. She thought that might develop into something much warmer, in time, but it was unlikely her feelings would ever be reciprocated. The Viscount had told her he had no intention of taking a mistress, but would not any prospective suitor say as much? And if he did, she was not at all sure how she would cope.

She said carefully, 'I believe he is an honourable man, Papa.'

'And *I* believe he will do his best to make you happy,' he told her.

'I am sure of it,' she said miserably.

'My love, can it be that you do not like Lord Austerfield?'

'Oh, no, no. I like him very well. I respect him, too, which I believe to be equally important.'

'Then what is your dilemma?'

She felt the emotion welling up and eventually it burst out.

'I do not want to leave you, Papa! Who will look after you if I am not here? Who will keep you company, watch over your health, ensure that the dinners each night are to your taste? I have been thinking and thinking and decided that I cannot leave you here at Morwood!'

'My love—'

She put her hands on his knee and interrupted him. 'I thought, perhaps, Lord Austerfield might allow you to live with me. He has said I need not make my home at Auster with him and can choose from any of his properties—'

'That is very kind, very thoughtful, my love, but it would never do. Morwood has been my home for sixty years, I am too old to move now. And there is no need.' He caught her hands and shifted in his chair to face her. 'Carenza, I did you a disservice all those years ago when I took a second wife. I know now that I was still grieving for your mama and sought company and comfort in the arms of a pretty woman. Alas, I did not see it at the time, but Gertrude's beauty does not extend to her character. However, she has been a faithful wife to me and I have no complaint, except in regard to her treatment of you. I should have done more to prevent it.'

'No, no,' she cried, distressed. 'How could you have done so? When we were younger you tried to be fair to every member of your family. If we have grown apart since then it is not your fault. Indeed, until the Viscount arrived it was not so very bad, you know.'

'You have been bullied and browbeaten into the role of a servant, Carenza. Over the years you have taken more and more upon yourself and I know full well that it is you who keeps Morwood running so smoothly.'

'Yes, but I do not mind that, sir! I am very happy managing the household for you.'

'But my health is failing rapidly, Carenza. I cannot help but worry what will become of you when I am gone. If only I had given you your mother's jewels, you would have had something to sell, to buy your independence. Instead, like a love-struck fool, I passed them on to Gertrude! As it is, when I die you will have only your mama's coral necklace and the pearls I bought you when you turned one-and-twenty, plus a pittance each year to live on.'

He sat forward, reaching for her hands and clasping them tightly.

'My darling Carenza, you do not know how cruel the world can be to an impoverished gentlewoman. Let me urge you most strongly to think upon His Lordship's offer. He will make you a kind and considerate husband, I am sure. You will have wealth, position and consequence. You will have more comfort than I could ever give you.'

'But what of you, Papa? I cannot leave you here. I should be forever wondering if you are miserable.'

'Ah, now, I have been giving it some thought.' His brow cleared and he sat up straighter in his chair. 'I have Evans and Mrs Trudby and an army of loyal servants here who will ensure my comfort. With the exception of Grimshaw, their families have worked at Morwood for ever and their loyalty to me is beyond doubt. Your stepmama would have the greatest difficulty in removing them, even if she was unwise enough to try.

'When you go, I shall retire to the east wing and leave Gertrude to live and entertain in the rest of the house, although for the next year or so she will be busy taking the girls out and about as she tries to find husbands for them. After that, I think she may well prefer to hire a house in London rather than remain buried here in the country. Your stepmother may do as she pleases, with my blessing. And I have thought, you know, that once you are married, I would invite Hubert Crossley to take up residence here. There is ample room for him here in the east wing. I have already mentioned the idea and he is all in favour of it. We would be company for one another. So, you see, my love, I shall go on very comfortably here.'

'You make a convincing case,' she said, smiling a little.

'The matter of your future has been on my mind for

some time now. I am aware that you do not get on with your stepmother.'

'I have *tried*, Papa, truly,' she told him earnestly. 'And I do not blame her for wanting to find good husbands for Letty and Adelaide. Any mother would want the best for her children, but she believes I wish to thwart her at every turn and it is not true. I promise you, I do my best to please her, even though...even though we cannot like one another.'

Her father sighed. 'Gertrude is not a bad woman, my love. I believe her dislike of you springs from jealousy, although heaven knows I have done my best to treat you all equally. Once you are married there will be no need for her to try to cut up my peace.' A sudden twinkle appeared in his eyes. 'And she has every incentive to keep me alive, because once I am gone, she will have to vacate this house and live on what little I can leave her! You see, my dear, I am being quite selfish when I urge you to take the Viscount's offer. What do you say?'

It was nearing the dinner hour and the thunder that had been rolling around all afternoon sounded much closer as Ross left his bedchamber. He paused for a moment in the corridor, waiting for a crash that never came. Then he gave his head a little shake and forced himself to walk on.

He was descending the final few stairs when Carenza appeared in the hall and begged for a few moments in private with him.

'Of course.'

Ross followed her into the morning room, feeling unusually apprehensive. He was unable to decide if he most wanted her to accept or to reject his offer. She was looking so nervous that he buried his own doubts and smiled at her, saying as he closed the door upon them,

'I hope, Miss Bettridge, that you have made a decision in my favour.'

One dainty hand fluttered. 'Will you not be seated, my lord?'

Did that signify a yea or a nay? He moved to a chair opposite the one she had chosen and waited in silence for her to continue. She wore a single string of pearls around her throat but even so she looked particularly severe, her grey silk gown more suited to a governess than a young lady about to be married. Perhaps she was going to refuse him, after all. Ross was surprised he did not feel more relief at the thought.

'My lord.' She folded her hands in her lap. 'I have discussed the matter with Papa and I am minded to accept your offer. However, before you commit yourself irrevocably, it is important you know a little more about me.' She added, a touch of bitterness in her voice, 'If *I* do not tell you, someone else is sure to do so.'

'Lady Bettridge, perhaps?'

Her shoulders lifted a fraction and fell again, but she made no answer to that.

'You may have wondered why I look so different from the rest of my family,' she said. 'I inherited my dark eyes and hair from my mother. She was a Cornishwoman, but of Spanish descent.'

She stopped, waiting for a response, and he said lightly, 'I see nothing reprehensible in that.'

His words won no answering smile.

'Some say Papa married beneath him. That Mama bewitched him. He saw her first at a mop fair in Truro and hired her for his housekeeper, but by the time they arrived back at Morwood they were betrothed. Papa says they spent seven blissful years together. I barely remember her: I was but four years old when she fell sick and died.'

'I am very sorry,' he murmured. 'I believe your life would have been very different, had your mother lived.'

She acknowledged this with a little nod. 'Papa says my mother always maintained she was of gentle birth, a good family that fell upon hard times. It never mattered to him and it has never troubled me, until now.' She looked up and met his eyes. 'It is not the noble lineage your family will require in a bride.'

'But my family are not choosing my bride. If I am satisfied that you will make an admirable viscountess, then that is all there is to it.' He rose and went over to her, taking her hands and coaxing her to stand. 'Now, Miss Bettridge. Carenza. Will you do me the honour of becoming my wife?'

He felt her tremble and instinctively his grip tightened. He wanted to protect her, but it was his scarred face that was upsetting her and how could he ever protect her from that?

'I beg your pardon!' He dropped her hands and turned away. 'I had quite forgot how difficult my hideous visage must make this for you!'

He strode to the window, staring out at the storm clouds billowing up in the west, black as the mood that was swiftly descending upon him. He was a monster to inflict this upon her. How could she be expected to accept his offer? He should leave, go back to his room and stay there until he could quit this house and return to Auster.

He felt a hand on his shoulder. Under its insistent pressure, he turned back. Carenza was standing very close, gazing up at him quite steadily.

'I do not see the scars when I look at you, my lord,' she said quietly. 'I see a good, kind, honourable man whom I would be proud to call husband.'

Her words banished the darkness and his heart leapt. He wanted to laugh aloud with pure joy, but he only allowed himself to believe for a fleeting moment that she meant it. She was merely being kind, but he appreciated it, enormously. He wanted to pull her into his arms and kiss her, but fear of seeing the horror in her eyes held him back. He contented himself by placing a chaste salute upon her fingers.

'Thank you. But there must be no misunderstanding. Tell me plain, are you accepting my offer?'

'Why, yes, my lord, I am.'

She sounded nervous and he watched, fascinated, as she ran her tongue over her lips. How would it feel to kiss that sensuous mouth, or to have those red lips pressing kisses on his skin? He was still grasping her hand and he quickly dropped it. These thoughts, these feelings, had no place in his plans!

'Excellent.' The word came out as a croak and he cleared his throat. 'I believe we shall deal very well together.' He pulled her hand onto his arm and managed to say with a smile, 'Shall we break the news to your family? Best to get over that hurdle as soon as possible, don't you think?'

Chapter Nine

What have I done?

The question rattled through Carenza's head as she accompanied the Viscount to the drawing room. She was finding it difficult to move one foot in front of the other, and suddenly thought the condemned must feel like this, on their walk to the gallows.

The family were all present, awaiting the call to dinner. The windows had been thrown wide but the heat was still oppressive. Lady Bettridge was waving her fan vigorously and her two daughters were wilting on the sofa, although they sat up when the door opened.

Carenza's eyes went first to her father, who was sitting in his usual chair. He looked a question, to which she gave the faintest nod, and was comforted by the beaming smile that spread across his features. Only then did she turn her attention to the rest of the room.

Her stepmother had stopped fanning herself, Letty and Adelaide were sitting bolt upright and all three of them were staring to see Carenza come in on the Viscount's arm.

'Ah, Lord Austerfield.' Her father struggled to his

feet. 'Come in, sir, come in! I believe there is something you wish to say.'

'There is, sir.' The Viscount paused. 'I am delighted to tell you that Miss Bettridge has consented to become my wife.'

At that moment lightning flashed, accompanied by a crash of thunder. It almost drowned out the screech from Lady Bettridge, who jumped to her feet.

'Your *what*!'

Beside her, the Viscount froze and Carenza glanced up quickly. His face was very pale, his eyes glittering, and she said anxiously, 'My lord?'

He seemed to recollect himself and gave her a little smile before turning to her father, who had come up to congratulate them.

'What is the meaning of this?' demanded Lady Bettridge, her bosom quivering.

'I would have thought it quite obvious, my dear,' replied her husband. 'Lord Austerfield has proposed to Carenza and she has accepted him.'

'That's impossible!' shrieked Letitia. 'She shan't have him!'

A cuff around the ear from her mother silenced her.

'Well, well, she is to be congratulated, to be sure,' declared Lady Bettridge, a strained smile fixed on her thin lips. 'But this is very sudden.'

'Yes, isn't it?' The Viscount appeared to have recovered himself and replied quite cheerfully. He put his free hand over Carenza's, which was clinging to his sleeve. 'I count myself honoured that Miss Bettridge has accepted my offer.'

There was a stifled squeal of rage from Adelaide but Carenza kept her eyes fixed upon her father, who really did look delighted by the news. He even insisted on taking his wife's arm to go into dinner, so that the Viscount could escort his fiancée.

There was no more thunder, but heavy rain began to lash the house as they crossed the hall. Carenza thought one might put the atmosphere at dinner down to the violent storm raging outside, but she knew that equally violent emotions were at work inside the dining room. Lady Bettridge kept a smile on her face and tried to maintain a little social chitchat, but Letty ate her food in sulky silence while Adelaide scowled across the table at her half-sister. Carenza knew that look of old and waited for an attack.

It came just after the servants had removed the chicken fricassee and hare collops and replaced them with the second course, which included roast duckling and artichoke bottoms, chosen especially by Carenza because they were her father's favourite.

The Viscount was behaving like an attentive suitor and helping Carenza to a small portion of the apricot compote when Adelaide addressed him.

'My lord, has Carenza told you about her mama? No one knows her lineage, of course, but families often make up stories of having noble ancestors, do they not? The truth is usually something far more scandalous.'

It was a calculated insult. Carenza saw her father frown, but the Viscount only smiled.

'Yes, Carenza has told me the tale,' he said easily. 'I can well believe she is descended from Spanish royalty. I myself saw many highborn ladies very like your sister when I was in the Peninsula. However, I should be equally delighted to discover her ancestors were Barbary pirates.'

Her father laughed gently. 'Nothing quite so romantic. I understand Carenza's grandfather met and married a Spanish lady. All quite respectable.'

'Your foreign looks will draw a great deal of attention when you are presented, Carenza,' remarked Letitia with a false smile. 'It is a pity you should be so *swarthy*, when the fashion is for skin as white as milk.'

Carenza's confidence wavered but the Viscount only laughed.

'Your sister will certainly attract notice, Miss Letitia. Beautiful women always do. I cannot wait to show her off at Court, where I have no doubt she will do me great credit. And there are other advantages to having such exquisite colouring, you know. We shall be spending most of our time in the country and she will not suffer any ill effects from the strong sunshine, when we ride out together.' He turned to smile at Carenza. 'That is, I hope you can ride? I am impatient to show you Auster, my dear, and it is much better seen from horseback than in a carriage.'

'Yes, I ride, my lord, and shall look forward to you showing me every inch of it,' she replied, smiling back at him.

It was all a game, she knew that. A happy charade for the benefit of her family, but the way he defended her was cheering.

When it was time to withdraw, Lady Bettridge rose from the table and escorted the three younger ladies from the room. As they walked across the hall, Carenza felt the air fairly crackling with anger and she braced herself for what was to come. No sooner had the drawing room door closed upon them than Lady Bettridge turned upon her.

'Well, miss, I hope you are pleased with yourself! I

blush to think what tricks you used to snare His Lordship.'

'None, ma'am, I assure you.'

Letitia broke in. 'The scheming hussy has been lying
in wait for him, taking every opportunity to insinuate
herself!'

'Yes, the sly little cat,' hissed Adelaide. 'She stole
him from under our noses!'

Carenza had expected them to be angry. They were
disappointed and she could understand that, so she tried
to be patient.

'There was nothing to steal,' she replied calmly.
'Lord Austerfield had no intention of making an offer
to anyone when he came here.'

Letty gave a little scream and stamped her foot. 'That
is not true! He was most attentive at Almack's. Is that
not so, Mama?'

'Yes, my love, it is. Why, he almost begged me for an
invitation!' Lady Bettridge rounded on Carenza again.
'And why would he come here, if not to propose?'

'His family has been pressing him to take a wife, but
he really did not want one.'

Letitia pounced on the words immediately. 'Then
why has he offered for you?'

Because he feels sorry for me.

'He has known you for less than a week!' exclaimed
Adelaide. 'He cannot have fallen in love with you.'

'I know that,' Carenza replied quietly.

'It must be expediency,' Lady Bettridge declared.
Her eyes narrowed. 'Yes, that's it. He must marry, so
he has chosen a dowdy, mouse-like creature whom he
can bury at Auster.'

'He will set up a mistress before the year is out,' said

Letitia, tittering. 'How will it be then, Carenza, to have your nose put out of joint by a lightskirt?'

Carenza hunched a shoulder and turned away. She would not engage in their petty quarrel. Letitia caught her arm.

'You little wretch! You have always thought yourself superior to Mama, and to us! How dare you flaunt yourself in front of Lord Austerfield.'

'You are being ridiculous,' she retorted, pulling free.

Her scorn infuriated Letty, who flew at her, grabbing at her hair and tearing it from its neat braid. Carenza pushed her away, but as she did so Letty's fingers caught her necklace, breaking the string and sending pearls flying in all directions.

And at this inauspicious moment, the gentlemen came in.

Following his host into the room, Ross took in the scene at a glance. Carenza's hair was in a tangle around her shoulders and the scratches even more evident on her pale cheek as she watched in dismay the pearls dancing across the floor. Letty glowered mutinously while her sister looked on in ill-concealed glee. However, it was the expression on Lady Bettridge's features that concerned him most. There was no mistaking the malice with which she regarded her stepdaughter.

'What is going on?' demanded Lord Bettridge, his tone unusually severe. 'What has happened here, madam?'

Ross guessed exactly what had occurred and was about to say so when Carenza's beseeching look made him pause. He remembered how anxious she was about her father's health and held his tongue. For her sake.

Lady Bettridge gave a little laugh. 'It was nothing

more than high spirits, my lord. You know what girls are like when they are excited. It was a little accident, nothing more.'

She waved to her daughters, ordering them to help Carenza pick up the pearls.

'We can use this to hold them all,' suggested Ross, taking out a fresh handkerchief which he unfolded and held between his hands. When all the errant pearls had been dropped into it, he tied the corners together to form a little pouch. 'You see how useful a clean handkerchief can be, Miss Bettridge.'

Carenza's eyes flew to his. She understood him. A shy twinkle put to rout the troubled look, but when she tried to take the makeshift bag, he stepped back and pushed it into his pocket.

'I shall have them restrung for you.'

She smiled at him. 'Thank you, my lord.'

Not only would he get them restrung, he decided, he would buy matching drops for her ears, too. Anything to see her smile at him again.

Lord Bettridge interrupted his thoughts, saying heavily, 'My lord, I must apologise for the shameful behaviour of my younger daughters.'

It was clear the old man was seriously displeased. He dismissed Letitia and Adelaide, who stammered their goodnights and hurried away, faces flaming. Lady Bettridge, visibly smarting from this unwonted harshness towards her darlings, bade the Viscount an icy goodnight and followed them out of the door.

Carenza took her father's arm and guided him to his chair. 'I am sorry, Papa. I never meant to distress you.' She glanced at Ross. 'And you, too, my lord. I am very sorry you had to witness such a scene.'

'I confess I did not expect them to react quite so violently,' muttered Lord Bettridge. 'I am quite ashamed of them.'

Ross put up a hand. 'They are not entirely to blame,' he said. 'By coming to Morwood, I raised expectations that have been most cruelly dashed. As soon as I realised my mistake I should have left. Or at the very least made the position clear.'

'I doubt they would have believed you, unless you had been blunt to the point of rudeness,' Carenza told him. She touched her hair and gave a little start.

'Heavens, I am not fit to be seen! I shall bid you both goodnight, sirs.'

She kissed her father's cheek, and as she passed Ross, he hoped she might do the same to him. She merely nodded, and he was surprised at the strength of his disappointment.

'Perhaps I should retire, too, sir,' he said, when she had gone. 'This evening has been rather eventful and I have no doubt you are fatigued.'

'Not at all. In fact, I would be obliged if you would take wine with me, Lord Austerfield.'

Even as he was speaking, the butler came in with a decanter and glasses and announced, his voice and countenance devoid of all emotion, that he surmised it might be more acceptable to Their Lordships than tea.

'Indeed, it is, Hutton,' replied Lord Bettridge. 'Leave the wine on the sideboard. Lord Austerfield shall pour it.'

'Very good, m'lord. And you might wish to know, sir, that Mrs Trudby has made up a bed for the maid in Miss Carenza's room.'

'Yes, yes. Good idea, Hutton.'

Ross was busy with the wine and, once the butler

had made his stately way out of the room, he carried a glass across to his host.

'Am I to understand from the housekeeper's actions that I am now considered a threat to your daughter?' he asked bluntly.

'Not you, my lord. The servants have got wind of the little contretemps that has occurred and are taking steps to prevent any further mischief. It is not the first time, I'm afraid. Never anything too serious, just pranks, you know. But if the younger girls put their minds to it, they can make Carenza's life uncomfortable.'

'Then the sooner I take her away from here the better.'

'I admit the violence shown towards Carenza this evening has surprised me. It is as if they actively dislike her.' Lord Bettridge was hunched in his chair, his face creased with dismay. 'I confess I had not realised the depths of their animosity. I removed all signs of my first wife from Morwood when Gertrude came to live here to avoid causing her distress. I tried not to have favourites amongst the girls and treated them all the same. Save that Carenza never had a come-out. I fell ill soon after she left the schoolroom, you see, and she refused to contemplate being presented. She insisted on staying here to nurse me, and after that, there never seemed to be a convenient time. Now I wonder if I could ever have persuaded Gertrude to bring her out.'

'It seems unlikely, given the hostility I witnessed here tonight.' Ross drew up a chair and sat down near his host. 'The question is, sir, what are we going to do about it?

Chapter Ten

'Good morning, Miss Carenza. It is going to be a lovely day, and that's a fact.' Mrs Trudby came into the bedchamber, crockery rattling on the tray she was carrying.

Carenza opened her eyes, her heart missing a beat. It was her wedding day. Just over a week ago she had accepted Lord Austerfield's offer, and since then everything had happened at such speed that she was still reeling at the thought of it all.

The reason given for a quiet wedding, and such a hasty one, was Papa's health. Mr Crossley helped to arrange the licence so they might be married at the parish church without the banns being read and, directly after the wedding breakfast, the newlyweds were to leave for Auster.

She sat up and looked about her as the housekeeper placed the tray on her lap. This was the last time she would sleep in this bed. The last time she would see Morwood or her father for many months. Later today she would be going off to Devon with a man she had known for little over a week. Her stomach turned over at the thought.

'Mrs Trudby, I do not think I can eat or drink anything this morning.'

The housekeeper gave her a searching look, then she put the tray on a side table and came to sit on the edge of the bed.

'This is just nerves, my dear,' she said, giving Carenza a motherly smile. 'Perfectly understandable on your wedding day.'

'But it has happened so quickly! What if it is all a mistake? What if—'

'Now, now, my love, it's not like you to get into a taking. Your father thinks this is the right thing for you and you can be sure he would only ever want your happiness.'

'I know that, Mrs Trudby, but what about *his* happiness? I cannot bear to think of Papa being uncomfortable.'

'Now don't you be worrying yourself about that, Miss Carenza. His Lordship will be very happy in the east wing and, between us, Evans and I will make sure he is well looked after. Also, he will have Mr Crossley living here soon to keep him company. What could be better than that?'

Carenza sighed. The housekeeper squeezed her fingers.

'My dear, 'tis my belief that Lord Bettridge will sleep much easier at night, knowing that you are settled in your own home, with a good man to look after you.'

'But how do we know the Viscount is a good man?' she persisted. 'We had never heard of him before Lady Bettridge invited him to stay!'

'Lord, but you're in a rare panic, and no mistake!' Mrs Trudby chuckled. 'A body can tell a great deal about a man from the way he treats others, especially those of a lower standing, my dear. I've heard no complaints about Viscount Austerfield below stairs, and that's a fact. Now.' She picked up the tray again. 'You'd best eat that toast and drink your tea before it grows cold, Miss Carenza!'

The clock was striking eleven when Carenza joined her father in the hall, ready for the short carriage journey to the church. She was wearing a gown of her mother's that had been packed away in an old box along with a host of other clothes. It had lain forgotten in one of the attics, until the housekeeper had remembered it three days ago. The ivory satin dress was too plain for current fashion, but it fitted Carenza's figure perfectly, so she had worked through the night with Mrs Trudby and Hetty, remaking a petticoat of silver gauze into an overdress and adding a deep flounce of Brussels lace to the skirts. Knots of ivory ribbon were sewn on to the sleeves and matching ribbons threaded through her thick black curls.

Lord Bettridge was waiting for her at the bottom of the stairs. His blue coat with its gold buttons hung a little loose about him, for the years of illness had taken their toll, but Carenza was heartened by his smile and the proud set to his shoulders when he saw her.

'You look enchanting, my dear.' He held out his hand to her and she saw him blink. 'So very like your dear mother.'

'Thank you, Papa.' She stretched up to kiss his cheek.

'Everyone has gone ahead to the church,' he said, pulling her hand onto his arm. 'Our carriage is at the door, shall we go?'

* * *

Ross tugged at his cuffs. From the tower above came the joyful peal of bells, while the crowded little church thrummed with anticipation. He had asked himself more than once this morning what the devil he was doing, offering marriage to a woman he barely knew. How in heaven's name had he convinced himself that this was a solution to his problems as well as hers? The unhappiness of her situation had touched his heart, but it was not only that he hated the idea of walking away and leaving her to the mercy of her uncaring family, he liked the lady. He enjoyed her conversation. She had wit and intelligence, when she was not cowed by her stepmother. Of all the women he had met, he thought he could bear her company more than any other. Damnation, that was insufficient reason to offer marriage! He put his hand up to his neckcloth, which suddenly felt suffocatingly tight. Too late to go back now.

A sudden commotion at the door and murmured voices made him swing around, thinking the bride had arrived. He was astonished to see his sister sailing up the nave in a flurry of lavender cambric and ostrich feathers.

'What the devil are you doing here?' he said sternly as she slipped into the empty pew directly behind him.

'I wanted to assure myself this was really happening,' Dido whispered. 'When I showed your letter to Beatrix, she thought it might be all a hum, to keep us off your back, so I set off post-haste to see it for myself!'

He scowled at her. 'Then I wish I had not written until after the event!'

Beside him, Brisco, whom he had brought with him as his groomsman, gave a little cough.

'She's here, m'lord.'

Ross forgot all about his sister and looked towards the church door. Carenza and her father were no more than black shapes against the sunlight, but as they came closer, he caught his breath.

The bride was dressed in a glistening, creamy gown with a clinging bodice that accentuated her full breasts. One dainty hand rested on her father's arm, the other clasped a small bouquet of ivory roses. She was a little pale, but perfectly composed, her dark eyes large and luminous in the heart-shaped face.

She came closer, her skirts shimmering and swaying with every step. By heaven, she was beautiful! Why had he never noticed that? He had never looked beyond the matronly cap and ill-fitting clothes, but as he gazed now at this lovely exotic creature, desire slammed through him, followed quickly by dismay.

A marriage in name only. Friends. Separate rooms. Separate lives. How the *devil* was he ever to keep those promises he had made her?

It is like a dream, thought Carenza. To be married on a summer's day, in her village church and surrounded by so many familiar faces. Who could want more? The feeling of unreality persisted throughout the service. She made her vows in a calm, clear voice and watched with detached interest as the Viscount placed the ring upon her finger. It was not until she emerged from the church that the enormity of what had happened rushed in on her.

'Steady now,' murmured the Viscount as she suddenly clung to his arm.

She summoned up a smile for him. 'It is nothing, a momentary spasm of nerves. I am quite well now.'

There was no time for more. The villagers were pouring out of the church, all wanting to congratulate the bride and groom. Carenza was glad of Lord Austerfield's support as she smiled and said all that was necessary. Lady Bettridge bustled up, her daughters at her side. In the days before the wedding they had ceased their hostilities, realising the advantages of being related to a viscountess and they each came forward to kiss her cheek.

'I hope you will not forget us, now that you are a great lady,' declared Lady Bettridge, with an arch smile.

'I do not think I could ever forget you,' she replied with perfect honesty.

She heard Ross give a little choke of laughter, which he quickly turned into a cough before drawing her attention to the tall, fashionably dressed matron in a lavender gown standing beside him. He introduced her as his sister and Carenza found herself being drawn into a scented embrace.

'My dear, I am all astonishment and delight to meet you. Come and tell me something about yourself!'

Ross could only watch as Dido walked off with his bride, because Lord Bettridge was waiting to introduce him to more of his neighbours. It was a full ten minutes before he could return to Carenza.

'I have just left your father,' he said, drawing her away from the little crowd. 'He wanted me to inform you he is going back to the house now.'

'Yes, of course. Thank you. I have invited your sister to join us for the wedding breakfast.'

'The devil you have!'

She shook her head. 'It will be no trouble to set another place at the table.'

'Damned impudence, Dido turning up like that.'

'It is only natural she should want to see you mar-

ried. I was very glad to meet her.' She tucked her arm
in his. 'I think we should be going back, too. The servants will be wanting to serve the meal.'

'The sooner that is over and we can be on our way
to Auster the better,' he muttered. 'I have had quite
enough of strangers gawping and goggling at my face
as if I was part of a freak show!'

'It is not your *face* that makes the villagers gawp at
you,' she replied, her eyes full of mischief. 'You might
have two heads for all they care. Your novelty is that you
are a viscount, and they have never seen one before!'

He gave a crack of laughter. 'By heaven, I hadn't
thought of that!'

'No, you were too busy feeling sorry for yourself.'

He was taken aback at that. 'You have burst that bubble of self-pity most effectively, ma'am!'

'I am glad. You are much better company when you
are cheerful.'

He stared at her smiling face, confounded by the
mixture of wrath and laughter swirling within him.
What the devil did she know of his troubles, what *right*
had she to tease him?

But as he escorted her away from the church, he
walked with his head just a little higher.

The slowing of the chaise woke Carenza. She opened
her eyes and sat up. Her maid was sitting opposite, her
face a pale oval in the darkness, but through the window she could see the glow of torches. The door opened
and Ross held out his hand to her.

'Welcome to Auster, my lady.'

His black outline filled the doorway, a wide brimmed
hat shadowing his face and his broad shoulders en-
hanced by the caped driving coat. Fighting down a sud-

den attack of nerves, Carenza took his hand and allowed him to guide her down the steps. After so many hours in the swaying carriage her limbs were stiff and she took a moment to steady herself.

The torchlight showed they were on the gravelled drive of a large, stone-built house. Two short flights of balustraded steps led up to a terrace, where the main door had been thrown wide and welcome light spilled out.

There was considerable bustle. Ross's curricle was already being driven away and servants were unloading trunks and baggage from the large travelling carriage that had followed them all the way from Morwood.

Ross guided her up a short flight of steps to the door, where a black-suited figure was waiting for them. Ross presented him to Carenza as Stoke, the butler, before leading her on to the drawing room. She was too tired to notice much except the welcome fire burning in the hearth.

'Oh, how comforting,' she exclaimed, moving towards it. 'I am very glad to see this, although I know one should not need a fire in July.'

'Not in Hampshire, perhaps,' he replied, stripping off his gloves, 'but here on the North Devon coast a fire is welcome almost any evening, except on the very warmest days.'

He removed the travelling cloak from her shoulders and she sank down on one of the chairs flanking the fireplace, holding out her hands to the flames. Not that she was cold, but nervous. Morwood seemed a lifetime away and all she could remember was endless hours in the swaying carriage. Ross had made the journey in his curricle, but she had not been alone; Hetty had accompanied her, overjoyed to be promoted to lady's maid.

'You must be exhausted from your journey,' said Ross. 'I am sure you want nothing more than to retire to your bed, but we must give your maid time to prepare.'

'Yes, of course.'

She smiled and accepted a glass of wine from him, thinking how considerate he was, how keen to ensure her comfort. It had been the same at each of the stops *en route*. Ross had sent his man ahead to bespeak a private parlour and separate bedchambers, but despite his best efforts to put her at her ease, there had always been dinner to negotiate and a little polite conversation before she retired and fell into a deep, exhausted sleep.

'Would you like supper?' he asked her now.

'No, thank you. I had sufficient when we stopped to dine on the road.'

He dropped into the chair opposite and another awkward silence developed. They sipped at their wine, looked into the fire, studied their hands. The Viscount cleared his throat.

'It will get easier.'

She looked up. 'I beg your pardon?'

'Living together, in the same house. It will become more comfortable, once we are accustomed to each other's company.'

'Yes. Of course.'

Carenza had finished her wine and she carried her empty glass over to the sideboard. She stood there for a moment, looking at the decanter and glasses.

'We were never this ill at ease at Morwood,' she said. 'Before you... Before we...'

'This is uncharted territory for both of us.'

She heard him approach and turned to face him.

He said, 'I want you to be happy here at Auster.'

'Thank you, my lord.'

'Ross,' he corrected, reaching for her hand. 'I believe we are friends enough for first-name terms. Are we not, Carenza?'

She jumped at his touch. Her heart began to race, thudding against her ribs as he rubbed his thumb gently over her wrist. He was smiling down at her and for one frightening, wonderful, heart-stopping moment she thought he would kiss her. The thought made her blush hotly and pull her hand free, even though she was aching for him to do just that.

Before either of them could speak, the door opened and a woman came in. Her black stuff gown and the white cap over her grey hair suggested she was an upper servant.

Ross said easily, 'Here is our housekeeper come to escort you upstairs, my lady. You received my message, Mrs Stoke, regarding the bedchambers?'

'I did, my lord, and everything is prepared as you instructed.' The old woman turned a beaming smile upon Carenza. 'Your maid is waiting in your room for you, ma'am.'

It was the excuse she needed to leave, but she hesitated, wondering if Ross would think she was running away from him. As if reading her mind he took her hand again and raised it to his lips.

'Off you go, my dear. Sleep well.'

Murmuring something incomprehensible, Carenza followed the housekeeper out of the room. She felt hot, troubled and very sure that the last thing she would do tonight was sleep.

Surprisingly, Carenza awoke the next morning feeling refreshed and optimistic. She lay very still for a while, enjoying the sense of well-being. The sunshine

undoubtedly contributed towards her happy mood, as
did the luxurious bed that had allowed her such a good
night's sleep. Also, the warmth of her welcome yesterday and the kindness with which the housekeeper had
received her had certainly helped.

But it was not only the comfortable surroundings,
it was the Viscount's forbearance. He had told her at
the outset how it would be and he was keeping to his
word. Last night she had been shown to a sumptuously
appointed bedchamber, where Mrs Stoke had handed
her a key to the door.

'There is no other way in or out of this room, ma'am.
His Lordship was anxious that you should be assured of
that,' the housekeeper had told her. 'He said I was to be
sure you understood that no one will trouble you here.'

Ross meant that *he* would not trouble her here, and
Carenza was touched by his thoughtfulness. She was
no innocent, even though she had lived all her life at
Morwood. She knew that marriage was an institution
many women endured rather than enjoyed.

Being an old maid, and of no consequence to her
stepmama, Carenza's presence in the corner of a room,
engaged with a book or at her sewing, often went unnoticed when Lady Bettridge was entertaining her friends
at Morwood. Whenever her daughters were not present,
the conversation became much more free, ranging from
the latest scandals to the delicate matters that beset married ladies. From these conversations Carenza learned
a great deal about the tribulations of the married state.
There were of course the advantages of position, security and, if one was fortunate, a generous allowance of
pin money at one's disposal, but the consensus amongst
Lady Bettridge's friends appeared to be that sharing

the marriage bed was at best inconvenient and uncomfortable. At worst, it could be painful and humiliating.

No, thought Carenza, throwing back the covers, she could very well do without that side of the marriage contract.

She dressed quickly and went downstairs, eager to explore her new home. Even the meagre selection of gowns she had brought with her could not dampen her mood, and she was further heartened by Hetty's approval of the household. The young woman had been nervous to be moving so far from her home and family, but she reported to her mistress that although she found the Devon accent a little difficult to understand, everyone was very friendly and treated her with the respect due to her as Her Ladyship's maid.

Dressed in the grey gown which she considered the most suitable of her morning dresses for a viscountess, Carenza went downstairs to the small parlour, where she found Ross already at the breakfast table. He rose as she entered and escorted her to her seat.

'I trust you slept well, ma'am?'

'I did indeed,' she assured him and it was true, although sleep had been a long time coming.

The key sitting snugly in the lock was reassuring, but it made her feel ashamed of her behaviour in the drawing room, that moment when the Viscount had smiled at her and she had reacted as if she had been scalded. She was so unused to receiving kindness from anyone save Papa that she had behaved most foolishly over a trifle. Having finally decided that Ross had only been trying to put her at her ease she went off to sleep, full of optimism for the future.

'I am glad of it,' said Ross. 'I am glad, too, that you have taken my suggestion and left off your caps.'

'I believe it was more of a command than a suggestion,' she murmured, keeping her eyes downcast. 'You said you'd be damned if you'd have your wife looking like a dowd.'

He laughed. 'Did I say that? I beg your pardon, but I am not one for pretty speeches.'

'No. I have come to realise that. Caps are *de rigueur* for married women, my lord, but I am happy to oblige, if you truly do not like them.'

'I don't. You have glorious hair, and I like to see it.'

She blushed at the compliment but decided it would be safer to talk of something else.

They chatted amicably over breakfast and afterwards she went off to meet with Mrs Stoke for a tour of the house. The housekeeper was quite ready to hand over all her keys but Carenza refused, saying with a smile that she would prefer to leave the running of the house in Mrs Stoke's capable hands.

'Lord Austerfield's comfort is paramount,' said Carenza. 'There is so much I have to learn that, for the present at least, things will run much more smoothly if you are in charge.'

She could not have said anything better. Relief was writ large in the older woman's countenance and she promised every assistance to help the Viscountess settle into her new role.

The tour of the house was very instructive for Carenza. It was not so very different from Morwood, although Auster was a much older property. It had been mostly rebuilt in the reign of Queen Anne and later additions made it a well-appointed and comfortable residence. She knew it was not the largest of Ross's properties, but she learned now that it was the most remote.

'The Viscount told me he prefers Auster because he spent so many happy times here as a child,' said Carenza, as she followed the housekeeper from one room to another.

'Aye, he did, my lady, but 'tis not only that,' replied Mrs Stoke, in a burst of confidence. 'His Lordship feels comfortable here, away from everyone, out of the public gaze.'

'I suppose the staff are accustomed to him,' observed Carenza.

'Most of us have known him since he was a boy. We don't even notice his poor face.' Mrs Stoke smiled and ended simply, 'It's part of who he is, my lady.'

Carenza did not see the Viscount again until she joined him shortly before the dinner hour. She was wearing her wedding gown and his brows rose as she walked into the drawing room. She felt her colour rising.

'I hope you do not think me overdressed, sir, but the ivory silk is the only one I consider suitable for evening wear.'

'Ah yes. We must buy you some new clothes.'

'I was thinking about that today, my lord. Mrs Stoke tells me there is a very good seamstress in Bideford who could furnish me with suitable gowns.'

'Are you sure you would not prefer to go to Exeter? I can put the carriage at your disposal.'

'Would you come with me?' She read the answer in his face, the shuttered look in his eyes and an almost imperceptible withdrawing into himself.

'Unnecessary,' he said. 'You can take Robert with you. Or Henry. Both footmen can be trusted, I assure you.'

'I shall bear that in mind, my lord, when the time comes for me to venture there, but for now I only need a few gowns in which I may receive visitors, and a local woman will do well enough.'

'Very well. But talking of Exeter, I have something for you.' He pulled a small velvet case from his pocket and held it out. 'Your pearls. I sent them on there to have them restrung. The jeweller delivered them earlier today.'

'Oh, thank you.' She opened the box and looked up, a question in her eyes.

He smiled. 'I asked him to include a matching pair of ear drops for you.'

'You are too kind.' She put a hand on her bare neck. 'May I wear them now?'

'Of course. I was just thinking how well they would look with that gown.'

There was a large mirror above the pier table between the windows and Carenza moved across to it. She fixed the pearl drops in place, but as she picked up the necklace, Ross stepped up behind her.

'Here, let me.' He reached past her to take the pearls and drape them around her throat. She held her breath as his fingers brushed the back of her neck. Her spine tingled; she could feel the heat from him, his breath on her skin. His body was like a magnet, drawing her closer. It was a conscious effort not to lean back against the hard, solid wall of his chest.

'There.' He rested his hands on her shoulders. 'As good as new.'

She touched the gleaming pearls and looked up to meet his eyes in the glass.

'Better,' she murmured, smiling. Impulsively, she reached up to cover his hand. 'Thank you, my lord.'

Immediately he pulled free, stepping away from her, but not before she saw a shadow flicker across his face. She had gone too far. He did not wish for such intimacy.

'Shall we go in to dinner?'

His voice was polite but cool and Carenza felt a little of her happiness drain away. Silently she placed her fingers on his proffered arm and accompanied him to the dining room.

Ross sat through dinner barely knowing what he said, what he ate. The food tasted of nothing. He was in danger of succumbing to her exotic beauty and he had to fight it. He had promised her security, a comfortable home. Even friendship, perhaps, but nothing more. His face was bad enough, but the scars on his body were much deeper, and ugly. She would never be able to forget them.

Chapter Eleven

The first weeks at Auster passed in a flurry of activity and Carenza had no time to feel bored or lonely.

She ordered her new gowns and the obliging seamstress promised to have at least some of them ready within a se'ennight. While she was waiting, Carenza worked with the housekeeper, getting to know the servants and learning the ways of the house. She tried to be out of doors for part of each day, exploring the grounds and talking to the gardener. She even ventured into the stables, only to learn there was no suitable ladies' mount. She made a mental note to talk to Ross about that.

Not that she saw much of the Viscount. They met at breakfast and dinner, and spent an hour in the evenings making polite conversation, but the rest of the day they went their own way. Carenza was very much aware that Auster was his home, his lair, and she was anxious not to make him feel she was intruding.

The staff had been instructed that Lord and Lady Austerfield would not be at home to callers for the first two weeks they were in residence. If anyone thought this odd, it was passed off with a laugh and a sly wink.

No one suspected it was because Carenza lacked suitable clothes. However, there was one visitor who was not to be gainsaid.

It was their third week at Auster and Carenza was in the morning room when Ross came in with a letter.

'This has just come for you from Morwood.' He handed it over and moved away a little, giving her time to read her letter. 'I hope it is not bad news?'

'Oh, no, quite the contrary,' she told him, smiling. 'It is from my father. He writes to tell me everyone is very well and that Mr Crossley has now settled in. They play chess or backgammon every day, take walks in the grounds, and yesterday Papa was even persuaded to drive to the village in an open carriage, which his doctor says has done him the world of good!'

'Good news indeed. That must relieve your mind.'

'Yes, it does. I would not wish him to fret.' She spoke cheerfully, but in truth her heart was a little heavy. She had to acknowledge a small pain at how well Papa was getting on without her. He would be missing her, she knew that, but it was also plain now that her presence was not necessary to his comfort.

'Talking of carriages,' said Ross, 'I thought I might drive you out one day, while the weather holds. It is time you saw something of Auster.'

'Oh, yes, I should like that very much!'

It was easier to smile now, for she was genuinely pleased with the idea. They were interrupted by sounds from the hall. Footsteps approaching and voices, one belonging to their butler, the other much louder and more forceful.

'Well, I ain't a visitor, Stoke. I am sure they will see me!'

'Damme,' muttered Ross. 'Amos Paston.'

Carenza knew that name. It was Ross's cousin and heir. She rose quickly as the door opened.

Even after such a short time, Carenza was well enough acquainted with the butler to know that the colourless fashion in which he announced the visitor signified disapproval. She could see nothing to disgust in the appearance of the gentleman who came into the room. He was a large man, solid-framed and dressed in a brown riding jacket, buckskins and top-boots. His short brown hair was greying at the sides and was brushed back from regular features that might be considered handsome.

Ross nodded to him. 'Welcome, Amos. What brings you here today?'

'I had business in Bideford and, since I was so close, I thought I should come and make the acquaintance of your new bride!' Mr Paston turned and bowed to Carenza. 'Forgive my coming in upon you without notice, ma'am, but I was sure you would understand, my being family!'

'You are my lord's cousin, I believe,' she said, holding out her hand to him. 'You are very welcome, sir.'

'Your servant, Lady Austerfield.'

The smile never wavered but she felt their guest was studying her thoroughly. She was very conscious of her unflattering gown, a pale pink muslin that had been chosen to show off Letitia's fair prettiness and did nothing for Carenza's olive skin. It had also been altered considerably, the skirts taken up and the bodice increased to accommodate Carenza's fuller figure. She suspected Mr Paston noted every detail although he was far too polite to mention it.

Once initial pleasantries had been exchanged, they all sat down and Carenza prepared to fill an awkward silence, but Mr Paston was before her, saying his wife sent her regards.

'Fanny is very sorry she could not come herself to meet you, Lady Austerfield, but she is in an *interesting state*. Too nervous to come.' He gave a self-conscious laugh. 'I know it is all superstition of course, but...' He trailed off, his eyes moving to Ross, who finished the sentence for him, the bitterness in his voice unmistakable.

'She is afraid being in my company will harm the baby.'

Carenza gasped, shocked that anyone could still believe such nonsense. She was even more astonished that Mr Paston should mention it, instead of saying the journey would be too much for his wife.

'Well, there is no denying your injuries are quite shocking, Cousin,' he said now. 'Do you remember the first time you met Fanny? Poor little thing, no sooner had she looked at you than she dashed well fainted off!' He gave a heavy sigh. 'And it was no good my telling her she would soon grow accustomed. Quite upset her, it did. She had nightmares for weeks afterwards.'

Carenza had heard enough.

'Where are my manners?' she exclaimed, jumping up and crossing the room to tug at the bell pull. 'I have not offered you any refreshment, Mr Paston. What shall it be, sir, tea? Or perhaps you would like a little wine?'

The subject of Ross's scars was abandoned while their guest decided upon his preference and, after wine had been served, she was relieved that the conversation moved on. Mr Paston asked her how she liked Auster but did not give her time to answer.

'I was a little surprised when Ross said you were settling in Devonshire. He has other properties that are far more suited to his rank. Not Comers, of course, although that has always been the principal seat of the Austerfields. Perhaps my lady does not know but that was where poor Sebastian met his demise.'

'We shall visit Yorkshire in good time,' Ross interrupted him. 'And all the other properties, too. There is no rush.'

'I like Auster very well,' replied Carenza. 'It will make a very comfortable home.'

'But you have not yet been here many weeks!' Amos laughed and picked up his glass. He sat back, crossing his legs as if very much at his ease, and yet she felt he was watching her closely. 'I confess, Mrs Paston and I were astonished when Austerfield wrote to tell us he was married.'

'I do not know why that should surprise you, Amos,' said Ross. 'You knew my family were hounding me to take a wife. It was the reason I went to town.'

His cousin gave a soft laugh. 'Good heavens, man, your manners have gone abegging today. That is hardly flattering to your bride!'

'The Viscountess is well aware of the situation,' barked Ross as Carenza's cheeks flamed. 'You know I am not one for balls and parties. Neither is my lady. Once we had decided we should suit, there seemed no reason to delay.'

'You met in town?'

'No, at Morwood. Miss Bettridge was living there with her father.'

'And you did not wish for a large society wedding, ma'am?' He laughed again. 'Then Ross is a lucky dog! I'd wager most men would prefer a quiet little ceremony, but the ladies do like to have their day, what?'

It was beginning to feel like an interrogation and Carenza replied more coldly than before.

'My father's health is not good. A large event would have been a sore trial for him.'

'Ah, I see. My dear Lady Austerfield, forgive me, I did not mean to pry.' His tone was apologetic, even remorseful, as he continued. 'And, of course, Ross would not want the world and his wife coming to gape—'

'No, I did not want that!' Ross jumped up and went over to refill his glass. 'I understand, Cousin, you called here more than once while I have been away.'

'Why, yes, I thought I should drop by, you know,' he said, 'just to keep an eye on the place for you.'

'That was good of you, but unnecessary. Jarvis keeps everything in good order here, as did his father before him.'

'Oh, I am well aware of that, but my business brought me so close I thought I might as well stop here for the night as put up in Bideford. But you are right, of course. Your steward needs no help from me.' He turned back to Carenza. 'You will soon discover, my lady, that everyone working here has been with the family for generations.'

'Apart from His Lordship's valet and groom,' she corrected him, eager to show that she was not totally ignorant of her new husband's establishment.

'Ah, yes,' replied Paston, nodding. 'Brisco and Rigby served under you in the army, Cousin, and I imagine you went through a great deal together. You must have been very thankful they were both spared that last battle, which was especially bloody. It cost you so many good comrades.'

Carenza was watching Ross. His face was impassive but she noticed the tightening of his jaw, as if he was bracing himself.

'So many fatalities,' Amos went on, shaking his head. 'Your family could do nothing but wait and hope. It would have been too much, especially after poor Sebastian's tragic accident, but the reports coming in were so despairing that we feared the worst.'

Ross flinched. His hands were clenched so tight the knuckles shone white and when Amos opened his mouth to continue Carenza broke in quickly.

'I must say, I am excessively pleased with Auster. Everyone here has been most kind. I could not have received a warmer welcome! But it is so very different from my old home. Do you know Hampshire, Mr Paston?'

Ross found himself relaxing as Carenza chattered on, shifting the conversation away from the dark subject of war. She described Morwood to Amos, then asked him about his own house in Kilburn and engaged in an exhaustive discussion of domestic concerns. He was surprised at how easily his wife moved on to the delights of London's musical concerts, theatres and even the British Museum.

Eventually Amos took his leave, but not before he had secured an invitation to join them for dinner that evening. The door closed behind him and Carenza sank down onto her chair, as if exhausted.

'*Brava*, my lady, you dealt with my cousin admirably.'

She opened one eye and looked at him. 'I confess I should have liked more notice of his visit.'

'Yes, it was unfortunate, and the one situation I wished above all others to avoid. I beg your pardon. I should have made sure he knew not to call unexpectedly. Amos has always been used to coming and going very much as he pleases in our properties,' he explained. 'He was an only child and his mother often sent him to join the family for the summer. Being older, he was always more Sebastian's friend than mine, but he has gone out of his way to help me since I inherited the title.' Another thought came to his mind and he looked at her. 'I thought you said you had never been to the capital?'

'I haven't.'

'Then where the deuce did you learn so much about it?'

'Papa's newspapers, and from books we have in the library at Morwood.' She sat up straighter in her chair. 'I was so afraid that at any moment he would catch me out in some inaccuracy.'

'I do not think my cousin cares a great deal about theatres or museums. That is,' he temporised, 'he cares about them in so much as they provide fashionable venues where he may see and be seen.'

Carenza did not respond to this, but privately she thought how much she would like to see performances of the plays she had read, or attend the concerts occasionally announced in the newspapers.

'I must thank you, too, for keeping my cousin so well entertained,' Ross went on. 'He is apt to dwell upon the more unsavoury parts of our family history.'

'I could see you were not enjoying it. In fact, I thought much of his conversation quite…insensitive.'

He waved a hand. 'Amos speaks plainly. I cannot hold that against him.'

Carenza was not so sure. She thought some of Amos Paston's utterances had been brutally callous.

She hesitated, then said shyly. 'If you would like to talk about your brother I would gladly listen, Ross. Or if you want to tell me about your life as a soldier, although I do not think anyone who was not there can fully understand the horrors of battle.'

'Thank you, but these are not subjects with which I would want to trouble you. I am fortunate to have Brisco and Rigby with me, should I need to talk.'

'They were with you a long time?'

'Aye. Sam until he lost an arm at Salamanca and Dan Brisco was beside me almost to the end. He was wounded at Quatre Bras, and taken back to Brussels, otherwise he might well have perished with the rest of my men at Waterloo.' He turned away and walked to the window. He said, staring out, 'If ever I am out of temper or shout at you, Carenza, pray forgive me. I will try not to do so, but sometimes I cannot help myself. It is as if a black cloud descends upon me. I know how unreasonable I am being, but I cannot speak of it. Try as I might, at such times, the words will not come out!'

'Thank you for explaining it to me,' she said quietly. 'I will try to understand. At least I shall be prepared now.'

She waited, hoping he might confide a little more, but he merely nodded.

'Aye, well. I shall leave you now. I am sure you will want to explain to Cook that we have a guest for dinner.'

Mr Paston returned in good time and made himself so agreeable that Carenza began to wonder if she had been too hasty in her initial judgement of the man. He ate heartily and complimented every dish.

'The praise really must go to Cook,' Carenza told him. 'She is very experienced and runs the kitchens with the discipline and efficiency of a general.' She chuckled. 'Between them, Cook and Mrs Stoke leave me with very little to do.'

'You are fortunate in your staff,' he said. 'Which reminds me, Lady Austerfield, would you have room in your household for another maid? I know of a young woman who is looking for work, my man Windle's niece. She had a spot of trouble at her last position and was obliged to leave, to save her honour. I thought she'd be better away from Kilburn, at least for the moment.'

'I leave all such matters to Mrs Stoke,' replied Carenza. 'However, I will see what I can do. If that suits you, my lord?'

Ross nodded. 'Hiring of domestics is your domain, my dear. We will write to let you know, Amos.'

'I was hoping we might resolve it quickly,' replied his cousin, looking a little sheepish. 'Thing is, we have the gel with us. Windle couldn't very well leave her in Kilburn and we were going to try to find her a position in Bideford, only since I was coming across here, I thought I'd ask…'

Carenza glanced at Ross, who laughed.

'It seems to me your man has dragged you into a pickle, Amos! Very well, bring her over in the morning. Mrs Stoke must talk to her and, if she is agreeable, the girl can start immediately.'

Amos Paston beamed, thanked them and continued with his dinner.

By the time Carenza left the men to their brandy, she was once again exhausted. It was not that Amos Paston had said and done anything to cause offence, but still she could not like him. Despite his smiles she had felt he was watching her, weighing up every word she and Ross spoke to one another. Also, he encouraged Ross to dwell upon his injuries and what he could not do, rather than what he could.

In defending the Viscount, Carenza had forgotten the shortcomings of her appearance and conversed with her customary ease. She hoped it was enough to convince Mr Paston that even if the marriage was not a love match, both parties were perfectly content with the arrangement.

When Carenza had gone, Ross waited until the brandy had been poured and the servants withdrawn before asking his cousin about the business that had brought him to Devon.

'I have acquired more shipping interests in Bideford,' Amos told him airily.

'That is a long way from Kilburn.'

'Aye, but I need to secure my income, now that you have taken a wife.'

'I thought I had been quite plain in my letter. You are still my heir and will remain so.'

'I am merely the heir *presumptive*, Cousin,' said Amos, toying with his wineglass. 'You are not incapable of fathering a child.'

Ross said, his lip curling, 'I might as well be.'

'You mean your scars, I suppose.' Amos gave a long sigh. 'One cannot deny that it would be difficult for anyone to overlook them and women are such delicate creatures, are they not? Female sensibilities are too nice for the horrors of war, the sight of such wounds must overset any lady. However, I am sure your Viscountess would endure it.'

'I would not have her *endure it*,' Ross ground out. 'Carenza and I discussed this. She knows what is expected of her. And what is not.'

'She does?' Amos looked at him, brows raised. 'Forgive me if I seem impertinent, Cousin, but you are still a young man, your wife is not unattractive. It would not be surprising if you were to feel...tempted.'

'No.' Ross spoke with finality. 'I shall make sure the situation does not arise. You know full well this is not a love match, Amos. Carenza and I understand one another and we go on very comfortably as friends. There will be no heir of my blood.'

Paston put up his hands. 'If you say so, my lord. And, sadly, I think it is for the best. You are wise not to inflict the sight of your physical deformities upon your wife. Also, those moods of depression you suffer are showing no sign of abating, are they?' His smile was full of understanding. 'It would be wrong to burden any gently born young lady with the full horror of your condition. Females are such fragile beings, easily stirred to pity for some pathetic, wounded creature, but it never lasts. Intimacy would most surely jeopardise your friendship with Lady Austerfield.'

The words were kindly meant, but they grated on Ross's nerves. He wanted an end to the conversation.

'Quite.' He pushed back his chair. 'If you have finished your brandy, shall we return to the drawing room?'

Amos followed him to the door but before opening it Ross turned.

'One last thing,' he said. 'What we have discussed here, about an heir. It goes no further. Do you understand me?'

'Oh, indubitably.' Amos smiled and put his hand on Ross's shoulder. 'You know you can rely upon me, Cousin.'

* * *

Amos Paston took his leave shortly after and, when he had departed, Carenza cast Ross a rather guilty look.

'Should we have invited him to stay the night, my lord?'

'On no account. There is a good road and a full moon to light his way. He should know better than to interrupt a couple on their honeymoon.'

That brought the colour flooding to her cheeks, but she noted that Ross was also ill at ease, twisting the signet ring around on his finger.

'Not that we are actually—'

'You do not need to explain,' she interrupted him, her blush deepening.

'No. Of course not.' She thought she heard him sigh. Then, 'This situation is a novel one for both of us, my lady. I hope we can find a way through it, together.'

'That is my wish, too,' she told him earnestly. 'I shall do everything in my power to make a success of this, for both of us.'

He smiled at that. 'I do not doubt it.'

Their eyes locked and the silence became charged with so much energy that Carenza could feel it swirling around and between them. It was like a smouldering fire about to burst into flame any moment.

'It grows late,' he said abruptly. 'I have a meeting with Jarvis early tomorrow.'

The spell was broken and Carenza had the oddest sensation that some danger had been averted. For now. She dragged her mind back to more mundane matters.

'And I have to ask Mrs Stoke to consider taking on a new maid. It does seem a little odd that Mr Paston should have brought the girl so far in search of work.'

'Perhaps it was difficult for her to find a new post in

Kilburn, where all the families know one another. I'd
wager he always intended to ask if we might take her.
After all, I am in his debt.'

'You are?'

'Amos has been a good friend to me. He arranged
for a carriage to collect me from the hospital at Portsmouth and was waiting here at Auster to receive me.
He stayed for months, helping me with the business of
my brother's death.' Ross sighed and walked across to
the hearth. 'It was such a shock, Seb's dying like that.
I never expected to inherit, never wanted the title. I
was very content with my life in the army. I liked it. I
knew what I was about, whereas this…' He glowered
into the empty fireplace. 'Amos has spent more time
at the Austerfield properties than I have over the past
ten years. He probably knows better than I how they
should be run.'

The sadness in Ross's voice was very evident and
Carenza went across to him.

'You will learn, Ross. You have good people around
you who want you to succeed.' She put a hand on his
sleeve. 'I will help you, too. As much as I am able.'

He looked down at her fingers for a moment, then
covered them with his own.

'Yes, I believe you will be a great asset to me.'

Carenza's heart swelled and the breath snagged in
her throat when she looked up at Ross. The left side of
his face was shadowed, but even if the candlelight had
been blazing directly on his scars she would not have
noticed them. All she could see was the warm smile
in his eyes.

This is where I belong!

The thought came unbidden, surprising her with its
force. She felt suddenly shy in his company.

'It is very late,' she said. 'I should go.'

'Yes, I think you should.'

His smile had turned a little rueful and on impulse she put her hand on his shoulder and reached up to press a light kiss on his unmarked cheek.

'Goodnight, my lord.'

Ross could not move. Could not speak. He watched Carenza glide out of the room and close the door behind her. Only then did he put up his hand to where her lips had touched his face.

Chapter Twelve

There was a definite spring in Carenza's step as she left the housekeeper's room. She and Mrs Stoke had just interviewed Ruth, the maid who had arrived at Auster before breakfast, escorted by Mr Paston's valet.

'She certainly seems a bright, well-mannered girl and appears to know her business,' was the housekeeper's verdict and Carenza sent Windle back to his master with the news that Ruth had been taken on in the role of housemaid.

It was a promising start to the day, and more was to come. As she emerged from the service rooms she was met with the news that the dressmaker had arrived with the first of her new gowns, finished and ready to be fitted. It was gone noon when this worthy eventually departed and Carenza sallied forth in a day dress of lemon muslin. She had just reached the hall when Ross appeared and gratified her by immediately noticing her new gown.

'It suits you,' he said. 'Much better than those washed-out pastel shades you brought from Morwood.'

She was not sure if that was really a compliment,

but his next question sent her thoughts in quite another direction.

'Tell me, did she also bring your riding habit?'

'Why, yes.'

'Good. Because Sam has just returned with a mare for you to try.'

'Oh! I thought we were going to wait for the Barnstaple horse fair, in September.'

'Sam heard of a sale at Tawstock and I sent him along.'

'Alone?' she said, surprised. 'How does he manage…' She tailed off with a little gesture.

'Without his left arm?' He smiled. 'Very well indeed! He has served me faithfully since I returned to England and makes a damned good groom. Better than many men with two working arms, in fact! But about the mare. She is in the stables, if you would like to see her now?'

'Oh, yes, indeed,' cried Carenza. 'Give me but a moment to fetch my wrap!'

The mare was beautiful. Carenza sighed.

'I had a grey pony very like this when I was a little child. She was the sweetest-natured creature one could imagine.'

'I've put her through her paces, my lady,' Sam Rigby told her. 'She's a lively mare, and she has speed, which you'll need if you are riding with His Lordship.'

'We will try her in the meadow first, until you are sure of her,' said Ross. 'She is bound to be different from your hack at Morwood.'

'I did not have a hack,' she replied, running her hand along the mare's glossy neck. 'When I outgrew my pony, it was not worth the expense of buying me another.'

'Your stepmother's decision?' Ross asked her. She flushed a little and his brow darkened. 'I might have guessed it.'

Rigby gave a little cough.

'Perhaps, my lady, we should look for something quieter, if you are out of practice.'

'Oh, I am not out of practice,' she replied sunnily. 'Although my father no longer rides, he could not bear to part with his two favourite hunters. Fewston and I would take them out for exercise.'

Ross's brows went up. 'With a lady's saddle?'

'Well, no. The only lady's saddles were for the overfed slugs kept for my sisters' use. I managed well enough.'

Rigby smothered a snort of laughter and Carenza glanced anxiously at Ross.

'Oh, dear, have I shocked you?'

'Not at all,' he replied, the merest quaver in his voice. 'However, the mare comes with a saddle, so you will not be obliged to scandalise the neighbourhood. When would you like to try her paces?'

'Oh, as soon as possible, if you please!'

'Then shall we say an hour? That will give Sam time to prepare the horses while you change.'

Barely an hour later Ross escorted Carenza to the meadow. It did not take him long to realise that she was quite at home in the saddle. She rode well and he could not deny that she looked very good, too, in her new teal-blue riding habit, a matching cap fixed at a jaunty angle atop her glossy black curls. They trotted and cantered around the meadow, eventually pulling up in the shade of the copse at the boundary, where the meadow gave way to common land and a well-defined track led up to the distant moors.

'Well, my lord, may we keep this lovely creature?'

Carenza had turned a smiling countenance towards him and he was tempted to say how well that epithet would suit *her*. He pushed the thought away. He was not one for uttering flowery compliments.

'She is yours, if you really like her.'

'Oh, I do.' She leaned forward and patted the mare's white neck. 'She is beautifully mannered but—' Carenza glanced at the rangy chestnut hunter he was riding '—do you think we shall be able to keep up with you?'

There was laughter in her eyes, and a challenge that he could not ignore. He gathered up the reins and nodded towards the track.

'Let us find out.'

Both horses sprang forward and they were soon galloping across the common. Ross held his mount in check and allowed Carenza to pass him, wanting to assure himself that she was capable of managing a spirited animal over the rough terrain. He soon realised he need not have worried. It was clear she was very much at home, bent low over the mare's neck as they flew over the ground.

They had reached the stunted trees and gorse of the moors before the pace slowed and Ross brought his hunter alongside the mare.

'I think that answers the question,' he remarked, smiling at her.

'You allowed me to lead all the way!'

'True, I could have overtaken you, had I wished to do so, but it would not have been easy, and I was loath to push Aethon too hard in this heat.' He glanced up. 'Talking of the heat, shall we turn back?'

'By all means.'

They began to retrace their steps and Carenza remarked in some surprise how far they had come.

'I also did not realise we had climbed so high,' she continued. 'One can see Auster and its grounds quite clearly from here and, oh!' She brought her mare to a sudden stop. 'Is that the sea in the distance, beyond the house?'

Ross followed her gaze. The gardens around Auster ended at a belt of trees and beyond that was grazing land, smooth and green, with a dark blue smudge along the horizon.

'Yes, that is the ocean. The land there ends in a steep cliff we call Shepherd's Leap, because so many sheep have been lost there over the years.' He pointed. 'Do you see that small ruin? It was a lookout tower, built during the reign of Queen Elizabeth.'

'And how far is it?'

He shrugged. 'From here? A mile or two, perhaps.'

'May we ride there now?' she asked, adding shyly, 'I have never seen the sea, except paintings, or pictures in books.'

'Very well.'

He urged his horse on and they cantered down the hill, following the lane around the edge of the gardens and only slowing to take a narrow path that wound through the trees.

'It is not far now,' said Ross as they emerged from the small wood and he waited for her to come alongside him. 'Are you still happy with the mare?'

'Oh, yes,' she told him, her eyes shining. 'I should very much like to keep her, if you please. Only, she will need a name. I have been racking my brains to think of something suitable.'

'What about Elvira?' he suggested. 'I heard it used in the Peninsula. I believe it means white, or fair.'

'Perfect! Thank you.' She leaned forward to stroke the horse's neck. 'Henceforth you shall be known as Elvira—do you like that, my beauty?'

Ross watched Carenza murmuring softly to the mare and his heart swelled to see her so happy.

'We can still go to the Barnstaple fair and buy you a second mount, if you wish it,' he said as they walked on. 'You should have your own carriage, too.'

'Thank you, my lord, but Elvira will be quite sufficient for my needs, I assure you. What should I do with more horses eating their heads off? If I want to drive myself, I can take the gig.'

'The one used to collect provisions from the village?' He grimaced at the thought. 'I would sooner you used my curricle.'

'I *might* do so, if I did not know your temperamental greys are so very valuable!' She laughed. 'Be honest with me, Ross, you would not rest if I took them out alone.'

'True. After all, I have not seen you drive, and you might be thoroughly incompetent.'

She gave a gurgle of laughter. 'I might, of course, although I do not think I am quite that bad.'

'I could buy another pair for you to drive.'

'*No*, Ross!' She was adamant. 'You are very generous, but I would by far prefer to ride about the country, when I can. I will not let you throw your money away so recklessly, but it is very kind of you to think of it.'

He did not pursue the matter, although he decided he would tell Sam to keep his eyes and ears open for a pretty little carriage and pair, suitable for a lady. The thought of buying things for Carenza pleased him. She would appreciate his gifts, not like the lightskirts he had known, whose continued favours depended upon how much a man was willing to pay them.

He had been particularly generous, on the occasions when he had sought comfort or escape from his loneliness in the arms of a woman. It had been difficult to find any who did not flinch or grow pale at the sight of his scars. Some had looked at him with pity, which he hated even more. Now he preferred to hide away from the world, but although fine clothes concealed the ugliness of his body, nothing could disguise the scarring on his face. Even Lady Bettridge and her daughters, desperate to court his favour, could not totally hide their repugnance. The best they could manage was not to look at him.

Carenza is not afraid to look at you.

The thought jumped into his head. He had to admit she had managed very well, after her initial shock at that first meeting. His mind went back to the kiss she had bestowed on his cheek last night. That had been a surprise, but very welcome. When he was with her it was possible to forget his monstrous looks. He had come to enjoy her company and he hoped she felt the same. Ross smiled to himself. It was far more pleasant having a wife to share his house than he had anticipated.

'I can hear the sea!'

Carenza's excited cry brought him back to the present with a jolt. How long had he been lost in his own thoughts?

'I beg your pardon, ma'am. I have been neglecting you.'

'Not at all. It is not necessary that we should talk

all the time we are together.' She hesitated. 'In fact, it brings me to something I have been meaning to say to you.'

His eyes narrowed. 'Your tone suggests I won't like what you are about to tell me.' She looked at him warily and he said, 'Come along, madam. Out with it!'

'I wanted to say that I am grown quite accustomed to your appearance, my lord. There is no need for you to shield me constantly from the damaged side of your face.' She ignored his angry mutterings. 'For example, the way you insist I sit at your right hand for dinner.'

'But that is where I want you,' he replied, trying not to sound ruffled. 'The alternative is to sit at the end, which is such a dashed long way when there are only the two of us. It makes conversation well-nigh impossible.'

She laughed. 'I agree with you on *that*, my lord, but there are other times, too. As if you are constantly aware of your scars.'

'Of course I am constantly aware of them! How could it be otherwise?'

'Oh, pray, Ross, do not be offended! It is unnecessary to be so vigilant on my account. I want you to feel comfortable in my company.'

He scowled at her. 'You are being nonsensical. I am perfectly comfortable.'

The amused understanding in her eyes made him glower even more.

'But you are even now keeping to the left of me,' she pointed out. 'I cannot think you are truly at ease when you are always trying to present your finest side.'

Carenza held her breath. Had she gone too far? She wondered if Ross would shout at her, or turn Aethon and gallop back to the house.

'That is utter nonsense,' he bit out at last. 'I do nothing of the kind!'

'Then you will not object if I bring Elvira around to the other side.'

The hunter jibbed a little as she manoeuvred, while Ross kept his gaze firmly fixed on the horizon. His lips had thinned, which suggested he was keeping his temper in check with an effort, but she was not ready to give up yet.

'There,' she said cheerfully, smiling across at him. 'The damage to your face is not so bad, after all. It has completely missed your ear. You have particularly fine ears, I think. I do not believe it is my imagination that the scars are fading, too. The redness and swelling are definitely reducing.' She added kindly, 'You are nowhere near as hideous as you think, my lord.'

'Really?' he ground out, his tone menacing. 'Anything else?'

'Well, yes. The little scar that runs to the edge of your mouth—it makes you look as if you are smiling. It is most attractive.'

Again the dangerous silence, then Ross laughed and she allowed herself to breathe a little more freely.

'My dear, you really do not need to concoct such flummery to humour me,' he drawled. 'I am quite inured to my hideous looks by now.'

'You are *not* hideous and I am not humouring you!' she retorted. 'However, I do have a soothing cream that I think might well help your scars to look even less angry.'

'I don't want your damned ointments!'

'Well, I think that is very unhandsome of you, when I went to all the trouble of picking the herbs myself yesterday, and mixed them so carefully.'

'Then you have wasted your time!'

'Will you not even try it?' She sighed and her shoulders dropped a little. 'It may not do you any *good*, Ross, but it will not do you any harm, either.'

She bent a soulful gaze upon him and he returned her look, his own eyes narrowed, then at last he gave a growl of exasperation.

'Oh, very well, I will try it.'

'Thank you!'

'Happy now?'

She beamed at him. 'I am, my lord.'

His scowl deepened, but she saw a glint in his grey-green eyes.

'Damned scheming hussy!'

She laughed at that but decided not to tease him further. Instead she looked about her.

'Is that the old tower over there? Then we must be near the cliff edge by now.'

She urged her horse to a canter and, smiling, Ross followed her. At the tower he suggested they dismount.

'I'll not risk us riding closer,' he said. 'Horses are easily panicked, and it is a sheer drop of a hundred feet or so to the rocks beneath.'

'We shall most certainly dismount, then!'

She waited for him to lift her down and he found her surprisingly light in his arms. As he set her on her feet, he breathed in her scent, a heady mix of summer flowers, as clean and fresh as the breeze blowing in off the sea. How dainty she was, too, with her head barely reaching his shoulder. She was looking up at him, her eyes dark and warm, and he was tempted to hold on to her, to kiss the delectable mouth that smiled so invitingly. But hard upon the thought came the echo of his cousin's words.

I am sure your Viscountess would endure it.

He stepped away from her. 'Let us walk.'

'In a moment.' She turned to stare out across the rest-less blue water that stretched away to the horizon. Her breast heaved as she took in a long, deep breath. 'I want to savour this moment. I love the hills and fields around Morwood, but this…this surpasses everything. It looks so beautiful, with the sun sparkling on the waves!'

Ross laughed. 'It is not always thus, I assure you. On a rainy day it is as grey as gunmetal. Deadly, too, where it reaches the cliffs. Come and see.'

The wind grew stronger as they approached the edge of the cliff and Ross offered Carenza his arm. She slipped her hand onto his sleeve and they took a few more steps, until they could look down and see the waves crashing against the rocks beneath. Her fingers tightened.

'Don't worry, we will not go too close.'

'You called this Shepherd's Leap,' she said, shiver-ing. 'I cannot think any creature would survive, if they were to tumble over.'

'It is almost certain death.' He stared down. 'It would be the surest way to die. Short of blowing one's brains out.'

She gasped. 'Ross, you wouldn't…?'

He laughed harshly and shook his head. 'Of course not.'

It was a lie. Even now he could remember the agony of those first weeks in Portsmouth. His patched-up body was healing but he became prone to terrible dreams and guilt for those who had perished while he had survived. Dan Brisco had nursed him through it, with Sam's help, and he had returned to some sort of normal life, although the dark thoughts and nightmares still occurred. Far too frequently.

'I am glad,' Carenza murmured. 'I am very glad you are here with me.'

She was leaning into him, her head resting against his shoulder, and he became aware of a feeling he had almost forgotten stealing over him. Contentment.

'So, too, am I,' he murmured, and was surprised to find that he meant it.

They spent an hour walking along the cliff, looking out over the sparkling water and talking idly of anything and nothing. Ross could not remember when he had last felt so at peace and it was with some reluctance that he took out his watch and announced that it was time to return, if they were not to be late for dinner.

They cantered back to Auster and, having assured Sam Rigby that the mare was quite perfect for her, Carenza allowed Ross to escort her back to the house.

'What an excellent day,' she exclaimed happily. 'New gowns *and* a beautiful new mare. I consider myself very fortunate.' She squeezed his arm. 'Thank you, my lord.'

'For what?' he asked, amused. 'Sam Rigby found the mare; I cannot take credit for that.'

'But it was you who asked him to look out for a suitable mount,' she argued. 'And you allowed me to buy whatever I wished from our local seamstress.'

'Good God, why would I do anything else? What the devil do I know about women's fashions?'

'As much as I, no doubt,' she replied, laughing. 'I hope you like the new evening gown that I shall wear for you tonight. If so, it augurs well for everything else I have chosen!'

* * *

They hurried up to their rooms to change for dinner. Ross entered his dressing room to find one of the female servants setting down his jug of hot water on the washstand. He recognised her as the new maid his cousin had brought to them.

'Ruth, isn't it?' he said. 'How are you settling in?'

'Very well, my lord, thank 'ee.'

'Good. You will find Mrs Stoke is very fair, if you work hard.'

'Aye, my lord.'

He looked at the clothes Brisco had set out over the chair in readiness for dinner. The coat of olive merino wool had served him well but tonight he thought he would prefer something better, since his wife would be wearing a new gown. The Bath coating and his newest satin waistcoat, perhaps. Carenza deserved that he should make an effort.

'Will that be all, sir?'

'What?' He had forgotten the maid. She was still standing by the washstand, regarding him.

'Is there anything else I can do for you, my lord?'

'No, no, off you go.' He waved her away, his thoughts on what he would wear for his dinner with Carenza.

Chapter Thirteen

'A beautiful dress, ma'am,' Ross observed. 'Our local seamstress has done well.'

'Thank you.' Carenza flushed a little as she smoothed her hands over the shimmering, burnt orange skirts. 'It is a new colour for this season called *terra rossa*. I was afraid the shot silk might be a little…startling.'

'Not at all, that colour suits you very well.'

She was too shy to return the compliment but she thought privately that the Viscount was looking elegant himself, in snow-white linen and a dark coat so exquisitely tailored that it hugged his broad shoulders without the slightest crease. Elegant cream knee breeches clung to his muscular thighs and the whole was enlivened by a cream waistcoat, exquisitely embroidered with flowers.

In her opinion, the fine network of scars on his face did not at all detract from his handsome appearance. She remembered the salve she had prepared for him was still sitting on her dressing table. There had been no time to pass it on before dinner, but she would ask Hetty to take it to the Viscount's man when she went up to bed.

It was the most pleasant evening she had yet spent

with Ross. The ride out had put them very much at ease with one another and over dinner their discussions ranged widely, with Carenza eventually inviting Ross to tell her about his properties. It was a small step from there to the management of the farms and soon they were devising plans for improvement and discussing breeds of cattle. It was only when the covers were removed and the final sweetmeats placed on the table that Ross realised how the time had flown.

'We have spent at least an hour talking of farming,' he declared. 'You are very knowledgeable on the subject.'

'I know a little, because I used to help my father with running the estate and the Home Farm,' she told him, her hand hovering over a dish of sugared almonds. 'I took charge of the accounts when I left the schoolroom, and often accompanied Papa to market or to his meetings with the farmers. That is, until he became too ill to cope any longer and we were obliged to take on a steward.'

'When was that?'

'About five years ago. Mr Niven has proved himself a very able manager and now knows almost everything required to run the estate, although he still consulted me on various matters.'

'I think you will be sorely missed.'

She blushed. 'By Papa, perhaps, but no one else.'

'Oh?' His searching eyes were fixed upon her. 'You have been gone from Morwood for little more than three weeks and I know you have already received numerous letters, asking for advice.'

'Not numerous. Only three, sir. Mr Niven wrote to enquire about the housekeeping ledgers. Lady Bettridge insisted I should hand them to her, as soon as I accepted your offer and she knew I would be leaving. I believe she fell a little behind with the accounts and several tradesmen were pressing for payment. I am sure Mr Niven has it all in hand now. Then there was a note from Mrs Trudby, who had mislaid the receipt for the lotion I make for Papa's hands in winter.'

'And the third?' he pressed her.

'My sisters could not remember where we purchase the sheet music for the pianoforte.'

'Confound it, did they all rely on you for *everything*?'

'Not at all. These are very trivial matters and all resolved now, I am sure.'

Ross was frowning and she quickly changed the subject so that their earlier cordiality was soon restored. It was not until a yawn surprised her that Carenza realised how late it was.

'Goodness, half past eleven!' she exclaimed, looking up at the clock. 'It has been a long day, my lord. I shall go directly to my bedchamber, unless you wish me to order the tea tray for the drawing room?'

He shook his head and reached for the brandy. 'No need. I am not partial to tea drinking when I am alone.'

'Very well, my lord.' She rose and stood for a moment, feeling there was something more to be said.

Ross looked up. 'Goodnight, my dear. I shall see you in the morning.'

He was dismissing her. Politely, kindly, but it was still a dismissal. Carenza left the dining room and made her way slowly up the stairs with a heavy heart. She knew she had no right to be disappointed; they were not lovers, after all. It was a marriage of convenience for them both. Ross had explained it all so carefully and she had agreed to it. All the same, there was an ache in her body that she could not ignore.

She had been aware of it ever since he had lifted her down from the saddle. Suspended in his arms, she had felt a delicious feeling of helplessness. It had been over all too soon but some of that exhilaration had remained for the rest of the day, a buzz of excitement and a heightened awareness of Ross. A quickening of her pulse when he was near. Now she recognised it for what it was. Desire.

Single ladies were not supposed to know anything about such matters, but Carenza had learned a great deal from Lady Bettridge and her friends. Their gossip was always conducted in tones of hushed outrage and they had believed that while lust in a gentleman was considered to be quite natural, any woman who exhibited similar desires was a wanton hussy, beyond redemption. Well, she could not deny it: she wanted Ross to take her to his bed.

By the time Carenza reached her bedchamber she was far too restless for sleep. She allowed Hetty to help her into her flowered silk wrap, another new creation of the seamstress, then she dismissed the maid and paced the floor, trying to bring some order to her jumbled thoughts.

She had never considered herself a bad person, but surely, if all she had heard was correct, she was as wicked as any wretched female for feeling such desire, such lust, for a man, albeit her husband. She could not even blame Ross for encouraging her. He had been excessively kind today, but he could also be morose and angry, either ignoring her presence or snapping at her. He had given her no reason at all to feel the way she did.

At last she gave up her pacing and climbed into bed, thinking she would read for a while. She picked up her book but the words jumped before her eyes. All she could think of was how much she had enjoyed herself today. Ross lifting her down from the saddle, holding her arm as they walked along the cliff edge. Ross smiling at her, causing her heart to thump and her body to ache with longing.

With a little cry of frustration, she threw the book down and blew out her candle. If this was the result of spending time with her husband, then she would have to find reasons to avoid his company. It was as simple as that.

Carenza took her breakfast in her room before dressing in her new gown of apricot muslin, but even then she did not venture out for another half an hour. She would give Ross plenty of time to remove himself from the house before she went downstairs.

It wasn't until she had shaken out her skirts and was on her way to the door that she noticed the alabaster pot on the mantelpiece. It was the cream for Ross which she had intended Hetty to give to his valet, only she had been so caught up in her own selfish thoughts this morning that it had gone clean from her mind.

She considered ringing for her maid but thought better of it. She might as well take the pot herself to Mr Brisco, then she could explain just what it was. She left her bedchamber just in time to see the valet disappearing down the backstairs. Chasing after him would be undignified and he would only have to carry the ointment back to Ross's bedchamber. No, the simplest thing would be to leave the preparation there herself.

Carenza was sure the room would be empty but she took the precaution of knocking softly before going in. The door opened noiselessly on well-oiled hinges and her slippered feet made no sound. She was halfway across the room before she saw Ross, staring out of the window. He had stripped off his shirt but was still wearing his buckskins and boots, suggesting he had just returned from an early morning ride.

'Oh, I beg your pardon!'

He swung round and roared at her.

'What the devil are you doing here?' He snatched up his shirt and threw it over his head. 'Get out!'

But Carenza could not move. The vision of his naked torso had burned itself into her mind. Not the welts and scars on his left shoulder and ribs, but the other side of his body, the side that was all honed muscle with only a few very old scars on the smooth skin.

'I said get out!'

'I beg your pardon,' she repeated, dragging her eyes up to his face. 'I saw Mr Brisco leaving and assumed you were not here.' She held out the jar. 'I brought you the salve I mentioned.'

'You might have saved yourself the trouble. You have seen my body. No cream will make a difference now.'

She trembled a little under his fierce glare, but she stood her ground.

'Yes, I saw your body, and I do not think the damage is quite as bad as you believe.'

He gave a snarl of anger. 'Damn you, madam, will you leave, or must I throw you out?'

'My lord, the wounds are deep, the damage severe, yes, but I saw nothing to disgust me.'

'Then you did not see it properly, or you have an unnaturally ghoulish disposition! My wounds are… repulsive.'

'Who has told you that?'

'Never mind who said it,' he ground out. 'Just leave me. Get out. Now!'

There was no sign of the friendly, courteous companion of yesterday. His voice was icy, the eyes more grey than green now and hard as granite. Her knees felt quite weak in the face of his rage but she still held her ground.

'This preparation will help, Ross. It will soothe and cool the angry skin.' She held the pot up again. 'Please try it, my lord. There is nothing in it that can harm you, I swear, and it might do a great deal of good.'

He glowered at her, his powerful chest heaving. It was a battle of wills and Carenza kept her head up and refused to look away from his angry gaze. Finally, he threw himself down on a chair and folded his arms.

'Very well. Apply it.'

'I b-beg your pardon?' She had not foreseen this.

'*You* apply it.' He put up his chin. 'To my face.'

She swallowed hard and went towards him, both hands wrapped about the alabaster jar to stop them shaking. He would only give her one chance at this. She must get it right.

Carenza pulled a small table closer, put down the jar and removed the lid. The subtle scents of the mixture drifted up to meet her, hints of jasmine, chamomile and elderflower. Her confidence grew. It was the duty of any housewife to look after her people and over the years she had treated many of the staff and tenants at Morwood with her salves and lotions. This would be no different.

Or so she tried to tell herself.

'It will not hurt,' she murmured, scooping a small amount of the preparation onto her fingers.

'You think I care for a little pain?' he barked, 'Get on with it!'

He presented his cheek to her, sitting with his back ramrod straight, his arms folded and one foot tapping impatiently.

His Lordship was nervous!

Carenza started by applying the salve to his temple. She could feel the fine, rigid lines of the scars beneath her fingers and worked the cream into the delicate tracery, gradually moving down to his cheekbone and on towards the jaw. She worked slowly, carefully. The room was silent; the only sound came from the birds singing outside the window. Ross was relaxing beneath her touch. She noted how his breathing had slowed and that booted foot had stopped tapping.

Encouraged, she continued, smoothing the sweet-smelling preparation along the line of his jaw and down the side of his throat, where she felt his steady pulse against her fingertips. She hesitated a heart's beat when she reached the open neck of his shirt, then slid her fingers under the fine linen and along his collarbone.

Ross's hand shot up and trapped hers.

'That is enough for today!' He pulled her fingers away and rose abruptly. 'Thank you, madam.'

'How does your skin feel now?' she asked him.

He shrugged. Carenza waited.

'It does feel a little more pliant,' he conceded at last.

'I believe it will help, over time, my lord. I suggest you rub in a little of the salve every night before you retire. You might also apply some to your body.'

'We shall see.' He had turned away from her and was staring out of the window again, arms folded, tension in every line of his body. 'I should be obliged now if you would leave me.'

His voice was hard, the words clipped. It was a command. Carenza put the lid back on the jar and silently left.

* * *

Ross heard the whisper of skirts as she crossed the room but not until the door had clicked shut behind her did he allow himself to breathe. He closed his eyes and rested his forehead against the glass, reliving the gentleness of her touch. Her fingers had caressed his face, soothing the skin, relaxing him. Until she had slipped her hand under his shirt and his body had jumped to attention.

Just the thought if it set his blood pounding again. If he had not stopped her, he had no idea where it might have ended. He had been tempted to pull her onto his lap and cover her face in kisses before carrying her to the bed and—

'No!' He groaned and dropped his head in his hands. He must not give in to this. He and Carenza had been getting on so well together. He valued the friendship that was growing between them and could not risk losing it, as they surely must if he took her to his bed. At some point she would look properly at his body and she would recoil. She would never again see her husband as anything other than a pitiful wreck of a man.

And of all the people in the world, he did not want to see fear and revulsion and *pity* in Carenza's face.

When they met next at dinner time neither mentioned their earlier encounter. Ross remarked upon her new gown and Carenza told him the seamstress had delivered the remaining clothes from her order that afternoon.

'They have been very industrious, finishing everything so quickly,' she told him as they went into the dining room. 'I now have gowns that are fit to wear when receiving visitors. I hope I shall not disgrace you, my lord.'

He wanted to kiss her hand and tell her she could never disgrace him. Instead he gave her a perfunctory smile and took his place at the table. It then occurred to him that Carenza might think he was ignoring her and that would not do.

'I have had a letter from my sister. You will remember she attended our wedding.' He grimaced, recalling how Dido had arrived unannounced and uninvited, having travelled from London and put up at the local inn.

A smile twinkled in her eyes. 'How could I forget such a determined lady?'

'She is a dashed managing female and should have stayed at home!'

Carenza laughed. 'She told me that if you were going to be married out of hand and in such a hurry, it behoved at least one member of your family to be present to give the union their blessing. I *think* she approved of me.'

'She does approve of you. She wrote to ask when we are coming to town.'

'Oh. We decided to remain at Auster, did we not?'

'*I* decided that,' he corrected her. 'Dido knows I detest London and she has invited you to join her there, if you would like to go.' He glanced up, adding roughly, 'I have no objection, if you wish to spend some time in town.'

He saw her eyes widen in surprise and there was a heartbeat's pause before she replied.

'That is kind of you, and of your sister, but I think I should prefer to remain here.' His spirits lifted, then she added, 'Until we can go to London together.'

'That might be a very long time, my dear.'

'We shall see.'

He looked up, suddenly suspicious, but she only gave him a bland smile and asked him to pass the dish of buttered peas. He thought then that Carenza was proving to be every bit as determined a female as his sister.

By the time the meal was over they were friends again, at ease with one another, and when it was time to retire, Ross escorted Carenza to her door and kissed her hand as he bade her goodnight.

'And you will use the salve I made for you?' she asked, holding on to his fingers.

'If you think it will help.'

'I do. I believe it is helping already.'

Her hand dropped to his shoulder as she raised herself on tiptoe and kissed his scarred cheek.

'Yes,' she murmured. 'That is a definite improvement! Goodnight, my lord.'

With that she whisked herself into her room and left Ross staring at the closed door. It was the second time she had kissed his face. She had not flinched; she had been calm, almost playful. What the devil was going on here?

Chapter Fourteen

The Viscount having approved her new gowns, Carenza was ready for the bridal visits. Cards were sent and received, local families called and visits were made. Life suddenly became very busy.

'With the result that I have hardly seen you for the past two weeks,' grumbled Ross, at breakfast one morning.

'You know I must not be backward in my attention to your neighbours,' she replied. 'You are very welcome to accompany me.'

'No, I thank you! That is, unless my absence is considered a slight upon you?'

'Since you are notoriously reclusive no one thinks it odd that I make the calls alone.' A mischievous twinkle gleamed in her eyes. 'You have started to attend church with me on Sundays, which is taken as a very good sign that you are not quite beyond redemption.'

He laughed at that. 'You are very good for me, you know.'

She coloured, inordinately pleased with his response.

'Why, thank you, my lord. I am very glad you think so! Now, if you will excuse me, I am promised to visit the squire's wife this morning, then there is a meeting of the parish Widows and Orphans Relief Fund. But before I can go out, I must speak to Cook.'

As she rose from the table Ross caught her hand.

'Have you anything planned for tomorrow? I thought, if this good weather holds, you might like to come riding with me.'

He was absently rubbing his thumb over her wrist and tiny arrows of heat shot through her arm. Her skin burned from the contact, even though his grip was light. She was obliged to concentrate hard in order to answer calmly.

'I have no plans that cannot be changed, my lord, and I confess that I should dearly like to ride out with you.'

'Good, then we shall spend the day together.' He released her. 'There, it is settled. Now off you go about your duties, my lady!'

'Thank you, my lord, I shall!'

She swept him a deep curtsy and he laughed. 'Away with you, baggage!'

She left the room and Ross turned back to finish his breakfast. It occurred to him that he laughed a great deal more now than before Carenza had arrived.

He had spoken true; she was good for him.

'I am sorry I have kept you waiting. Jarvis had an urgent matter to discuss with me this morning.' Ross apologised as he hurried into the hall, where Carenza was waiting for him.

'If he needs you, my lord, we can always postpone our ride.'

'No, it is resolved now.' He ushered her out of the door. 'He wants to hire more men to help with the harvest.'

'Do we need them?'

'Extra hands are always useful.' He hesitated. 'There are a number of ex-soldiers in the area. Men turned off after the war and now destitute.'

'Then we must certainly help as many as we can,' she replied. 'In fact, we might even keep them on through the winter, if you do not object.'

'And what would they do?'

She tucked her hand in his arm. 'I was meaning to talk with you about this, my lord. You see, the rector has plans to set up a school for the village children and he says there is an old ruin near the church that could be used for the purpose. It is part of the Auster estate.'

'I see.'

'If you have no use for it, perhaps we could have the building restored as a schoolhouse. The work could be carried out over the winter.'

'Let me see if I understand you, madam. You want me to retain these extra workers and pay them to build a schoolhouse.'

'Well, yes.'

'On land that I presume you would have me make over to the village for the purpose?'

'The rector says it is a very *small* plot and has been standing idle for years.'

She waited in silence for his reply, unable to tell from his countenance what he thought of the idea.

'I know the piece of land you mean,' he said at last. 'Amos mentioned it when he was here. Suggested we should turn it to some use.'

'And what better use could there be than a school?'

'He was thinking more of something profitable. Even selling it.'

'Oh. Yes. Of course.'

'No *of course* about it,' he replied. 'I think your suggestion is a much better one. I had been wondering what more we might do to help those poor devils.'

They had reached the stable yard where Sam Rigby was waiting with their horses. Ross threw Carenza up into the saddle and held on to the bridle until she was settled.

'The idea of putting them to work on the schoolhouse is an excellent one,' he went on. 'They will learn crafts other than fighting that they can use to support themselves.'

'You agree, then?' she asked him, wanting to be sure she had not misunderstood.

'Yes, I agree.' He swung himself up into the saddle. 'It shall be a gift to the village, to celebrate our wedding. Now, shall we go?'

They spent the rest of the morning riding around Auster, stopping often for Ross to introduce his bride to the labourers and tenant farmers that they met. He had sent word ahead to the George, the coaching inn on the Exeter road, and they stopped there at noon to enjoy a cold collation before riding up onto the moors. It was a glorious day and Carenza turned her face up to the sun, closing her eyes as she listened to a skylark trilling joyously in the clear blue sky.

'Thank you,' she said impulsively. 'I am enjoying this so very much.'

'We can go a little further if you wish,' he said, amused. 'We have the whole day to ourselves.'

He led the way to the edge of an escarpment and waved his hand at the landscape spread out before them. 'This is mostly Auster lands. Where would you like to go, my lady?'

She pointed at the trees covering the steep slope below them. 'I should like to explore the wood. It is very warm up here on the moors and I am sure the horses would welcome the shade.'

'Come along, then.'

They made their way into the wood, which was indeed cooler with a thick canopy of leaves providing cover from the hot sun. Ross led the way through the trees and was about to turn for home when Carenza halted.

'What is that?' She tilted her head to one side. 'I am sure I can hear water.'

Ross listened. 'The Hidden Pool,' he said. 'I had quite forgotten. Would you like to see it?'

He forced a way through the undergrowth and soon they found themselves on the edge of a large pool. It was surrounded by trees on three sides and a waterfall cascaded noisily from the high cliff on the fourth.

'But this is so beautiful, Ross!'

'Sebastian and I used to come here as boys.'

'Can we dismount and walk a little?' she asked him.

'By all means.'

He helped her down, then reached out for her hand. 'The ground here is uneven and I would not want you to fall in.'

Carenza doubted there was any real danger but she was happy to put her hand in his as they explored the glade. There was little breeze here and she tugged at her neckcloth.

'This must be ideal for bathing,' she remarked, looking wistfully at the water.

'It is, but the rocks fall away quickly a few feet from the edge and it is too deep to stand. One must be able to swim.'

'I can swim,' she told him. 'At least, I could. Papa taught me. But that was years ago. I have most likely forgotten how.'

'I doubt it.'

'I hope you are correct, because I am so hot and the pool looks so inviting. What do you say, my lord, shall we try the water?'

It was madness, of course. Carenza was surprised at herself for suggesting it, but they were so at ease together the words had slipped out before she had a chance to consider.

'Out of the question.'

She had expected that, but having come this far, she decided to pursue the idea a little further.

'If you are thinking it would be improper, I believe it is quite the thing now for ladies to bathe in the sea,' she argued. 'I do not have a bathing gown but I am sure my shift will do the trick.'

'It is not *your* body that needs to be hidden!'

'Ross, your damaged skin is not so very bad, I promise you.'

'Do not lie to me!'

'I do not lie. Surely, your mirror must tell you—'

'I only ever look at my face in the mirror. That is bad enough!'

'As a consequence, you have allowed your imagination to make the situation far worse than it really is.'

He was still frowning. 'You sound like my old nanny.'

'I have no doubt she was a very sensible woman so I shall take that as a compliment, my lord.'

That evoked a genuine laugh from him. 'Then you are easily pleased.' He gave her hand a slight tug. 'Come along. It is time we were heading back.'

They remounted and Carenza followed Ross out of the glade, disappointed but not surprised by his response. He had come to believe himself grotesque and unlovable. She was determined to show him it was not true.

Once they were clear of the trees, Ross glanced up at the sky. Dark clouds were billowing up in the west and he thought they would be lucky to reach home before the storm broke. He should not have extended their ride. His lips tightened. Certainly, he should not have taken Carenza to the Hidden Pool. When she had invited him to swim with her, looking up at him through those long, dark lashes, for one heady moment he had been sorely tempted. It was only the thought of exposing his ragged and distorted flesh to her gaze that had stopped him throwing off his clothes and joining her in the cool water. He closed his eyes and cursed inwardly.

'Ross?' Carenza had brought the grey mare alongside Aethon and was looking at him anxiously. She reached out to touch his arm. 'Are you ill?'

Her concern flayed him. It felt too much like pity and he shook off her hand. 'Leave me be, madam. It is nothing.'

He shut his lips firmly against saying anything more. He was being a brute and hated himself for it. He desperately wanted to explain the pain and bitterness and self-loathing that tormented him but it was all trapped inside his head. He clenched his fists on the reins.

'Pay me no heed, Carenza.' He forced out the words. 'I...regret... I cannot be a perfect husband.'

He had managed to speak but his voice sounded cold, heartless. She must think him a monster.

They rode together in silence for several minutes, then she spoke quietly.

'Perhaps we are well matched, then. You and I,' she said quietly. 'Neither of us is perfect.'

'What a dashed foolish thing to say, madam!'

'No, I am being honest. I have always known that I am no beauty. That is why there was really no point in my having a come-out. Without a fortune no one would offer for me and it would have wasted a great deal of Papa's money.' She sighed. 'I am not tall enough, you see. My figure is best described as generous and I have it on good authority that my mouth is too wide, my brows too black and my nose is not quite straight.' She hesitated. 'Papa has told me many times how much I look like my mama, but she was so ill-favoured her portrait is not displayed anywhere at Morwood. It is hidden away in an attic, if it still exists at all. So, there it is. I am far from perfect.'

That is not true at all. You are perfect, Carenza. You are beautiful!

Damn the black devil inside that stopped him from telling her!

Ross thought how sultry it had become. The air was close and heavy around them, adding to the deepening mood of gloom that had him in its grip.

'What a good time for us to return to the house,' remarked Carenza, gathering up her reins. 'The clouds have quite obliterated the sun.'

At that moment a low rumble of thunder sounded in the distance.

'A storm is coming,' he muttered, urging Aethon to a canter. 'We must get back.'

They had just reached the road back to Auster when the first fat drops of rain fell and soon it was a steady downpour. Ross slowed and looked about him.

'We should seek cover.'

'We cannot be more than a mile from Auster,' said Carenza, stopping beside him. 'Let us ride on.'

'If you wish, but you will be drenched.'

She laughed. 'I am already drenched. Come on!'

After the heat of the day, Carenza did not mind the rain, although soon her clothes were wet through, the skirts hanging heavily around Elvira's flanks. Ross rode beside her, the brim of his hat low over his eyes. Despite the wet, Carenza felt a fizz of happiness as they cantered back towards Auster. She had enjoyed her day with Ross and felt they were growing closer. It augured well for the future.

As if to contradict her a growl of thunder rolled around the darkening sky.

'We need to hurry,' Ross muttered, crouching lower in the saddle and increasing the pace.

Carenza urged the mare on but she could not keep up. Auster was in sight now at the far side of the meadow and she was quite happy to let the hunter surge ahead. She smiled, thinking how she would tease Ross later for being so ungentlemanly as to abandon her.

A flash lit up the sky. At the same time there was a crash of thunder and Elvira threw up her head. Carenza steadied the mare, and when she looked up again, she saw that Aethon had stopped his headlong gallop and come to a stand, snorting and sidling nervously.

As she rode up Carenza saw that Ross was gazing blankly ahead of him, the reins slack between his fingers. Quickly, she reached out to grab the bridle. The chestnut jibbed at the unfamiliar hand and she was obliged to soothe the horse before turning her attention back to the rider. Ross was very pale and she asked him quickly what was wrong. He turned his head and his wild, burning gaze looked right through her, as if he had been struck by a lightning bolt.

'Ross! *Talk to me!*'

The urgency of her tone had an effect. He took control of the reins.

'Thank you, I can manage now,' he told her. 'Aethon was alarmed by the noise, that was all. Come on, we must get indoors.'

He set off again and Carenza followed, but her little bubble of happiness had gone. It seemed to her that it was Ross who had been startled, not the horse.

The thunder continued to crash above them as they rode into the stable yard. Sam Rigby ran out to take the hunter's head while one of the stable lads came forward to help Carenza. By the time she had dismounted Ross had disappeared. She ran inside to Aethon's stall, wondering if he was helping to unsaddle his horse, but she saw only the groom, murmuring softly to the restless creature.

'Where is His Lordship, Sam?'

The man looked up, a frown clouding his usually cheerful countenance.

'He'll have gone into the house, my lady. To get out o' his wet clothes.' Aethon snorted and stamped and Sam turned back to him. 'Hush, my beauty, you're all safe now.'

Carenza fixed her gaze on the horse. 'There was a thunderclap.'

'Aye, that'd do it, my lady. Loud noises unsettle him, but he'll come round, you'll see. Just give him time and he'll be right as rain.'

She turned an angry gaze upon the groom.

'Surely that is very unsatisfactory,' she declared. 'His Lordship could be seriously hurt, if Aethon is so easily panicked.'

Sam had been frowning at her, but at this his brow cleared. 'Nay, His Lordship is a fine rider, ma'am. He'll not come to any harm on old Aethon. This horse'll bring him home safe every time, you mark my words.'

He smiled, touched one finger to his hair in a salute and went back to his duties, leaving Carenza to make her way indoors.

When she reached the hall there was no sign of the Viscount, but there was an unusual amount of activity. An assortment of trunks and bags were piled at the bottom of the stairs and two footmen were running back and forth, carrying them upstairs.

Carenza looked an enquiry at the butler, who informed her that His Lordship's sister had arrived.

'I have shown Mrs Burnley into the morning room, my lady, and supplied refreshments while Mrs Stoke is making ready the guest rooms.'

Carenza blinked. 'Oh, dear, and I was not here to receive her!'

She flinched as a particularly loud crash of thunder burst over the house. Stoke's impassive countenance relaxed slightly into a look of understanding.

'A real heavy storm this is, ma'am, and no mistake. Sets everyone on edge.'

'Let us hope it passes soon,' she said, heading for the stairs. 'Give Mrs Burnley my compliments, Stoke, and tell her I will be with her as soon as I have changed.'

Carenza quickly exchanged her sodden clothes for a day dress of embroidered orange sarsnet, but her thick hair was still damp when she made her way downstairs

again and she threw a muslin fichu about her shoulders
to catch the water that obstinately trickled down from
the neat braids.

She entered the morning room to find Dido flick-
ing through a copy of *The Gentleman's Magazine*, a tea
tray as well as a glass of ratafia and a plate of sweet
biscuits on a table at her elbow. When the door opened,
she dropped the periodical and rose to her feet.

'My dear Carenza, forgive me for descending upon
you in this way!' Dido enveloped her in a warm, scented
hug. 'Austerfield's letter incensed me so much that I set
off immediately to see you.'

'You did?'

'Why, of course! As soon as my foolish brother wrote
to say you would not be coming to town, I decided that
I must come to *you*!' She kissed Carenza's cheek and
drew her over to the sofa. 'Come and sit down, my love.
I had them cobble together a small fire in here as soon
as I heard you were out riding, for I knew just how it
would be with this rain. You would be soaked through
and no way to dry that glorious hair! Ross has never had
any consideration for the weather, you know.'

Carenza uttered a mild protest. 'It was hardly his
fault that we were caught in a storm, ma'am.'

'Nonsense. He should know it always rains after a
dry spell!'

This was so unarguable that Carenza's lip quivered
as she murmured, 'You are quite right.'

'Well, well,' Dido exclaimed, looking about her. 'You
have made improvements already, I am pleased to say.'

'Thank you, but truly, I have done very little.'

'Rearranging the furniture out of its old, formal setting, fresh flowers on the table and the best Meissen tea
service in use again? I call that a vast improvement,'

declared her sister-in-law. 'And there is an air of liveliness about the house that has been absent for too long. Auster has been missing a lady's touch.'

Carenza knew not what to say to that, but soon realised an answer was unnecessary. Her guest was in full flow.

'Now, I hope you will not object, but I have had to make use of several of your guest rooms—I was sure you would not have visitors yet and I hoped you would not object.'

'Not in the least, ma'am, but why do you need so many?'

'My dear, pray, do call me Dido. We are sisters now, after all! Where was I? Oh, yes. One of the reasons you should be going to town is to procure clothes more suited to your rank. What you are wearing is perfectly charming, my dear, but you are not accustomed to moving in the first circles and can have no comprehension of the number of dresses you will need to fulfil your role! I decided, therefore, that my wedding gift to you would be an introduction to Collette, my own modiste, and the purchase of several suitable gowns. Heaven knows I had such short notice of your wedding that there was no time to buy you anything in advance! And I have not the slightest doubt that it was Ross's idea to bury yourselves away here, but it will not do, Carenza! He has obligations, as I shall tell him when I see him. Where is he, by the way? He did come back with you, did he not?'

'Why, yes, Mrs—I mean Dido.' The image of Ross's white face and burning eyes flashed into her mind. 'Perhaps I should go and find him.'

'No, do not trouble yourself. Stoke sent up word that I was here and I am sure Ross will appear when he is ready.' She pursed her lips. 'I suppose he thinks he need not stand upon ceremony with his sister. Ah well, we shall go on very well without him.'

Mrs Burnley drained her glass and Carenza carried it over to the sideboard to refill it with ratafia, pouring a glass for herself at the same time. She felt in need of something stronger than tea to sustain her while she was in the company of her sister-in-law.

'Now, as I was saying,' Dido continued, when they were both seated again. 'I was quite put out when Ross wrote to say you would not be in London, but I am not one to be easily turned from my purpose. I have brought Collette with me, along with two of her assistants, dozens of fashion plates and a whole carriageful of materials! I described you to her and together we decided upon the colours that would best suit you.'

'I—I am quite overwhelmed,' stammered Carenza. 'I am sure I cannot accept such munificence.'

'You can and you shall, to oblige me. When Mr Burnley died, he left me with no children, sadly, but more money than I shall ever require. It is quite delightful to have someone else to spend it on. I am sorry I did not give you notice of my arrival, but I thought it more important to set off for Auster, that we might rig you out in style as soon as possible.' She looked searchingly at Carenza. 'You look uncertain. If you are concerned that Ross will object to having so many people staying here, then I have thought of a solution, should he decide to turn us out. We shall put up at the King's Arms in Bideford!'

Carenza sipped her wine and wondered what the hapless landlord would think if the lady and her entourage were to descend upon him that evening. She doubted he would be able to withstand the widow's fearsome de-

mands and had a sudden image of guests being ejected
from their rooms without notice.

'I have no idea what the Viscount will think of your
arrival,' she said frankly. 'But it would be absurd for
you to put up at an hotel when we have so many empty
rooms. For my part I am delighted to see you.'

'Of course you are!' Dido beamed at her and clapped
her hands. 'We shall have such fun together, my dear.
I cannot wait to show you all the lovely things Collette
has brought with her.'

She rattled on and Carenza did her best to concentrate, but she could not help wondering why Ross had
not appeared. She was on the point of excusing herself
to go and find him when Dido rose, saying she must
change for dinner.

'La, I had not realised how the time has gone on.
No need to come with me, my dear. I know my way
perfectly well.'

She swept out and Carenza waited, giving her guest
time to reach her bedchamber before she left the morning room and went in search of the Viscount. The butler
informed her that His Lordship had not come downstairs, so she made her way to his bedchamber, steeling
herself to knock firmly upon the door. Brisco appeared
and stepped out into the passage.

'How may I help Your Ladyship?' he enquired, pulling the door closed behind him.

'I wish to see His Lordship.'

'I regret that is not possible at present, ma'am.'

'Is he ill?'

'No-o, not exactly.' His eyes slid away from her enquiring gaze.

'Let me talk to him—'

She went to pass him but he blocked her way.

'I'm afraid not, my lady. The Major gave me strict instructions that no one's to go in.' He looked at her uneasily. 'I beg ye, ma'am, leave him be. He don't like anyone to see him when he is like this.'

Carenza regarded him with narrowed eyes.

'You were a soldier in his regiment, were you not, Mr Brisco? You obey his commands implicitly.'

'I'd give my life for His Lordship,' he said simply. A rueful smile appeared. 'And he'd take it, too, if I was to let you in.'

'Very well, I shall not enter his room. But you must tell me what ails him.' He looked even more alarmed at that. She put up her chin. 'I shall not leave until you have done so!'

He sighed. 'It comes over him now and again, you see, the dark mood when he will see no one. Too much soldiering, ma'am. Too many battles. It's worn him out.'

She did not understand, but the man was sincere, she was certain of it. She nodded slowly.

'Very well. I will not disturb him tonight.'

The valet looked relieved. 'Thank 'ee, my lady. He'll be himself again in a day or two, you'll see.'

As he turned to go back into the room she stopped him. 'Tell His Lordship I was asking after him.'

Chapter Fifteen

'So my brother is not joining us for dinner.' Dido shook out her napkin with a snap. 'I should not be surprised to learn he has contracted a chill after his drenching. I do not believe he has ever fully recovered from his injuries.'

'Was he very ill?' asked Carenza, deciding this would be a good opportunity to learn something more of her husband.

'Oh, at death's door, my dear,' replied Dido. 'At first we thought he had perished at Waterloo, because there was no word for weeks after the battle. That was a blow, of course, coming so soon upon his brother's death. However, he survived, despite the most appalling injuries that have left him horridly disfigured. But as his wife, you will know that better than I.'

All the servants except the butler had withdrawn and Carenza could only hope Stoke was accustomed to Mrs Burnley's forthright speech. The temptation to learn more was too great to resist.

'Was he…is he much changed since he returned to England?'

'Oh, yes. Well, I *believe* so, but I was married at one-

and-twenty, when Ross was seventeen, and I have seen very little of him since then, so I really cannot tell you when the change occurred.' Dido considered this while she helped herself to the rice. 'As a boy he was adventurous, even reckless. No horse was too strong, no fence too high. The army proved a good choice for him. He loved the life, and as we discovered when we sought news of him after Waterloo, not only was he respected by his superiors but his men thought very highly of him. Those that were left, that is. There was such chaos and confusion after the battle and it was weeks before we discovered he was alive.'

'How did you learn of it?' asked Carenza.

'A letter, quite out of the blue, saying he was coming home.' Dido tutted. 'If that isn't just like Ross! Brisco nursed him until he was well enough to be shipped back to Portsmouth where they chanced upon another of his old comrades who is now his groom. They accompanied him to Auster and here he has stayed ever since, save for his trip to London to find a wife, but you will know all about that, my dear!'

Carenza blushed but Dido did not notice and carried on cheerfully.

'Ross says there is nothing more the doctors can do for him. I suppose it is hardly surprising he is so reclusive, but I hope that will change, now he is married. I live in hopes his temper will improve, too. One never knows if he is going to rip up over something. You must not let him bully you, my dear.'

'I won't,' Carenza assured her, smiling a little. 'But it is understandable if he is a little short-tempered, with all that has happened to him.'

'Perhaps you are right. He was very attached to Sebastian, of course; I think his brother's death hit him

very hard.' Dido sighed. 'I believe he would happily
have passed on the title to his cousin, if it had been
possible.'

'That would be Mr Amos Paston.'

'Yes. Do you know him?'

'We have met,' said Carenza cautiously. 'He called
here, soon after we arrived.'

'The devil he did!' exclaimed Mrs Burnley, in a
very unladylike manner. 'The impudence of the man!
No doubt he sees the inheritance slipping from his
grasp. And a good thing, too, for I cannot like him,
even though I am told he did help to bring Ross back
to Auster.'

Carenza was silent, remembering how uneasy she
had felt in Amos Paston's company.

'But all that is past now,' Dido continued, beaming.
'I am sure we are all looking forward to Ross having
a family of his own. Which reminds me, Collette has
included several deliciously fine nightgowns for you to
choose from. All lace and froth and *scandalously* sheer.
Designed to drive a husband wild, my dear! Since Ross
is not joining us this evening, what say you we go to see
Collette after dinner and set her to work immediately
on your trousseau?'

It was near midnight when Carenza eventually
climbed into her bed. She and Dido had spent a couple
of happy hours with the modiste. They admired the
nightgowns, pored over fashion plates and inspected
the part-finished dresses, several of which met with
Carenza's approval. After a quick fitting, the modiste
promised that her assistants would work through the
night to have some of them completed by the morning.

Images of the gowns floated past her eyes as Carenza

lay in the darkness. The styles were far different from anything she had ever owned before. Dido had told her they were all the highest kick of fashion and Carenza could not help a little tremor of excitement at the thought of wearing such creations. If Collette was as good as her word, then one of the first gowns to be finished would be a stylish morning gown of emerald green tamboured muslin, which Dido assured her was particularly becoming. Carenza hoped Ross would agree.

She turned onto her side and snuggled one hand against her cheek, imagining a time when her husband might look at her with admiration and, thinking of those scandalous nightgowns, perhaps something more.

Mrs Burnley was already breaking her fast when Carenza sat down at the table the next morning.

'How is our invalid?' Dido asked, after bidding her a cheerful good morning.

'Better,' she replied slowly. 'He is gone out riding.'

'Riding? Is that wise?'

That had been very much Carenza's reaction when Brisco had given her the news. Now she held her peace as Dido continued to animadvert at length upon her brother.

'If ever there was such a headstrong, contrary man I have never met him!' she declared, reaching for another bread roll. 'Even as a boy he would never listen to anyone's advice. How he ever managed as a soldier, taking orders, I have no idea. Although I suppose as an officer he was more used to *giving* the commands. And from all I have heard he acquitted himself well, which was quite unexpected, because as a boy he was always in a scrape and flouting the rules. Papa maintained he was born to be hanged!'

Listening to the Viscount's loving sister holding forth in such a manner amused Carenza and did much to cheer her. They were both worried about Ross, but there was little they could do about it and, as Dido told her, while he had the loyal Brisco and Sam Rigby to look after him, he would not come to much harm.

When they had broken their fast, Dido carried Carenza off to see the modiste and her assistants. The fabrics they had brought with them yesterday had now been unpacked and spread out around the room. Silks, satins, bolts of lustring and sarsnet jostled with lengths of merino cloth and Indian muslins. A small table was spread with ribbons, frogging and braid while a trunk stood open under the window, a treasure trove of reticules, fans, shawls and gloves of every hue.

Carenza was requested to stand in the middle of the room while the modiste and Mrs Burnley circled slowly around her.

'Now you have seen her in daylight, Collette, do you think I described her correctly to you? The first time I saw Lady Austerfield I knew she was not quite in the usual style.'

'You are right, madam,' agreed the modiste, her face alight with enthusiasm for the task ahead. 'We shall make more of that, not less. We will choose colours that will flatter her black hair and olive skin. My lady will look superb!'

'But am I not a little…' Carenza bit her lip. 'Am I not too short to look well in these fashions?'

'By no means!' Collette assured her earnestly. 'You have a figure to be envied, my lady. It does my heart good to have the dressing of one who actually has a shape, rather than a mop stick!'

Flattered and a little dazed by such unaccustomed praise, Carenza submitted to the modiste's ministrations. Pattern books were consulted, fabrics draped around her, while Mrs Burnley and Collette discussed the merits of gold or silver frogging, Vandyked lace and Mameluke sleeves. It was all very new and exciting and it was past noon before she looked at the clock and recollected she had not yet agreed tonight's dinner with Cook.

She left Dido with the modiste and made her way along the corridor to the stairs. When she passed one of the windows she stopped, enjoying the fine view over the shrubbery and the belt of trees beyond it to the distant cliff. A movement caught her eye and she could see a rider galloping towards the ruined tower. A rider in a dark coat and with a chestnut-coloured horse. Was it Ross? Carenza strained her eyes to watch. The horse and rider passed the tower without slowing and, for one heart-wrenching moment, she feared they were not going to stop, that they would plunge over the cliff and onto the deadly rocks beneath. It seemed to her that the horse was dangerously close to the sheer drop before it finally turned and began to canter along the cliff.

Perfectly safe, she told herself. If it was Ross, he was merely enjoying a gallop. Sam had told her Aethon would always bring his master back safe and she must believe that. She had no choice. She pushed aside the little worm of fear gnawing away inside and continued down the stairs.

Carenza was making her way across the hall later that afternoon when Ross walked into the house. For a moment she went giddy with relief. He was mud spat-

tered and very pale, but she concealed her anxiety behind a smile as she stopped to greet him.

'You are back. How was your ride?'

He barely broke his stride and glanced at her as if he
had not understood the question.

'Good,' he muttered at last, taking the stairs two at
a time.

'Is that all?' She hurried after him but said no more
until they had reached the deserted corridor leading to
their bedchambers. Then she reached out and caught
his arm.

'Will you not talk to me, my lord? I have been very
worried about you. I thought I saw you at Shepherd's
Leap.'

He swung around, shaking off her hand.

'I do not want you to worry over me!' he snapped.
'I know my duty. There was no danger of my taking
my own life.'

She recoiled and prayed he had not read her thoughts.
'No, of course not. Oh, Ross—'

Instinctively she reached out again but he jumped
away, snarling at her.

'For God's sake, leave me alone, woman. I do not
want your pity!'

With that he disappeared into his room, slamming
the door behind him, and Carenza was left staring at
the empty space.

She was still fretting over their encounter when she
joined Mrs Burnley in the drawing room before dinner,
but tried to put it out of her mind and said instead how
much she had enjoyed her morning with the modiste.

'I cannot thank you enough for all you are doing for
me, Dido. I thought I had no interest in my attire, but

I was quite wrong!' She added shyly, 'It was very different when Lady Bettridge provided all my gowns. I was never called upon to give an opinion.'

Her sister-in-law gave an unladylike snort. 'Pale pastels might look well on those washed-out daughters of hers but they do nothing for you. It is no wonder you had no interest in clothes, if you never had the pleasure of choosing them for yourself. Well, that will change now. You can spend a fortune on your back if you wish to do so.'

Carenza was a little startled by the thought and said, laughing, 'Good heavens, would you have me ruin His Lordship with my extravagance? No, no, you have been more than generous, providing me with so many gowns. I have sufficient now for years to come.'

Dido looked at her sternly.

'Sufficient for this year, perhaps, but in the spring I shall insist you come to London with me to buy more,' she said. 'I am sure Ross will agree with me!'

The Viscount came in at that moment. Carenza thought he still looked pale and tension made the web of scars on his face more prominent than they had been of late.

'Ah, so there you are at last, Brother,' cried Dido, in her usual acerbic manner. 'I was beginning to think you were avoiding me.'

'I would not be so uncivil,' he said, bestowing a perfunctory kiss on her cheek before walking over to the sideboard to help himself to a glass of wine. 'How long do you intend to stay?'

'I see marriage has not improved your manners,' she retorted.

He scowled at that. Carenza broke in quickly.

'Dido has come with fabrics, patterns and even

seamstresses to make up the gowns for me. Is that not kind of her?'

She fixed Ross with a bright smile and was relieved to see his frown lessen.

'Yes, I had heard.'

'You are not to be worrying that my carriages and cattle are filling up your stables,' declared Dido. 'I would have sent them off to the village, but Jarvis told me there would be room for them all in the barns at the Home Farm for a week or two. Once Collette and her minions have gone back to town there will only be my travelling chaise to accommodate.'

Ross lifted his glass to her and drawled, 'You appear to have thought of everything, my dear sister.'

He wandered over to the fireplace and rested one foot on the empty grate.

Dido graciously inclined her head. 'I shall be here some weeks,' she announced. 'There is a great deal of work to do to turn your wife into a viscountess, Austerfield. Also, I shall be able to help you with the arrangements for the ball.'

Ross looked up. 'There is not going to be a ball.'

'Pray do not be so teasing, Brother. What is the point of Grandpapa adding the ballroom here if you do not use it? You know your new Viscountess must be introduced to the neighbourhood.' Dido laughed. 'It will be like the old days. We had such magnificent balls here when we were younger. Of course, once I was married and you were in the army we only managed to attend occasionally. Do you remember, Ross? The world and his wife were invited. Those parties were *such* a crush and everyone would talk of them for weeks afterwards!'

His lips thinned. 'I have raised no objection to morning callers, but I will not have the house filled with hordes of people. It is out of the question.'

'But you must have a ball!' Dido could not hide her astonishment. 'Your neighbours expect it, even if they have not said as much. Think, Brother! It would be taken as a slight upon your new wife if you do not celebrate your marriage with a party.'

Carenza leaned forward. 'I assure you, Dido, I do not want—'

'It is not a case of what you *want*, but what is due to our family name,' Dido interrupted her. 'It is bad enough that Ross married you out of hand and refuses to take you to London. If he fails to introduce you properly to his neighbours it will look very odd indeed. They may well assume you are not worthy of the position.'

Carenza was inclined to think that was the truth and she was astonished when Ross agreed with his sister.

'Dido is right, damn her! We must hold a ball. I would not have anyone think I am ashamed of my wife.'

'But, Ross,' Carenza objected, 'Auster is your refuge. I know how much you abhor crowds. You would have no peace.'

'Only for the one night,' said Dido crisply. 'Ross need not trouble himself with the details. We shall arrange the whole.'

Carenza was not convinced, but before she could muster her arguments, the Viscount came across to sit beside her.

'Do you dislike the idea so much?' he asked gently.

'Not for myself, sir, but for you. To have so many people invading your home, I know you would greatly dislike it!'

He took her hand. 'Bless you for your concern, but it must be done. I have not behaved well to you, marry-

ing you in haste and bringing you to this out of the way
place. You have borne it all with admirable calm and I
hope this will be some recompense, especially for my
black moods and irascible temper.'

Carenza realised he was acknowledging his earlier
anger. His rueful look was as close to an apology as she
would receive from him, but it was enough. She gave
a little nod and he kissed her fingers.

'You are too good to me, Carenza!' The mischievous gleam was back in his eyes as he added, 'Besides,
with you and my sister to arrange everything, there
will be precious little for me to do save to be present
on the day!'

'Excellent.' Dido gave a satisfied nod. 'The Bet-
tridges will be pleased to see how comfortably their
daughter is settled.'

Carenza looked up, alarmed at the prospect, but it
was Ross who spoke first.

'I should be delighted to welcome Lord Bettridge
here, if he is well enough to travel.'

'Alas he is not, my lord,' Carenza replied sadly. 'Anything more than a short, gentle drive is too much for
him these days.'

'I suspected as much,' he replied. 'I would rather
your stepmother and her daughters did not come here
without him. Unless you particularly want to see them,
Carenza?'

She gave him a little smile, grateful for his understanding.

'No,' she murmured. 'I am not quite ready to face
them yet.'

'What is this?' demanded Dido, looking intrigued.

Ross turned to her. 'My wife was not treated kindly
at Morwood and I find that very hard to forgive. They

shall have time to reflect upon their behaviour before we invite them to stay with us and, when they do, I shall expect them to treat my wife with the respect she is due.'

Carenza felt a little glow of happiness at these words and the look that accompanied them. It was full of pride and affection, and she squirrelled it away like a rare treasure.

Chapter Sixteen

'That will be all, Dan. Goodnight.' Ross fastened his banyan and walked across the room to the armchair.

'It is early yet, Major, are you sure you don't want me to stay?'

'No, I thank you. I shall read until I am tired enough to sleep.'

With a nod, Brisco reluctantly left the room and Ross tried to settle down with his book. He knew his man was anxious for him, and with good reason. There had been times in the past when he had drunk himself into oblivion to stop the nightmares, but he was determined not to take that course tonight. Not only because waking up was even worse, but since his marriage he had not enjoyed sitting alone in the dining room, lingering over his brandy. Thus, when the ladies had retired early this evening he had accompanied them, escorting his wife to her door and bidding her goodnight with a chaste kiss on the cheek.

Carenza.

Her image rose in front of him and he felt again the tug of desire. She had looked delightful tonight; the new gown of amber silk had given her skin an added glow and he had found it hard to keep his eyes off her. She was unaware of her allure and thought herself quite unworthy of him, but he found her ever more attractive. He had glimpsed a strong, mischievous spirit in her. It cheered him to see her eyes twinkling with laughter and at such times he wanted to pull her into his arms and enjoy the sweet intoxication of her kisses. He shook his head to dispel the distracting thoughts and fixed his eyes resolutely on his book.

Ross read a page, maybe two, before his mind drifted again. He remembered their ride together and how at ease they had been in each other's company. So much so that she had made that outrageous remark about bathing together at the Hidden Pool! He would have enjoyed that, the freedom of swimming with her, teasing her. Pulling her naked body against his and kissing her...

He shifted uncomfortably. Confound it, that must never happen! He had already risked their delicate friendship with his damnable temper. They had been getting on so well until that clap of thunder had made him take leave of his senses. On that ride they had talked together, laughed together. She had made him forget his injuries and believe that at last he could conquer the madness that came over him at times, those black clouds of guilt and misery so thick he could see no future for himself. He had begun to think that he might have a chance of happiness, after all.

Then came the thunder and in an instant he was transported back to the battlefield. His head rang with the boom of the cannon, the urgent, shouted orders and screams of the dying, while the acrid smoke filled his nose and mouth. He was drowning again in sweat and blood and fear.

The thud of the book landing on the floor roused

him and he bent to retrieve it. His physical recovery had been swift this time and riding out on Aethon had done much to clear his head. But his nerves were still shredded and he had lashed out at Carenza. She did not deserve that. It must not happen again and for her sake, as well as his own, he must keep her at a distance.

Ross climbed into bed and spent a long time lying in the darkness, thinking about Carenza. When he eventually fell asleep, he was not troubled by terrifying nightmares. Instead he was disturbed by dreams of his wife, scenes where he gave in to his desires, only to have her push him away in disgust.

When Brisco came into his master's bedchamber at seven o'clock with his hot water, he took one look at Ross and frowned.

'Another bad night, Major?'

'I've had worse.' Ross threw back the bedclothes and walked over to the washstand. 'Send word to the stables to saddle Aethon. And apologies to the ladies that I shall not be joining them at breakfast.'

'You are going riding again, Major?'

'What is it to you if I am?' He rubbed a hand over his eyes and let out his breath in a long sigh. 'I beg your pardon, Dan. I am in the devil of a mood.'

'It ain't that bad if you can apologise to me,' said his valet cheerfully.

'No, you are right. This is different. I need to think, without being distracted by female chatter.'

Dan nodded, understanding writ large on his countenance.

'Before you go, sir, will you be using the cream Her Ladyship left for you? She charged me yesterday to remind you about it.'

Ross hesitated and Brisco gave a slight cough. 'If you'll forgive me, Major, I do believe the scars have receded somewhat since you've been applying the ointment.'

'Do you now?'

Brisco was in no wise deterred by his master's scowl or the menacing note in his voice.

'Aye, I do,' he replied, meeting his master's gaze. 'I think it was a good day when you married Her Ladyship, Major, and that's a fact.'

The Viscount returned to the stables shortly before noon, no closer to deciding whether it was better to share a house with Carenza, knowing he could never take her in his arms, or to set up a separate establishment and avoid the temptation. The problem was, he thought as he strode back to the house, he wasn't sure he could live without her now. Brisco was quite right, damn him: his life seemed so much better since he had married Carenza.

As if he had conjured her from thin air she appeared before him on the path. She was carrying a basket and over her black curls she wore a straw bonnet with deep lemon ribbons that were tied in a jaunty bow beneath one ear. She was wearing the matching lemon gown that rivalled the sun and he fancied he could see the luscious curves of her figure through the thin muslin.

It was clear she had not been expecting him, because her step faltered. She gave him a little smile, dipped a curtsy and slipped away through the gate into the flower garden. Ross berated himself silently, knowing she wished to avoid a repeat of his boorish behaviour yesterday. Quickly, he followed her.

'Good morning, my lady!' She stopped and waited for him to come up. 'May I walk with you?'

Her response was polite but wary. 'I am come to gather flowers for the drawing room, my lord.'

'Then let me help you.' She looked surprised and he added, 'If you recall, I am rather good at finding the best blooms.'

She flushed a little and his spirits lifted to know that she remembered.

'I am not collecting roses today, but if you are not too fatigued, you may carry the basket for me.'

A peace offering. He took the basket from her and they set off towards one of the colourful flower borders. He enjoyed walking slowly from plant to plant, watching her make her selection, carefully snipping the stems and placing each new bloom gently in the basket. It took little more than half an hour to gather all the flowers she required and he would happily have spent as long again.

'There, I am done.' She straightened and turned to smile up at him. 'Thank you, my lord.'

His brows rose. 'Are we so formal today?'

A shadow flitted across her features. 'I believe you want to keep some distance between us.'

'It is not what I *want*, Carenza, it is what I must do, for both our sakes.'

'I thought we were friends now.'

'We are.'

She shook her head. 'Friends talk to one another.'

'We are talking now.' He wanted to turn the conversation, but nothing occurred to him.

'On our ride the other day it was different,' she argued. 'You allowed me to tease you. Since then, I feel you have been pushing me away.'

'I am.' He added bitterly, 'I must.'

She stopped. 'But why? I do not understand you.'

'Because if I do not keep you at arm's length, I will not be able to help myself!'

Her eyes widened. Nervously she ran the tip of her tongue over her lips and desire, hot and urgent, pounded through his blood.

Turn and walk away, man. Now.

'Do you mean you would like to…to kiss me?' she stammered.

'Oh, more than that, Carenza,' he muttered, the words wrenched from him. 'Far more than that!'

'Then why not?' She stepped closer and rested her hand against his chest. 'We are man and wife, after all.'

Why not, indeed? He closed his eyes. Why not give in to temptation and take her in his arms? His fists clenched. Either that or take refuge in anger and storm away.

As if aware of his struggle, she clutched at his coat. 'Ross, there is a seat here. Will you not stay and talk with me?'

He gave in to the pressure of that tiny hand and walked with her to the bench. They sat down, a small gap between them. He fidgeted, putting the basket on the ground, removing his hat and placing it gently over the cut flowers, all the time trying to think how best to begin.

'Waterloo left me…scarred. Inside as well as out. I cannot forget what I saw, what I experienced, on the battlefield. The scenes are burned into my memory. I am haunted by them, especially at night. The dreams are so real that I am living those times, all over again.'

He rubbed his eyes, suddenly feeling very tired. He had never tried to put it into words before. He had never needed to do so. Dan Brisco and Sam Rigby were soldiers, they understood. Carenza, however, was watching him, hands folded, waiting for him to continue. Something about her gentle patience made it impossible for him to send her away without at least trying to explain.

'I am constantly on my guard against the memories and the pain they induce, but even that is not always enough to prevent them overwhelming me. Laying me low. That is what happened on our ride the other day.'

She said slowly, 'Was *I* responsible for that, was that why you were so cross with me the next day?'

'No,' he said emphatically. 'It was not your fault. I should never have allowed myself—' He broke off, raking his fingers through his hair. 'You were not to blame, Carenza. I should not have ripped up at you, forgive me. My temper is unpredictable, dangerous. Sometimes my mood is so black I want to strike out at everyone around me. Riding hard helps me to shake off my angry thoughts. That was what I was doing yesterday, when you saw me near Shepherd's Leap. There was no danger then, but I confess, there have been times when I was tempted to end it all.'

There. The words were out. He had voiced the unforgiveable. She would leave him now, shocked and disgusted by such an admission of weakness.

But instead Carenza moved closer and tucked her hand in his. 'Oh, Ross, I am so sorry. Tell me how I may help.'

Relief that she had not shunned him was swamped by the notion that she pitied him, and he could not bear that. He gently removed her hand from his sleeve and twisted away from her.

'You can help best by staying away from me.'

'I do not believe that!' He felt her arms go around

him and she rested her cheek on his back. 'I am your wife, Ross. Will you not let me comfort you?'

'No!' He shook her off and jumped to his feet. 'Confound it, madam, do you know what you are risking? You are cursed with me for a husband, Carenza, but I'll not make bad worse. At present, it is still possible to have our marriage annulled.'

He heard the quick indrawn breath and she said, in a small voice, 'Is that what you want?'

'No, but I offer it to you as an alternative to this sham of a marriage.' She was silent and he said roughly, 'I suggest you return to the house, madam, before your absence is noted.'

'Does that matter? I am not ashamed to be alone in the gardens with you.'

'How can you say that, now you know the truth about me?'

'All I know is that you are feeling very sorry for yourself!'

His brows snapped together. 'I beg your pardon?'

She jumped up from the bench. 'Your years as a soldier have left their mark on you, I know that, but I am your *wife*, sir. We made solemn and unbreakable vows to one another. My place is here with you, in sickness and in health.'

'Carenza—'

'Do not shut me out, Ross,' she begged him. 'Talk to me, tell me how to help you when you are not well.' She added shyly, 'Let me be a proper wife to you, Ross. We might even have a child—'

'No! How can you even think of it?' he demanded wrathfully. 'I will not pass on my tainted blood—'

'Who told you such nonsense? Your blood is not tainted.'

'You cannot be sure of that!'

'Brisco said you had done too much soldiering. You have seen too many horrors. *That* is what has affected your spirits; it is nothing to do with your blood.'

'You know nothing about it!'

'And you do? Have you had this from a medical man? No, I thought not.'

'That is *enough*, madam!' he said icily. 'These matters are not within your province. By God, I wish I had never brought you here!'

She reeled back as if he had struck her. He saw the blood drain from her cheeks.

'Now we are getting to the truth,' she whispered. 'You wish you had never married me.'

Unable to bear the stricken look in her eyes, Ross turned away.

'That is true,' he muttered, 'but not for the reasons you might think.'

An uncomfortable silence swirled about them. He dare not break it. He must keep his distance, not succumb to the temptation to beg her pardon, to sweep her into his arms and lose himself in her kisses.

'I know I am not the bride you deserve,' she said quietly. 'You are a hero, a soldier who gave everything to serve his King and country. But because of your scars you do not think yourself worthy of a perfect, beautiful wife. Instead, you chose to honour a very imperfect specimen. One who could never turn a man's head, who would pass unnoticed in company. You told me as much, when we first met.' He heard her moving away. 'You have been poorly served, sir, and I am sorry for it.'

There was a whisper of skirts and her firm, brisk steps on the gravel as she left him.

Chapter Seventeen

When Carenza had gone, Ross sank back down onto the bench and raked his fingers through his hair. What a crass fool he was! He had been so caught up in his own concerns he had not realised how she would interpret his words. Curse it, he would not hurt her for the world. He must find her, put things right with all speed.

He picked up his hat and the forgotten flower basket and hurried back to the house, but Carenza was nowhere to be found. He guessed she was avoiding him but he was determined to make his peace with her. He stationed himself in the hall and when she came down the stairs shortly before the dinner hour, he humbly requested a private word with her.

She looked as if she wanted to refuse, but after a heartbeat's hesitation she walked briskly into the morning room.

'You found the flowers?' he said, shutting the door behind them. 'I gave the basket to your maid.'

'Thank you, yes.' She spoke crisply, clearly not in a mood for idle chatter, so he came straight to the point.

'It was not my intention to upset you,' he said, taking her hand. 'Forgive me!'

She gently but firmly removed her fingers from his grasp.

'If I was upset it was quite my own fault,' she told him. 'I was determined that we should talk and I only have myself to blame if I did not like what was said. You have made no secret of the fact that you were barracked by your family into taking a wife. It should have been no surprise to me to learn you are now regretting it.'

'What I *regret* is trapping you into a loveless marriage.'

She flinched. 'Yes, but unless you wish to go through the indignity of an annulment, we must both make the best of it, my lord.'

She turned on her heel and stalked to the door.

'No! Carenza, wait!'

She turned and gave him an icy stare. 'Let me remind you we have a guest, sir. Your sister may very well be in the drawing room by this time, and wondering what has become of us.'

Carenza made her way across the hall, aware of Ross's firm tread behind her. He was regretting their marriage. That was hardly a surprise, but she was shocked at how much it hurt. Pride kept her moving. Not by the flutter of an eyelash would she admit how much it had cost her, when he asked for forgiveness, to not throw herself onto his broad chest and cling to him.

His slightest touch made her skin tingle, her body positively ached for him to kiss her, but earlier, in the flower garden, she had as good as offered him her body and he had refused her. She was too proud to ask again.

For the remainder of the evening Ross and Carenza were icily civil to one another. She was thankful for

Dido's presence because it obliged them to maintain society manners, manners that were going to have to sustain them through this pretence of a marriage, at least in public. A restless night brought little comfort because of the knowledge that this was how her life would be from now on. She and Ross would be polite acquaintances sharing a house.

'And why not?' she asked her mirror, as she brushed out her hair. 'He told you at the outset what was required and you agreed to it.'

Day after day Carenza presented to the world a calm façade. She and Ross behaved with impeccable politeness to one another, both aware that Dido was watching them closely. Occasionally one or other would relax their guard and there would be a little teasing, an inadvertent smile, before the shutters came down again.

At first, Carenza found some diversion in trying on Collette's final creations, but even that small solace ended when the modiste announced that her work was done and returned to London.

'We must be thankful she could come here at all,' remarked Carenza, the evening Collette departed. She smoothed her hands over the skirts of another new gown, this time a plum-coloured silk with an overdress of silver-striped French gauze. 'She is so good, I am sure she must be extremely busy.'

'She is one of the best,' Dido affirmed. 'I must say that she has excelled herself with the gowns she made up for you, my dear. Do you not agree, Ross?'

He gave a faint smile. 'My lady has never looked better.'

Carenza inclined her head in acknowledgement. All very polite, very cold. Stifling a sigh, she turned again to her sister-in-law.

'I can never thank you sufficiently for arranging it all, Dido. I believe I have more clothes than I can ever wear!'

'Which is as it should be,' Dido replied. 'The only item outstanding is your ball gown and Collette can make that up in London, now we have decided upon the fabric and the style.'

'You will oblige me, Sister, by having it put to my account,' said Ross, without looking up. 'You have already lavished a fortune on my wife.'

'But it is my money, and I have thoroughly enjoyed spending it,' replied Dido, laughing.

'I do not doubt it, but on this point, I insist. Pray instruct your modiste that no expense is to be spared in making my lady's gown.'

He called for more wine and Dido threw such a knowing look at Carenza that she blushed.

'I—I thank you, my lord,' she stammered. 'I hope I shall not disappoint you.'

'You could never do that.'

The fierce glow in his grey-green eyes was quite unexpected and hope flared again in Carenza's breast. Nothing more was said, and they parted as usual with a brief 'goodnight,' but she went to bed in considerably better spirits than she had enjoyed for some time.

Scarcely had the impromptu sewing rooms been returned to a state of readiness than one of them was required for another unexpected guest.

It was the end of August and Ross was in his study, working on his accounts. At least, he was trying to do so, but his mind kept wandering to Carenza. She was out with Dido and he was glad she had someone to accompany her as she made her calls upon the neighbouring families. It had never been his intention to accompany Carenza and, to her credit, she had never asked it of him. It would be bad enough having everyone staring at his disfiguring scars at the ball!

Carenza had been as good as her word concerning the arrangements for that event. Apart from agreeing the invitation list, he had had very little to do with it. She had even assured him that one room would be kept private for him, should he wish to escape from the bustling crowd of guests.

He put down his pen and sat back in his chair. He was lucky to have found such a wife, one who worked hard to make Auster a comfortable home and was content to remain living here so retired. He knew the reason for that, of course. She considered herself somehow inferior. His hand clenched into a fist. She was nothing of the kind! She was a lady, through and through, and with her new stylish gowns, she would rival any of the beauties seen in London. Perhaps this ball would prove it to her.

An hour later and he had managed to concentrate sufficiently to complete most of his tasks for the day when he was interrupted by a visitor. He looked up impatiently as the door opened.

'Amos!' Ross put down his pen and rose to greet him. 'Is aught amiss? We had no word of your coming.'

'No, no, nothing amiss, my lord, save that I have business in the area and thought I might beg a bed here for a few nights.' He waved one hand. 'I believe Lady Austerfield is out driving with your sister or I should have laid my request before her.'

'Of course we can find room for you.' Ross bade him sit down and went over to a side table to pour two glasses of Madeira. 'How long do you stay?'

'Well, that depends....' Paston ran the brim of his hat restlessly between his hands.

'You know you may remain as long as you wish.' Ross handed him one of the glasses and hesitated, his brows raised. 'Well? What is it?'

'I heard tell you were holding a ball.'

'Word travels quickly,' exclaimed Ross, surprised. 'The invitations have not all gone out yet.'

'No, and that is why I thought I should just give you a hint, you see. Mrs Paston being in an, er, *interesting condition*, she cannot attend.'

What you mean is, she cannot bear to look at me!

Ross felt his jaw tightening.

'We had already understood that,' he said. 'I had scratched you from the list.'

'Oh, well, as to that—' Paston gave a rather sheepish laugh '—my business in Bideford is going to occupy me here for the next couple of weeks, possibly until after your ball, and, if you have no objection, I should very much like to attend. After all, it would not do to give the impression there has been any falling out between us, Cousin.'

'Falling out? Why the devil should anyone think that?'

Amos spread his hands. 'People might be forgiven for thinking your existing heir's nose has been put out of joint...'

'Nonsense! Let them think what they like,' he replied, irascibly.

He did not, however, give Amos firm assurances that his inheritance was secure, as he had done in the past. Why, he could not say. After all, he was as determined as ever that his marriage to Carenza would never be consummated.

Wasn't he?

Ross stirred restlessly. 'You will excuse me, Cousin. I must balance these ledgers before I can leave my work for the day. Have you had your bags taken up?'

'I have not. When this was a bachelor household I did not hesitate, but now the house has a mistress and I could not take it upon myself to order it.'

Ross nodded and rang the bell. 'I will have a room prepared and ask Stoke to bring refreshments to the drawing room for you. We do not stand upon ceremony with you, Amos, so I am sure you will be able to amuse yourself for a while.'

'Oh, yes, Cousin. Of course. You wish to work. I will take myself off and leave you to your accounts now.'

Ross watched him go, then picked up his pen again but he did not immediately set to work. He held it between his fingers, a faint, pensive crease in his brow. Strange, that Amos had heard of the ball. Perhaps Dido had written to Fanny about it, but he could not recall being asked to frank the letter.

He shrugged and dipped the pen in the standish. It was no matter. One more body here or there would make no difference when the whole house would be overrun.

When Carenza and Dido returned to Auster, Stoke informed them they had a guest.

'Mr Paston requested that his usual room should be prepared for him, my lady, and in your absence, His Lordship agreed to it.'

'His usual room!' Mrs Burnley sniffed. 'The man takes too much upon himself,' she muttered as the two ladies made their way upstairs. 'The Chinese Room is one of Auster's finest guest chambers!'

She said no more then, but when she learned from

Amos Paston that he was staying for the ball, her indignation would not be disguised.

'Impossible,' Mrs Burnley declared. 'Surely you are not planning to be away from home for Fanny's confinement?'

They were coming to the end of dinner; the good food and generous quantities of wine had relaxed everyone, but it had made Mrs Burnley more forthright than ever.

'My dear cousin, that will not be until October,' Mr Paston replied, selecting a filbert biscuit and dipping it into his sweet wine.

'You know such dates are unreliable,' she retorted. 'It might well be sooner.'

He laughed gently. 'If it is, then Fanny will be well looked after. You cannot believe that a husband has any role to play in these matters? No, no, far better that I should uphold the family honour by acknowledging my new cousin.'

He smiled and inclined his head towards Carenza, who wondered why she found his manners so unsettling.

'Very gallant, Amos, and I am sure you will not object to moving to one of the smaller rooms,' said Dido, all sweetness. 'I have already invited the Cathwaites to stay, and the Chinese Room is by far the most suitable for a marquess and his lady.'

'Of course, I shall be happy to give up my room,' he replied smoothly. 'But let us wait until they have accepted the invitation, shall we?' He paused, then added delicately, 'We must prepare ourselves for a few refusals, I think.'

Carenza's face flamed and Dido said wrathfully, 'Nonsense! There was some talk after the wedding, it is true, but nothing to warrant such a snub to my brother's bride!'

'You wrong Amos, dear sister. It is not my bride they wish to avoid,' drawled Ross. 'Our cousin means they cannot bear to look upon my disfigured visage. I experienced it for myself, firsthand, when I was in town.' He added bitterly, 'People either like to gape at a monster, or they cannot look at him at all.'

'But you *all* misunderstand me,' Paston protested, throwing up his hands and looking hurt. 'I meant neither of those things. Good heavens, when anyone has mentioned the Viscount's sudden marriage, I have been at pains to assure them there was nothing remiss there at all! And as for His Lordship, a hero of Waterloo must always be revered, whatever his...' He did not finish the sentence and Carenza did not miss the tiny grimace he gave before continuing. 'No, no, it is Auster's remoteness, the distance from town and lack of good accommodation that will be of consideration to *le bon ton*.'

'Which is why we have been at pains to assure our most important guests we can accommodate them here!' There was no doubting the triumphant note in Dido's voice as she said this, nor the satisfaction she took from her next utterance. 'You may be sure, too, that curiosity to see the new Viscountess will prove a very strong incentive to our guests. So, Amos, shall we move you to one of the bachelor chambers in the morning, before you grow too comfortable in the Chinese Room?'

Carenza felt quite wretched. However much Amos might deny it now, he knew she was not a worthy match for the Viscount and his insincere compliments confirmed it. Ross should have married someone from his own world, not a penniless creature with no beauty and of questionable birth. She glanced at her husband, thinking he deserved far better than this.

Damn Amos, thought Ross, observing Carenza's troubled gaze, the silly fellow always managed to make bad worse! He wanted to rebuke his cousin, but Carenza had already recovered her poise and was calmly discussing the allocation of rooms with Dido. He would let it go, for now, but he must have words with Paston. The man was no longer welcome here if he could not guard his tongue.

With the ball set for the end of the month, Auster was bustling with activity. As well as working with Dido, sending out the invitations, Carenza threw herself into household chores, inspecting the linen cupboard with Mrs Stoke, checking on the number of spare bedrooms that could be used for guests and making sure there was sufficient bedding, as well as discussing menus with Cook and deciding upon the extra supplies they would need. Mrs Stoke suggested they let the new housemaid, Ruth, help with compiling lists and writing orders for the local shopkeepers.

'She is making herself useful in the laundry room,' the housekeeper explained, 'but when I discovered how often she writes to her family I told her she should be looking higher than that. She is an inquisitive soul, rather prone to gossip, but I've told her if she proves herself useful here, then I would gladly give her a reference when she wants to move on.'

Carenza was happy to agree and left Mrs Stoke setting Ruth to work while she went about her daily business, thankful there was so much for her to do at Auster. She may not be required to fulfil all her duties as the

Viscount's wife, but she could and would run his house-hold for him. Looking after Morwood for Papa was now paying dividends, and her success gave her confidence, so much so that when she happened upon Amos Paston talking to Ruth in the hall, she did not hesitate to walk over and enquire if anything was amiss.

'Oh, no, no, dear lady,' he replied, while the maid bobbed a hasty curtsy and hurried away. 'I was merely enquiring how she was getting on. I feel somewhat responsible for the girl, you see.'

'Oh, does not Windle apprise you of her progress?' she asked him. 'I believe she writes home regularly.'

The expression that flitted across his face reminded her of a cornered animal. It was gone almost instantly and he laughed.

'Yes, yes, that is true, of course, but a word in person is always useful.' He looked past her and said in a louder voice, 'Ah, Cousin Ross, there you are! I am here and ready, as you see!'

With a bow he moved away from Carenza, who turned to see Ross coming down the stairs. He was dressed for riding with the curly-brimmed beaver hat already covering his brown hair and the riding crop and gloves in one hand. She thought he looked very handsome, despite the web of scars that shadowed one side of his face. Her throat dried and she felt the now familiar lightness in her stomach at the sight of him.

She had formed the habit of avoiding the Viscount but today, instead of hurrying away, she followed Amos to the bottom of the stairs. Ross checked when he saw her, then summoned a smile as he descended the final few steps to the hall.

'Something I meant to say, Ross,' said Amos. 'I noticed the Twigg isn't in the gun room.'

'That sporting gun of my father's?' Carenza thought it was with some reluctance that Ross looked away from her. 'I sold it. To the squire.'

'Sold it?' exclaimed Amos. 'Whatever for? It was the best gun in your collection!'

'Aye, and a pity for such a piece to be lying idle. You know I never shoot now.'

'But your guests will want some sport, man!'

Ross shrugged. 'There are plenty more for them to choose from.'

'Aye, but none as good as the Twigg.' He shook his head. 'Pity. That rifle was the best I have ever handled.'

But the Viscount was not listening. His attention had returned to Carenza and she felt herself blushing under his gaze.

'You are going riding, my lord?'

It was a foolish remark and she half expected Ross to tease her, but he replied soberly.

'I am taking Amos to see the new drainage work we are carrying out in Springs Field. You will recall we discussed it.'

Yes, she remembered. In the early days, when she had thought they might be happy together. Before he told her how much he regretted marrying her.

She glanced up to find his eyes locked on her face and she could not look away. Energy was thrumming between them, so strong it was almost tangible. It held her in thrall, unable to move or speak while molten desire flooded through her.

The power of his gaze and its effect was frightening but Carenza did not want it to end. She had never known herself so drawn to anyone before. A word, a gesture, and she would throw herself into his arms.

Beside them, Amos shifted restlessly.

'Well now, the horses will be saddled and waiting for us, Cousin. We had best be away!'

'What? Oh. Yes.' Ross turned away from her. 'Let us go.'

The magic was broken. Carenza felt chilled, bereft, but even as she struggled to gather her scattered wits, Ross turned back to her.

He said, with the ghost of a smile, 'Until dinner, my lady.'

The two men left the house. Carenza watched the door close behind them but still she did not move. She had no idea what had happened, why there had been that sudden jolt of awareness, but she had recognised it and so had Ross; his final words and the look he gave her confirmed it.

Carenza waited impatiently for the dinner hour and dressed with care in the orange shot silk that Ross had admired. She had spent an hour in the garden searching out a handful of deep apricot-coloured rosebuds for Hetty to nestle amongst her curls and she completed the ensemble with the coral necklace she had inherited from her mother.

'Well, Hetty, will I do?' She spun around on her toes, giddy as a schoolgirl.

'Lud, ma'am, you look beautiful!'

Carenza laughed. 'Perhaps not quite beautiful, but I hope His Lordship will approve!'

And with that, she sailed off to the drawing room.

Ross stood before the empty fireplace, sipping his wine and listening to Dido and Amos exchanging insincere pleasantries as they waited for dinner to be announced. He felt dog tired and wished he might give his excuses and retire to bed, but as host, that would be the height of incivility and one or other of them would be sure to ask him what was wrong.

He gave a bitter inward laugh. If only he knew the answer to that! Usually, the physical exertion of riding helped to clear his mind and calm him, but not today. The drainage work appeared to be coming on very well, so it couldn't be that, but somehow during the afternoon the old feelings of unease and restlessness had come upon him again.

Amos had talked incessantly, which had not helped. He had to acquit his cousin of malice; everything he said was designed to soothe or comfort Ross, but unfortunately it had the opposite effect and put him more on edge than ever. He shifted restlessly, struggling to refrain from pacing back and forth and drawing attention to himself.

It was at that moment that Carenza came in and stopped just inside the door, as if unsure of her welcome. She was wearing the orange silk with a simple strand of coral around her neck. One glossy black ringlet had been coaxed down to rest on her bare shoulder and for a moment Ross forgot his anxieties, forgot everything except the sheer beauty of the picture she presented.

Her shy smile and the starry glow in her dark eyes warmed his heart. Amos surged towards her and Ross tensed as his cousin took her hand and kissed it, following up with several flowery compliments. Carenza's response was gracious, if reserved, and Ross found himself breathing more easily when she declined Paston's invitation to take a chair and instead chose to sit beside Dido on the sofa. As she made herself comfortable, she glanced up at Ross, and when their eyes met he felt again that connection, strong as an iron chain, binding them together.

His fatigue disappeared and the restless energy within him turned into a wave of desire, but at the same time he was filled with alarm. In his head he heard the trumpeting of the field bugle sounding the retreat. He turned and walked away from everyone. He could never be a good husband. He was too much a soldier, a man of violence. He had seen how men reacted when their blood was up—God knows he had disciplined enough of them!—he could not risk allowing Carenza to get too close to him.

He did not want her to see how far his disfigurement went beyond the bodily scars. It was bad enough that she had fallen foul of his short temper. She must never know the full extent of the nightmares, the panic and self-loathing that threatened to overwhelm him, made him less of a man. He could not bear her pity.

Carenza watched Ross move to a chair in a far corner of the room, scooping up *The Gentleman's Magazine* from a side table as he passed. There had been no mistaking his welcoming smile when she came in. She had felt the tug of attraction when their eyes met but he was clearly determined not to let it go any further. He had now buried his nose in the magazine as if he was bored with the company.

'Carenza, Stoke tells me there were several letters today. Have there been any more replies to our invitations?'

Stifling a sigh, she turned back to reply to Dido's question.

'Why, yes. All acceptances. We have had only one refusal thus far, and that was from a dowager countess whose age and poor health make the journey impossible.'

Dido looked at Amos Paston and said triumphantly, 'You see, Cousin, the Auster Ball will be an outstanding success.'

'You cannot doubt my delight at the news,' he replied, with only the tiniest suggestion of gritted teeth.

Dido beamed. 'The house will be bursting with guests, there will not be a room to be had in any of the local hostelries and anyone with a bed to spare or an empty stable will be able to fill it that week. It will be quite like old times!' She gave a little trill of laughter. 'We used to dance until dawn!'

Ross looked up. 'Aye, we did. But we were very much younger then.'

'Pho! And you are in your dotage now!' she teased him.

'I feel it sometimes.'

'And no wonder,' put in Amos, 'when one thinks of all you have suff—'

Carenza cut across him. 'I thought we might turn the library into a card room for the night, Ross. I hope you do not object? We can then open the double doors between the yellow saloon and the drawing room to make more space for those who do not wish to dance. What do you say?'

'You and Dido are arranging the whole,' he said, shrugging. 'I am happy to leave it all to you.'

'I am sorry there must be such upheaval in your home, my lord,' she said, contrite. 'But it will not be for long, I assure you. None of the guests will be staying more than a few days.'

'And it must be done, Ross,' Dido reminded him.

'Yes, it must be done, and I suppose it will not be so

bad.' He put down the magazine. 'Do you remember, Dido? On fine nights, when the last of the carriages had gone, we would take cakes and wine onto the terrace to watch the sun rise.'

Carenza saw the reminiscent smile on his lips and wanted to ask him more, to encourage this mellow mood, but Ross pushed himself to his feet.

'Ah, here is Stoke come in to tell us it is time for dinner.' He walked over to Carenza and held out his hand to her. 'Shall we go in, my lady?'

Chapter Eighteen

Carenza watched Ross throughout dinner. There was a tension about him, as if he was afraid to let down his guard. She did her best to deflect the conversation away from him, keeping up a flow of inconsequential talk with the others until she could think of no fresh subjects and Dido stepped into the silence.

'I understand you rode out with Amos today, Ross. I hope you had good sport?'

'No sport, we went out to look at a new land drain. We took Jarvis with us. He has been most involved with the plans for draining the bog at the lower end of Springs Field.'

'It will improve the grass,' explained Carenza. 'There will be better grazing for the milch cows and, we hope, better yields.'

'Yes, indeed.' A gleam of appreciation glinted in Ross's eyes. 'We discussed it all in great detail, did we not?'

'My dear sir,' cried Amos Paston, 'surely you did not bore Lady Austerfield with such matters?'

'I did not find it boring at all, sir,' Carenza corrected him. 'I enjoy learning about these things.'

'I can think of nothing more tedious,' he returned, with a laugh. 'But I am more of a town creature.'

'Then I am surprised you should want to spend so much of your time at Auster,' remarked Dido. 'Have you heard from Fanny recently, Cousin—how does she go on?'

'I had a letter today. She is very well.'

'And not missing you at all, I am sure,' she replied affably.

Carenza hurriedly changed the subject. 'I have not ridden Elvira for some time now. If it is a fine day to-morrow I should like to see Springs Field for myself. Will you come with me, Ross?'

He hesitated. 'Are you not too busy with arrangements for the ball?'

'Nothing that cannot wait.'

'And if there is, I can deal with it,' added Dido.

Carenza fixed her eyes on her husband. 'I should dearly like to ride out with you tomorrow.'

She felt rather than saw his withdrawal.

'I cannot guarantee I shall have time,' he said. 'You will do well enough with a groom. Or take Jarvis with you, if you truly wish to see the drainage work. He knows everything there is about it, and he is far more knowledgeable about farming than I!'

He turned to address a question to his sister, indicating the subject was closed, and Carenza lapsed into silence. He had smiled at her, lessening the blow, but she recognised it as a snub and carried the disappointment to bed with her.

It was a warm night, but thankfully she fell asleep at once, only to wake up with a start some hours later. Perhaps it was the moonlight streaming into the room that had disturbed her. Then it came again. A faint cry coming in through her open window. She sat up, listening hard, and after a few moments she slipped out of bed and padded across to throw up the sash. Outside the landscape was bathed in the blue-grey light of the half moon. Everything was still, silent. It must have been the cry of a fox.

She was about to return to her bed when she heard it again. A man's voice, shouting. Then a stream of unintelligible words. She leaned out. Further along she could see that another window was open and it did not take a moment to realise it was Ross's bedchamber. More mutterings and another cry. Carenza did not hesitate. She picked up her wrap and ran out of the room.

'Ross?'

Carenza knocked softly on his door, straining her ears, but all she could hear through his door was agitated mutterings. She went in. The room was bathed in moonlight and beneath the canopy of the great bed she could see that the covers had been thrown back. Ross was naked, lying in a tangle of sheets, thrashing wildly as he issued orders and shouted out men's names between garbled unintelligible phrases.

She touched his shoulder. 'My lord—'

He flung out an arm and she jumped back, narrowly avoiding a blow.

'Ross, wake up!' She caught his fist and held it firm against her breast. 'You are at Auster. You are safe.'

He muttered incoherently and she leaned closer, smoothing the damp hair from his forehead.

'Hush now, you are dreaming.'

He grew still, then his eyelids fluttered. It was difficult to read his expression in the gloom, but his eyes were fixed, staring.

'Carenza.' He sat up and pulled his hand free from her grasp. 'You should not be here.'

'I heard you calling. I could not ignore it.'

He rubbed a hand over his eyes and groaned.

'You were having a nightmare, Ross.' She perched herself on the side of his bed and put a hand on his arm. 'Will you tell me? Sometimes it helps to talk of these things.'

'No!' He dropped his head into his hands, pushing his fingers through his already dishevelled hair. 'I cannot.'

'Because you do not wish to relive it?'

'Because you are a woman.'

She blinked. 'That is one of the silliest things I have heard you say! I am not a soldier, but I believe I have as strong a stomach as many men. In fact, I know it, having witnessed more than one horrid accident on the Home Farm at Morwood. I have seen strong labourers faint off at the sight of a little blood.'

He was silent and, after a moment, she shivered.

'My feet are cold. May I share your bed with you while we talk?'

She did not wait for a reply but climbed up beside him, pulling the covers over them both.

He drew in a ragged breath and said, with careful constraint, 'We are not going to talk. Go back to your room.'

'But we must, Ross. If you send me back now, who knows what horrors my poor, female imagination will conjure to account for your nightmares.'

'Do not joke about it!' He was fully awake now and edging his body away from her. 'What I have seen.' He shuddered. 'It would disgust you. Infect you with such terrors as you have never known.'

'I will risk that.' She turned and laid one hand on his bare chest. 'You have been led to believe women are very poor creatures, but you are wrong. You thought the mere sight of your damaged body would repel me but it is not so. The scars are far less prominent than they were the first time I saw them. Whether that is the result of my lotion I do not know, but I assure you they do not disgust me.'

Her fingers began to move over the jagged welts on his left side and his hand shot out to catch hers.

'Don't, Carenza!'

'Can I not help you? I promise I shall not try to… to seduce you.'

A laugh was forced from him. 'Just being here you tempt me, madam!'

However, he did not push her away and she took some comfort from that. He fell back against his pillows with a sigh of exhaustion and she settled herself more comfortably beside him.

'Will you not tell me something of what troubles you, Ross? Let me share a little of your burden.'

He was lying tense and still, tightly grasping her hand, and she waited, willing him to talk to her. After a moment he began to speak.

'It is always that last battle. Waterloo. We had formed square against the French cavalry. In the main, those around me were experienced soldiers. Many had served with me in the Peninsula. I knew them well. They wouldn't break under the cavalry charge, or the artillery, and by God we had to withstand both for what seemed like eternity!'

She listened while he described the sheer hell of the day. Wave after wave of cavalry, interspersed with deadly artillery fire that hurtled down and tore into the ground around them. There was no escape. His words conjured the thunderous noise and acrid smell, the gradual darkening of the sky as the sun was blotted out by smoke from the guns. He described the constant struggle to move the wounded to safety and keep the square intact. She closed her eyes, determined not to distract him with her tears as he described the carnage, the slaughter of friend and foe and even the horses. Finally, he told her of the exploding shell that had killed his comrades.

'I was buried beneath a suffocating pile of bodies and that was the last I knew of the battle. I woke up in a field hospital, dazed, confused, and no one knew who I was. Looters were at work even before the battle had ended, taking anything of value: rings, watches, calling card cases. It was a long time before I was well enough to tell anyone my name.'

'It is no wonder you are plagued by nightmares,' she murmured, shrinking against him. To her surprise, he put an arm around her and gathered her close.

'This summer I had not been plagued quite so badly,' he said. 'Until.'

He stopped. The silence was unnerving and when she could stand it no longer, she prompted him. 'Until?'

'Until that day we rode out together. When we visited the Hidden Pool. That was a disastrous misjudgement.'

'Oh.' She felt the hot prickle of tears behind her eyes. 'Did you dislike it so much, riding out with me?'

'No, not at all, but we tarried too long.' He shifted his position and raised himself on his elbow to look down at her. 'We should have turned back earlier. I knew there was a storm coming but I ignored it. I was enjoying myself too much. Enjoying your company, Carenza. I forget myself when I am with you. All the pain and guilt that haunts me fades away. I forgot about the danger. I thought myself safe, until it was too late.'

He sat up, turning away so she could only see his back.

'It wasn't Aethon who panicked in the storm,' he said in a low voice. 'It was me. One thunderclap and immediately I was back in the battle, trying to fight, trying to save my men. Only I could not move, could not speak. I was frozen with the terror, the horror, of it all. Afterwards there is always delirium and sometimes black moods of sheer despair. It can be hours, days, before I am in control of myself again. That is why, when I *could* move, I abandoned you. I raced back to the stables and fled to my room, to hide away until the madness had passed.'

Carenza knelt up and put her arms around him, resting her cheek against his broad back.

'Sam Rigby tried to tell me,' she murmured. 'He said you would be well again in a couple of days. I thought he was talking about your horse.'

'No, he meant me. Sam was at the hospital at Portsmouth, about to be discharged when I arrived. He and Dan Brisco nursed me back to some semblance of health, then they came here with me.' A long shuddering sigh broke from him. 'I have kept it hidden from everyone else. I especially did not want you to know what a pathetic creature you have married. You deserve a proper husband, not a broken shell of a man!'

'Hush!' Her arms tightened about him. 'You do not need to hide anything from me, Ross. I will help you.'

'No. I have Brisco and Sam Rigby. I do not need you.'

She flinched at his words but was not deterred. Not this time. She scrambled around on the bed and looked him in the face. It was pale and unclear in the moonlight, but she could make out his frown and guessed at the pain he was feeling.

'I do not mean *in place* of your groom and your valet,' she told him. 'I will work with them. Together we shall help you through this.' She smiled and cupped his face with her hands. 'Sam Rigby has learned how to manage without his arm, a much greater disability to overcome than your scars, my lord. As to your inner wounds, it is no wonder they plague you so, when you have kept them hidden for so long.' She ended with a plea. 'Let me help you, Ross.'

He sighed again but this time there was less anger and frustration. It was more of a soft exhalation.

'You have helped already, just being here and talking with me.' He covered her fingers and pulled them gently from his face. 'But you should go now, before I forget myself.'

He was still clasping her hands, his eyes glittering in the moonlight. Carenza caught her breath as a tiny spark of hope flickered.

'F-forget yourself, my lord?'

He released her and turned away.

'You look…very beautiful in the moonlight.' He spoke grudgingly, as if the words were forced from him. 'You must go, before I am tempted to break our agreement.'

She said daringly, 'I should like that.'

'Go, madam!'

'Would it be so very wrong?' she persevered. 'If I can help you forget your unhappiness, even for a short while, is that not a good thing?'

She touched his shoulder and he shrugged her off with a snarl.

'No! It would be wrong of me to take you merely

to satisfy my own desires! For God's sake, get back to your own room.'

He threw himself down on the bed with his back to her and dragged the bedding tight around him. Shutting her out. Carenza bit her lip, aware that what she said, what she *did* next, could change everything. For better or worse.

She slipped out of her wrap. The thin cotton nightgown she was wearing beneath it looked pale and virginal in the moonlight and she quickly threw it off. She lay down, measuring her length against Ross, moulding herself to him.

'You would not be *taking*, my lord. I would give myself freely.' She placed a gentle kiss on his shoulder. 'I am your wife, Ross. Who else should comfort you?'

A groan rumbled through him and she felt it against her body. She continued to press kisses over his back, until he whipped around and took her in his arms.

'Confound it, you have bewitched me!'

A laugh gurgled in her throat and she felt a huge sense of relief that he was not rejecting her. Then his mouth found hers and her whole being sprang into life, every nerve tingling deliciously. She returned his kiss, wanting it to go on for ever. When he finally stopped, she began to explore his body with her mouth. She ran her lips over the scarred flesh and the smooth, unblemished skin with equal pleasure until Ross pulled her back into his arms for another deep, all-consuming kiss. His hands caressed her body, which grew soft and pliant beneath his touch. The ache deep inside her became pronounced; she wanted more and pushed against him, offering herself to his caresses. She was melting with desire and gave a soft moan, her body shifting restlessly as his roaming hands roused sensations that were quite unfamiliar but deeply satisfying.

Excitement began to ripple through her, growing stronger by the moment. Ross shifted, moving on top of her, and her thighs parted to receive him. As he pushed into her she gasped, but the fleeting shock was immediately replaced by pure pleasure and she matched her movements to his. She gripped his shoulders, her fingers digging into the muscle as wave after wave pulsed through her. It could not go on or she would surely die of pleasure! Her body jolted, no longer under her control, and she cried out as Ross made one final thrust and they clung together in a fierce, suffocating embrace before rolling apart, breathless and exhausted.

Carenza was still in a daze, wondering what had happened, when Ross gathered her against him. She felt his lips on her neck.

'Thank you,' he whispered.

A long soft sigh of satisfaction escaped Carenza and, smiling, she fell into a deep sleep, wrapped in his arms.

Ross stirred and woke to a half-light, the first grey streaks of dawn lightening the sky. He felt rested, calm. Carenza was sleeping beside him, her dark lashes fanning her cheeks, and that glorious black hair tumbled over the pillow. Her naked shoulders were visible, but the rest of her luscious body was hidden beneath the covers. He remembered the thrill of running his hands over her skin, smooth and unblemished. And yet, for all her own perfection, she was not repelled by him.

There had been no pretence in the way she had responded to his caresses. She had returned them eagerly, wanting to give him equal pleasure. He raised himself on one elbow to look at the woman beside him.

He could not help smiling at the fact that she was truly his wife now.

As if aware of his scrutiny she opened her eyes, gazing at him for a moment. A slow smile spread over her face and his heart lifted.

'Good morning, my lord.' He moved closer to kiss her lips and she pushed her body against him again. Her smile deepened and she slipped her arms around his neck. 'You seem to be very much…awake.'

Her voice was a seductive purr that set the blood pounding through him.

'I am.' He rolled on top of her and began to cover her face with kisses. She laughed, a low, throaty sound that set his pulse racing even faster. 'And you are beautiful.'

'*You* make me feel so,' she replied, pulling him closer.

He had intended to take his time this morning, but his body, and Carenza, had other ideas. Their kisses quickly became frenzied and she was soon bucking and writhing against him as he drove into her until at last they collapsed together in a tangle of limbs, their passion sated. For the moment.

Ross gazed up at the shadowed canopy of the bed.

'You do realise,' he said, 'there is every possibility that so much…*activity* will result in a child.'

'Are you so set against it, my lord?'

'No, not now. I know my concerns were ill-founded. Except that I do worry about the effect of my…appearance.'

'Our children will grow up with it and see nothing amiss.'

He turned his head to looked at her. 'Children?'

She smiled saucily. 'I hope we will not stop at one, my lord.'

He laughed, enjoying this new, confident Carenza. He pulled her close for another kiss.

'I hope so, too.'

'One thing,' she said, becoming serious. 'You must tell your cousin, as soon as maybe. You have given him to understand that he would remain your heir and it is only right he should be informed of the change.'

'Yes, he should. He will be disappointed, but it cannot be helped. You need not worry. I shall break the news to him gently.'

'Good.' She paused, considering. 'Perhaps, until he has been apprised of the new situation, it would be best if we were discreet. Which means I should slip back to my own bed before the servants are abroad.'

His arms tightened. 'We need not worry about Brisco.'

'Perhaps, but I would not depend upon Hetty keeping such a tasty morsel of gossip to herself.' She made to push him away, then relented. 'One last kiss, then, and I will go. We must act as if we are nothing more than friends until you have told your cousin.'

The last kiss turned out to be a long one and it was some considerable time later when Carenza slipped out of bed and quickly donned her nightgown and wrap.

'I will see you to your room,' said Ross, reaching for his banyan.

'No! The servants will be abroad soon and may see you.'

'Nonsense, they will not venture upstairs for another hour yet.'

They went to the door, the Turkish carpet on the floor muffling their steps. As Carenza went out she saw a blur of white in the passage.

'Ruth?' she called out to the housemaid hovering

in the shadows. 'What on earth are you doing here so early?'

The maid held up a bundle of folded linen. 'Beggin' your pardon, I left these bolster covers up here yesterday. I wanted to get them back before Mrs Stoke discovered my mistake and gave me a scold.' She added anxiously, 'Pray, say you won't tell her, m'lady!'

'As to that, we shall see. Go on back downstairs now.' Carenza watched the girl hurry away and turned back to Ross, who was standing in the doorway behind her. 'Oh, dear, so much for our efforts to be discreet.'

'It is of little matter.' He shrugged. 'I will see Amos as soon as I can today. But more to the point, the girl should not have been here at this hour. Was she spying upon us, or did you believe her story?'

'It could be true, although I had heard she is very inquisitive. Which is a pity, because she is very bright and I was hoping she might be of use to any of our guests who need a maid, but I will not recommend a girl I cannot trust.'

'Indeed not. Tell Mrs Stoke to keep an eye on her. Now,' he said, his eyes glinting, 'you had best get to your room, before I drag you back into mine!'

Carenza floated down to breakfast on a cloud of happiness. Ross was already at the table with his sister and Mr Paston when she entered. Amid the flurry of greetings he met her eyes and gave his head a tiny shake, indicating he had not yet spoken to his cousin.

Ross stood and pulled out a chair for her. She thanked him politely and sat down, but as he moved away his fingers grazed the back of her neck. It was a fleeting touch but it sent a delicious shiver running down her spine. The now familiar ache of desire began to unfurl, deep inside. She selected a hot roll and buttered it, keeping her eyes firmly away from Ross. She hated this pretence and hoped that by the end of the day he would have found an opportunity to speak to Amos Paston.

After breakfast, Ross and his cousin went off together and, when Dido announced she had letters to write, Carenza occupied herself with household duties. They did not wholly occupy her mind, and she found herself wondering how Mr Paston had taken the news that he was unlikely to succeed to the viscountcy. Shortly after noon, she saw Ross coming down the stairs and stopped to speak to him.

'Have you seen your cousin?' she asked anxiously. 'How is he?'

Ross nodded. 'He was disappointed, naturally, but not surprised. He wishes us well and shows no desire to storm off in a temper.'

'I am relieved to hear it. I should not like to be the cause of bad blood between you.'

'Amos said something very similar,' said Ross. 'I am encouraged to think he was not too surprised by my announcement. I believe we shall go along very well.'

They were interrupted by Jarvis, who came in search of Ross to discuss estate matters, and Carenza went on her way, hoping very much that Ross was right about his cousin.

When they all met at dinner, Amos Paston did indeed appear to be quite at ease. She might not like his sly looks and innuendo but there was no doubting that he seemed unperturbed by the new situation.

As the evening wore on Carenza found her anticipation growing. Ross had been warmly attentive all evening—would he come to her room that night? Would he invite her to his? By the time the party broke up she was almost quivering with nerves, something that Ross remarked upon as he escorted her to her bedchamber.

They had stopped at her door and she looked up at him. 'We have not discussed our sleeping arrangements.'

Immediately she felt the change. His reply was almost curt.

'They must remain as they are.'

'Must they?'

'My habits would disturb you, Carenza. Sometimes I am awake until the early hours of the morning.' She waited, sensing there was more. 'And my bad moods. When the black cloud comes upon me, it is best I keep away from everyone. My temper is vile, my language intemperate. Brisco understands, but I would not subject you to that.'

'I suppose it is useless to tell you I would not mind it?'

'It is, because *I* should mind it, very much.' He raked a hand through his hair. 'At the hospital, in Portsmouth, one doctor told me he had seen such cases as mine before. There can be an improvement, in time.'

'Then I will be patient,' she said. 'But until then, what are we to do? Can you not come to my room, at least for a while?'

'Of course.' The glow in his eyes set her pulse racing. 'If you invite me.'

She reached out for his hand. 'Then, pray you, my lord, come in.'

The following week was Carenza's happiest yet at Auster. She was content to leave the preparations for the ball with Dido and Amos while she spent more of her time with Ross. They walked in the gardens, rode together over the estate and visited the vicar to discuss his plans for the village school. With each day his mood grew more mellow. He allowed her to apply the balm she had prepared to his face and body, a process which invariably ended in Ross taking her to his bed and driving her into a bone-melting passion with his kisses. She loved to look at his body now, to see the evidence of a lifetime of fighting. Of battles survived. It made her all the more thankful to have him with her and determined to savour every moment together.

Ross, too, was feeling ever more hopeful. Carenza was good for him; there was no doubt about that. She calmed his body and his mind. There had been only one recurrence of his nightmares and Carenza was there to hold him, to soothe away the terrors. By the end of the week he could regard his image in the looking glass without loathing and he no longer saw repugnance in every glance that was levelled at him. He could even look forward to the cursed ball with equanimity.

Chapter Nineteen

It was inevitable that the world would intrude upon this idyll. Two weeks before the ball Ross received a letter from London that put him into a state of frowning indecision for the rest of the day. However, by dinner time he knew what must be done. He wanted to tell Carenza first, but there was no opportunity to speak to her privately before they all went into dinner. His sister began to berate him for his reclusive habits because he refused to join them on a visit to an elderly neighbour and he was goaded into a retort.

'It is not that I do not wish to see Major Edwards, Dido. I shall not be here.'

Carenza looked up. 'You are going away?'

'Alas, there is no help for it.' He met her eyes, hoping she would read in his glance his reluctance to leave her. 'I have received a letter from Philps, my man of business, and it demands attention. I am afraid the matter cannot be delayed. I must set out immediately, if I am to return in good time for the ball.'

He observed Carenza's disappointment and continued, needing to make her understand.

'It concerns the manufactories we own in the north,'

he explained. 'More investment is required and it will be necessary for me to speak to my bankers before I sign the papers. However, it must be done quickly, or the mill will close and men will lose their livelihoods. Whole families will suffer.'

She responded as he knew she would. 'Then of course you must go, my lord, and as soon as maybe.'

'I shall send Sam off tomorrow with instructions for Philps to have everything in readiness for my arrival, that I may leave again the following morning. You might like to give me a note for your dressmaker; I could collect your ball gown.'

'Better still, why do you not go with him, Carenza?' Dido suggested. 'You might stay an extra day and do a little shopping while Ross is busy. In the evenings I am sure he would be free to escort you somewhere. Perhaps a visit to the theatre. What a treat that would be!'

'There is nothing I would like more,' said Ross quickly. 'Although I must warn you that most of the time will be spent travelling. We could have no more than two nights in London if we are to be back in time for the Auster Ball. We cannot cancel those arrangements now.'

'Indeed, you cannot,' cried Amos, 'that would give rise to no end of speculation amongst your neighbours. And yet I see your dilemma, my lord. The ton must be agog to see your new Viscountess.' He laughed. 'From your reluctance to show her off they will be expecting some sort of freak. They will be astounded to discover your bride is so very ordinary!'

Dido gave a screech of indignation. 'That is a shocking thing to say, Cousin, and not at all complimentary to Lady Austerfield!'

Carenza was flushing vividly and Paston put up his

hands, looking horrified. 'Oh, good heavens, I never intended—that is, I do beg your pardon, my lady. I meant it as a jest. I was teasing His Lordship, who knows what society is like for gossip! I meant you no disparagement, my lady. Oh, dear, oh, dear, now I am quite mortified. I would not offend you for the world. Pray, let us forget I ever spoke of it!'

Carenza nodded. 'Yes, let us do that, if you please.'

Her cheeks were still pink and Ross said furiously, 'Damn you, man, what are you about, to be so clumsy with your words? I've a mind to throw you out of the house this instant!'

'Good idea,' muttered Dido, but Carenza was quick to protest.

'Oh, no, no,' she cried. 'Pray do not do that, my lord. I do not want to be the cause of a rift in your family. And besides,' she added, with a tremulous smile that tugged at his heart, 'Cousin Amos is in some points correct, is he not? There *has* been much speculation about us. I do not think I am ready to face London society yet, Ross. We have invited a few of your close acquaintances here for the Auster Ball. That will be enough for me, for the present.'

'You will stay here, then?' he asked her, reluctant now to leave her behind.

'I will. There is plenty to do while you are away.'

'And she will have your sister and myself to help her,' put in Amos. 'Believe me, I shall be working very hard to regain Lady Austerfield's good opinion.'

Carenza inclined her head and began to talk of something else, indicating the subject was closed. With that Ross had to be content and after dinner he went off to write the letters for Sam to take with him. By the time he had finished and given the correspondence to his groom, along with his instructions, it was very late and the drawing room was in darkness. He went upstairs, pausing outside Carenza's room, but there was no light showing beneath the door. Much as he wanted her, she might not welcome his company and he would not climb into her bed uninvited.

Ross spent a restless night. His sleep was not troubled by the usual nightmares but with vague worries and unease. His cousin's words were still nagging at him, and although Amos was all politeness at the breakfast table, he could not be easy. Towards noon, he went in search of Carenza and begged her to be careful.

'Paston's comments last night went beyond what is acceptable,' he told her. 'I suspect he is more disappointed over our marriage than he admits.'

'It would not be surprising. Poor man, we have dealt him quite a blow to all his hopes.'

'That may be so, but I do not want you to be the object of his resentment while I am away. If Dido was not here to bear you company you may be sure I should send Amos to the rightabout—not that he has been anything other than a good friend to me,' he added quickly. 'He is not always tactful, but I believe he means well.'

Carenza was not so sure. She could not like Amos Paston. His bonhomie did not ring true and she thought many of his comments to the Viscount were barbed, designed to remind him of his injuries. But Ross did not see his cousin in that light and Carenza knew her own judgement might well be clouded by jealousy.

She had only realised it last evening at dinner, when Ross had announced he was going away. The searing disappointment was like a thunderbolt, and she knew then, without any doubt, that she was falling in love with her husband. She also knew her feelings were not reciprocated. Ross liked her; he respected her judgement and approved of the way she ran Auster, but he had never uttered one word of love. Not that she had ever expected any. She could only be grateful that she was able to share his bed and give him comfort, some small release from the dark thoughts that troubled him.

'Amos has gone off with my gamekeeper now,' Ross went on. 'They are taking out the shotguns but you know it is a sport I no longer enjoy.'

Shooting was so much part of a gentleman's world that she felt a moment's sadness he was not going with them, but there was no hint of regret in Ross's face. On the contrary, there was a definite gleam of laughter in his eyes.

'I have other plans,' he went on. 'I want you to come riding with me.'

'Now?'

'Yes, now!'

'But what about Dido? We cannot leave her alone.'

'My sister would be very much *de trop* on this occasion. She is perfectly capable of amusing herself until dinner time.' He took her hands. 'What do you say, will you come?'

She was unable to resist his smile. 'How can I refuse? I should like it above all things! Give me five minutes to change!'

It was rather more than five minutes later when they slipped off to the stables, where their horses were waiting for them.

'Where are we going?' she asked him as they trotted out of the yard.

'You will see.'

'Ross, you are most infuriating. Tell me!'

But he cantered away and she could only follow, intrigued.

Carenza soon guessed where they were heading, and as Ross turned Aethon towards the woods, she called out to him.

'Are you taking me to the Hidden Pool?'

'I am.' He glanced back at her. 'We have unfinished business there, my lady!'

She could not help a little jolt of excitement at his words. They pushed their way through the final bushes to the side of the pool, where he lifted her down from the mare.

'Do you intend to swim?' she asked as he tethered the horses.

'There will not be many more hot days this year and I thought we should make the most of it.'

'I am not sure we should…'

'You had no such doubts the last time we were here. In fact, as I recall, it was your idea that we try the waters.' He put his arms around her. 'I shall make sure you do not drown. What do you say?'

Carenza felt the laughter bubbling up inside her. It was as though the combination of the pool and the warm September sunshine had infected them with a sort of madness. Giggling like children they began to undress. Despite the nights they had spent together, Carenza felt a little shy and she averted her eyes when Ross stripped off his clothes and dived into the water. When she looked again, he was swimming across the pool with strong steady strokes. Quickly she removed the rest of her clothes, until she was wearing only her shift. By the time she was ready to enter the water Ross had returned. He grinned up at her.

'Well, madam, are you coming in?'

She stepped carefully onto the rocky ledge just beneath the surface and gasped as the cool water washed around her ankles.

'All or nothing, Carenza.'

His teasing voice stiffened her resolve. She climbed down into the water, blushing furiously as the cotton chemise floated up around her shoulders.

'This is no time for prudishness, madam,' declared Ross. 'You cannot swim in that.'

He came closer and caught at the material, dragging it up and over her head and throwing it on to the bank, while Carenza quickly dropped further into the water, trying to conceal her nakedness. Ross, she realised, showed no sign of wishing to hide his scarred body from her. She was surprised how pleased she was at that.

'Well now, will you try to swim?' said Ross, 'Don't worry, I will be here if you need me.'

Carenza discovered that she had not forgotten everything her father had taught her. She kicked out and began to move steadily away from the bank. Ross swam beside her as she rediscovered the joy of floating, weightless, in the water. They swam across the pool and Ross grabbed her hand, dragging her under the cascade with him. She squealed as the cold water poured down on them.

'My hair!' she protested, laughing. 'I was being so careful to keep my head out of the water. It will take hours to dry!'

They were behind the waterfall, where ferns clung tenuously to the cliff wall. Here, the pool was shallow

enough for her to stand and she put up her hands to push
the wet hair from her face.

'Let me.' Ross came closer and gently brushed aside
a stray tendril.

He hooked the curl behind her ear. Carenza stood
very still. A little thrill ran through her as his fingers
moved over her neck and rested on her shoulder. In the
dim, subaqueous light his eyes were shining like em-
eralds and she was no longer sure if the rushing sound
was the waterfall or the heated blood pounding through
her body. He lowered his head and she turned her face
up, inviting his kiss.

A heady excitement filled her as he captured her
mouth with his own. She put her hands on his shoulders,
pulling herself closer and eagerly returning his kiss.
He teased her lips apart and she felt his tongue dancing, exploring. She pushed against him, the hardness
of his body exciting her. His hands slid down her back
to cup her buttocks and he pressed her closer, then he
lifted her out of the water onto the ledge and climbed
up beside her.

Carenza had never felt so alive. Her wet skin was
sensitive to his every touch, yet when Ross gently eased
her down, she barely noticed the cold hard rock at her
back. She was aware only of his dizzying kisses and the
heat of his body. She clung to him as his gentle hands
caressed her, moving over her breasts, skimming her
waist and sliding down to make her arch with pleasure
as his fingers delved between her thighs, stroking and
teasing until she was writhing against them, her very
bones turning to water.

She threw her legs about his waist and tilted herself
up, inviting him to enter her. Ross needed no second
bidding and soon they were moving together as one.

She gasped and arched up against him. He gave a final, juddering push and she clung to him, her nails digging into his shoulders. With a wild cry, she felt herself tipping over the edge of ecstasy and toppled headlong into momentary oblivion.

Ross held her in his arms and Carenza snuggled against him.

'Thank you,' she murmured.

'For what?

'I thought, when you did not come to me last night...'

His arms tightened. 'It was late and I would not impose upon you, Carenza.'

'I wish you had come in. I missed you.'

For a moment he was silent, then he said slowly, 'I would share your bed every night, if it wasn't for the nightmares.'

She raised herself on one elbow and placed her hand on his chest. 'You told me they are not so frequent now. I could help you, if I was there, beside you.'

It was so tempting. She could help him, he was sure of it, but what of the price to herself? He needed to be sure she would not suffer.

'Perhaps it would work,' he said at last. 'When I return from town we will talk of it more.'

He pulled her close for another kiss; then, reluctantly, he twisted out of her arms and slid back into the water. 'Time we were moving, I think.'

They swam around the pool, ending back at the waterfall where, all restraint forgotten, they splashed each other mercilessly until the chill of the cascading water made Carenza shiver.

'Come along,' said Ross. 'Let's move out into the sun.'

They struck out again across the pool until they

emerged from the shadow of the cliff. Carenza turned onto her back and floated, head back and eyes closed, enjoying the sun's heat on her body.

Ross watched her, smiling. His wife. The creature he had thought so unremarkable when they had first met. How wrong he had been. She was clever and capable, and now her initial shyness had worn off, she teased him like an equal. He was so comfortable in her company that he could forget his scarred and battered body.

When they eventually reached the spot where they had left their clothes, Carenza hung back in the water as Ross climbed onto the bank.

'Will you pass me my shift?'

He looked back at her grinning. 'It is a little late for modesty, madam wife!'

'You are not the only one to be conscious of one's body. My shift, if you please.'

He dragged on his shirt before picking up the chemise and holding it out to her.

'It is too damp to put on.'

She snatched if from him and pulled the wet fabric over her head. 'It will do until I reach the privacy of yonder bushes.'

'You still want to hide from me, after what we have just done?'

He saw the blush painting her cheeks. She put out her hand for him to help her out of the water. 'But that is in the heat of the moment. I would not have your illusions shattered.'

Ross was perplexed by what she had said. He watched her walk away from him, noting how the wet linen clung to her skin, accentuating every curve. It was no illusion, he thought. She was a very desirable woman.

She disappeared into the shrubbery to dress and he began to don his own clothes.

He said, 'You have no need to be ashamed of my seeing you, Carenza.'

'I am not ashamed, exactly,' came the disembodied voice from the other side of the bushes.

'Your body is quite perfect. You should believe that.'

She appeared before him, still tying the strings of her bodice.

'Thank you, my lord, that is very kind.' She hesitated. He saw the colour mount to her cheeks and she said shyly, 'What we have just done—swimming in the pool, then afterwards, behind the cascade, I did feel truly beautiful then.'

'But you *are* beautiful, Carenza.' He ran a finger gently along her cheek. 'Beautiful, kind, wise.' Another kiss and he caught her hands, holding them against his chest. 'I wish I did not have to go to town in the morning. Are you sure you will not come with me? It is not too late.'

Carenza hesitated. She was well aware of the trials to be faced there. The gossip, the questions, the inevitable whispers. She could not compare with the fashionable London ladies, whatever Ross might say. Amos was right: people would wonder why he had married a drab little creature without fortune or looks to recommend her. It would be better for her to remain at Auster and prepare for the ball. Hopefully she would earn the Viscount's respect for her efforts.

She summoned up a brave smile. 'I understand that you must go and attend to your business, my lord. Pray do not be anxious for me. I shall do very well here with Dido to keep me company.'

'If that is what you wish, but I hope you know how much I shall miss you!'

* * *

They said no more on the subject until the following morning, when Carenza went out to the travelling chariot with Ross to see him off.

He kissed her and said, trying to make her smile, 'Do you know, I think I am glad now that you do not come with me to town? I should be very much afraid that while I was busy working, you would be swept off your feet by some dashing rake!'

She chuckled. 'There would be little chance of that. I am not nearly handsome enough!' She gave him a little push. 'Off you go now, my lord. Do your duty and come back safely!'

And Ross went, climbing into his carriage and giving her a cheerful wave as it lurched into motion. It was a pity she wasn't coming with him, but he knew in his heart that the time was not right. Carenza was too unsure of her own worth and, on this trip, he would not be able to give her the attention she deserved.

He was determined that when he did introduce his lady to the ton, it would be in a blaze of glory. A fanfare of trumpets, if it could be arranged. He would leave no one in any doubt that she was a worthy viscountess.

Chapter Twenty

Auster was very quiet without Ross. Carenza kept herself busy with arrangements for the ball, making sure the house was cleaned from top to bottom and working with Dido on the correspondence. Amos Paston was eager to help and he exerted himself so much that even Dido's hostility towards him lessened. Carenza now found herself looking forward to the evenings with her guests. She was persuaded to play for them on the beautiful piano in the drawing room, and although she took Amos's praise with a large pinch of salt, having an audience that was complimentary rather than quick to criticise every false note improved her performance considerably. Her happiness was increased when Dido urged her to play for Ross when he returned.

'He has always loved music,' she told Carenza. 'I have no doubt he will be delighted to hear you.'

Carenza was flattered and promised to bear it in mind, then she turned the conversation back to the forthcoming ball. She wanted to know about the previous parties at Auster, taking note of Dido's comments about what the guests had particularly enjoyed. She hoped that this ball would be every bit as successful.

* * *

'There is one thing that would raise this party above the ordinary,' Amos declared. 'A firework display! Coloured flares to light up the night sky and entertain our guests.'

'We never had fireworks at Morwood,' said Carenza. 'I cannot recall ever seeing a display, but I believe the patterns they make in the night sky can be exceedingly pretty.'

'Oh, yes,' cried Dido, clapping her hands. 'I remember we had them once at Comers. Ross was very young but he loved it! There is no doubt it would make Auster the talk of the neighbourhood for weeks afterwards. What a pity we did not think of it earlier; it will be too late to arrange for them now.'

'Ah, there might be a way,' put in Amos. 'I have a good friend whose business is fireworks. By chance, his last letter mentioned an order cancelled at short notice. I could send an express to him, if you wish, to see if he might help us?'

'That is an excellent idea,' exclaimed Dido. 'It would be something quite out of the ordinary.'

'Then with your permission I shall make enquiries.' Amos gave a little bow. 'Shall we keep it as a surprise for Ross?'

Carenza looked a question at Dido, who nodded. 'He was happy for us to deal with everything; this shall be his treat.'

'Very well, then.' Amos beamed. 'I will arrange the whole and you, Lady Austerfield, shall take the credit!'

'I must say, Amos Paston has surprised me this week,' said Dido a few days later. 'I have never known him so agreeable. He has proved himself a great asset in organising the ball. Although it is no more than he should, considering he has had the run of the house for years!'

Carenza said nothing, not wishing to be drawn into any criticism of Ross's cousin. Mr Paston could not have been more helpful, yet still she could not warm to him. She felt uncomfortable in his company and was at pains never to be alone with him. Somehow, his presence made her yearn for Ross even more. It had been a full week now and there was still no word. She missed him so much it was a constant, physical ache.

Dido noticed and tried to comfort her.

'I expect he has been delayed in town,' she said. 'Business matters can be unpredictable, you know.'

'But the ball is only days away now.' Carenza bit her lip. 'What if he is not back in time?'

'He will come, never fear.' Dido gave her arm an encouraging pat. 'Pray, Carenza, do not be imagining the worst. If anything had happened to Ross you would have heard by now. Bad news always travels quickly.'

Carenza knew her sister-in-law was right and tried to put her worries to one side. She went about her everyday tasks as if there was nothing wrong, but when Ross finally did arrive, she could not maintain her calm pretence.

It was just two days before the ball and Carenza was picking flowers in the garden when she saw the travelling chariot approaching with Sam riding along behind it. She ran around the house, reaching the drive just as the coachman drew up at the door. Her breath caught for a heartbeat until Ross jumped down, then with a cry she dropped her basket and flew towards him.

'You are come at last!' She threw herself into his

arms, saying between laughter and tears, 'Oh, Ross, I have missed you so much!'

Delighted and slightly winded by this reception, Ross laughed and bent to kiss her upturned face.

'Well, sweetheart, I had not expected such a warm welcome!'

'Oh, dear, I beg your pardon,' she muttered, blushing and giggling at the same time. 'I never intended to launch myself at you in that way.'

'You can be in no doubt now that you have been missed, Cousin!' tittered Amos Paston, appearing at that moment.

Ross gave him a slight smile but immediately turned back to Carenza,

'Don't apologise,' he told her. 'I hope you will always greet me thus!'

He pulled her hand onto his arm and escorted her into the house, Amos following behind them. They made their way to the drawing room, where Dido was waiting.

'I hope your business was concluded satisfactorily?' she said to Ross, as they all made themselves comfortable.

'Yes. The documents are signed, the investment secured.'

'Well done, Cousin.' Amos rubbed his hands together. 'I have no doubt your efforts will pay good dividends.'

Ross frowned. 'I did not do this for the profits.'

'No, no, of course not, but they will follow, nevertheless. I only wish my own business ventures required so little work from me. Especially now that I am unlikely to be your heir, Austerfield.'

An awkward silence fell. Amos gave a soft laugh.

'You must not think me bitter, my lord. My only wish is for your happiness, so let us talk of other matters. The ball is almost upon us and we have all been busy, but most of the credit must go to Lady Austerfield. She has overseen all the arrangements.'

Carenza disclaimed quickly. 'I could not have done it alone.'

'It has been quite like old times,' declared Dido, beaming. 'I am only sorry that Beatrix cannot be here, but she is presently touring the north country with her family and it would be too much to expect her to dash all the way south at such short notice.'

'Thank heaven for that,' muttered Ross. 'I have enough managing females at Auster without my aunt Malham adding to the list!'

His sister ignored this. 'I must say I have enjoyed myself enormously, helping Carenza with all the arrangements for the ball. Everything is in readiness now for the arrival of our first house guests tomorrow.'

'And then we shall not have a moment to ourselves.' Ross rolled his eyes in mock horror.

'It has been a long time since Auster saw such a party,' said Amos. 'We must make sure it is one your guests will never forget. Now, if you'll excuse me, I have letters to write. I shall see you all at dinner.'

He went out and Carenza cast a wretched glanced at Ross.

'I cannot help but feel for your cousin. He has been so helpful and obliging while you have been gone and yet one can only imagine how disappointed he must be! To think that one moment you are heir to a viscountcy and the next you have all your hopes dashed.'

Dido was less sympathetic. 'It is never wise to count

your chickens before they hatch. Amos is a fool if he truly thought Ross would never have a family.'

He gave a little shrug. 'I'm afraid I gave him assurances to that effect.'

'You were still on your sickbed and not thinking clearly when you made that decision,' his sister replied. 'Anyone but a zany would know you might well change your mind, once you were recovered.'

'Nevertheless, I think perhaps I owe him something for that.'

Dido frowned and pursed her lips.

'Perhaps,' she said reluctantly, 'but only once you are sure he is well and truly cut out of the succession!'

Carenza blushed fierily and she saw Ross's lips twitch.

'More, er, chickens to hatch, eh, Dido?'

His sister gave him a hard look. 'It is no laughing matter,' she said, rising from her chair and shaking out her skirts. 'Someone must consider the practicalities.'

With that, she went upstairs to prepare for dinner.

'Oh, dear, is she offended, do you think?' asked Carenza, as the door closed with a snap.

'I doubt it. Not enough to pack her bags and leave us in peace, at all events.'

'I would not wish her to do so,' Carenza told him. 'I could not have managed the ball without her.'

Silence fell and Carenza felt suddenly very shy to be alone with her husband.

'I collected your gown,' he said at last. 'I have had it sent up to your room.'

'Thank you. You are very good.'

'I also brought something else for you.' He rose and held out his hand to her. 'Come.'

Intrigued, she went with him to the morning room,

where she saw what looked like a large picture shrouded in a linen cloth and resting against the wall.

'Oh.' She glanced up at him, 'This is for me?'

'It is.' He waved her forwards. 'Uncover it.'

Carenza walked over and carefully threw back the cloth to reveal a large canvas fixed inside an elaborate gilt frame. She stepped back, eyes widening in surprise.

It was an almost life-size painting of a woman in a diaphanous cream gown, luxurious coal-black hair piled up on her head. She was standing beside a table on which was a vase filled with brightly coloured flowers and she held a single rose in her shapely hands. Her dark eyes stared out thoughtfully from the canvas and a gentle smile curved her red lips.

'I think...' Carenza peered at the coral beads around the smooth column of the woman's neck, then she looked back at Ross. 'Is it m-my mother?'

'Yes, it is. Lamorna, Lady Bettridge. It was painted shortly after her marriage to your father.'

'But how did you come by it?'

'You mentioned a portrait of your mother, so I wrote to Lord Bettridge, to ask him about it, and I stopped at Morwood on my way home. That is what delayed me for the extra day.' He smiled at her. 'Your father is in good health and sends you his deepest love, Carenza. I have given my word I will take you to see him before the year is out.'

She clasped her hands together. 'And you did all this, just for me?'

'Not *just* for you. For us.' He took her shoulders, turning her back towards the painting. 'Does she look familiar? She should, for you are her image.'

'There is a likeness, yes,' she admitted.

'Your half-sisters convinced you that you are not

handsome. But you *are*, Carenza. You are beautiful.'
She shook her head and his hands tightened on her
shoulders. 'Look at the painting, Carenza. *Look!* Apart
from the outmoded gown it could be you. And she is
beautiful, is she not?'

She could not deny it. Ross went on.

'Your father told me he put this painting away because it distressed his new wife to have it on display. It
was Lady Bettridge or your half-sisters who told you
the subject was ill-favoured, is that not so?' He gave a
little growl of annoyance. 'Your silence tells me I am
correct. It was wrong of them. Very wrong. They tried
to crush your spirit with their lies, Carenza, but you are
more handsome than any of them!'

She looked again at the portrait and something
stirred within her. A hitherto unknown confidence to
believe the evidence of her own eyes. She turned towards him.

'Do you truly think I am beautiful, Ross?'

He cupped her face in his hands and gazed down
at her.

'I do. But it is not just your physical attributes. It is
your kind heart, your goodness and generosity of spirit
that raises you above mere outward beauty.'

'Oh.' She put up her hands to cover his and smiled
mistily. 'No one has ever said anything like that to me
before.'

Ross felt the rumble of anger deep inside for the way
she had been treated. He wanted to hold her close and
promise to look after her, but guilt held him back. He
had not been able to protect his men and the shame of
it lay heavily on his soul. He knew better now than to
make promises he could not keep.

'They should have done!' he said sharply. 'You are a

diamond of the first water, Carenza. You will outshine everyone at the Auster Ball, I have not the slightest doubt of that. In the spring I shall take you to London and show you off to the world. Society shall see how proud I am of my new Viscountess!'

Ross glanced at the clock on the mantelshelf and gave an impatient sigh.

'I should very much like to carry you off to bed, but there is not time. We must do our duty by our guests. Oh, Lord, and we have even more arriving tomorrow! Well, before they arrive we shall decide what we do with your mother's painting. It must be displayed prominently, a constant reminder of how beautiful you are. At least until I have your likeness to hang with it.' She blushed adorably at his words and he kissed her, a hard, dizzying kiss that left them both breathless, before putting his hand on her waist and walking her out of the room.

'Are we still in separate bedchambers?' he asked, as they crossed the hall.

The timbre of his voice sent a sizzle of excitement running down Carenza's spine and her response was somewhat disjointed.

'We said we would discuss it when you returned, my lord, although it is what *I* should like...'

'It is too late to do anything about it now, but once the ball is over, we shall move your things to my bedchamber. There is a second small room off it that will do for your dressing room.' He stopped and pulled her into his arms. 'We will begin our marriage again, Carenza, and this time it will be a true marriage, of minds and bodies. I want you beside me. Day and night.'

Her heart sang, as much from the glow in his eyes as the words.

'Oh, Ross, I am so glad of that! I—'

She broke off as a movement beyond Ross's shoulder caught her eye. She was embarrassed that their intimate conversation might have been overheard, but as mistress of the house she felt obliged to speak to the servant who was hovering nearby.

'Should you not be below stairs—oh, is it you, Ruth? Is anything amiss?'

The maid had started to hurry away but she stopped and dropped a curtsy.

'No, m'lady. I was late back and didn't want a scold from Mrs Stoke so I took the quickest way through the house. I didn't think anyone would be in the hall at this time…'

Ruth trailed off, wringing her hands together and looking so woebegone that Carenza could not bring herself to reprimand her further. She waved the girl away and they continued up the stairs.

'That girl has a habit of appearing in odd places,' Ross observed.

'Yes. I must speak to Mrs Stoke if it happens again. Do you think she heard us?'

'Does it matter?' Ross's arm about her waist tightened in a squeeze. 'It is my experience that servants know almost everything in a household. What difference can it make if she tells everyone we are a happily married couple?'

The thought remained with Ross throughout the evening, because, much to his surprise, he realised he *was* happily married. He was almost silent at dinner and spent most of his time watching his wife. He had missed Carenza while he was away; he had felt it like a physical pain. He could not wait to take her to his bed again and lose himself in her body. He wanted to share long, lingering kisses, to breathe in the sweet scent of her that reminded him of summer.

His sister's voice broke into this pleasant daydream and he reluctantly dragged his thoughts back to the present to beg her pardon.

'I was saying, Austerfield, that your face is looking very much better.' The use of his title as much as Dido's glare was an admonishment. 'Did you purchase some new treatment while you were in London?'

'No.' Ross sent a smile over the table to Carenza. 'I have been using the balm my wife prepares for me.'

'Very effective, Cousin. Lady Austerfield is to be congratulated.'

'Well, your scars are much less in evidence,' said Dido, ignoring Amos Paston's comment. She turned her attention to her plate for a moment, then looked up again as another thought struck her. 'Or perhaps it is that you yourself are much less conscious of them.'

Perhaps that was part of it, Ross thought. He had given little thought to it while he was in town, but he could not recall people recoiling from him as they had before. Was he so much improved, or had he been too morbidly aware of his injuries? Had he imagined the looks of horror that had been cast at him?

The truth was probably somewhere between the two, he decided. What surprised him was how little it mattered to him now. He looked at his wife, sitting at the far end of the table, and felt his heart stir. Happily married indeed.

Chapter Twenty-One

Carenza was too busy to allow her excitement and happiness to bubble over. It was the day of the ball and the house was in uproar, with house guests arriving and the final touches being made to the ballroom. The kitchens, too, were a whirlwind of activity. Not only was a grand dinner to be prepared, but also a supper for the early hours of the morning. She had not a moment to herself until she went upstairs to change into her ball gown, an exquisite creation in cobalt blue silk, sparingly trimmed in gold Brussels lace.

Hetty arranged Carenza's thick dark hair into a knot high on the back of her head, with small curls framing her face. She had just finished when there was a knock at the door and Ross came in. Carenza thought he looked very handsome in his black evening coat and snow-white linen, and when he smiled at her, the breath caught in her throat.

'Am I interrupting you?'

'No, no.' She rose and dismissed her maid. 'I am ready now.'

'Not quite.' He came forward. 'I bought you these.'

He opened a velvet box and held it out to her. Nest-

ling on a bed of silk was a sapphire and diamond necklace with a matching comb and drops for her ears.

'Oh, how lovely,' she whispered, reaching out to
touch the necklace.

'I took the liberty of viewing your gown before Collette packed it away,' he told her. 'Much as I like your
pearls, I thought this might look better.'

'Oh, I shall look like a queen,' she breathed.

'A viscountess, certainly,' he replied, amused. He
picked up the necklace. 'May I?'

She quickly removed her pearls and turned, hardly
daring to breathe as his fingers skimmed the back of
her neck, setting her skin ablaze and firing little darts
of heat through her body. She closed her eyes, savour-
ing the moment.

'There.' She felt his lips on her shoulder.

It was too much. She twisted about and slipped her
arms around his neck.

'You are too good to me, Ross.'

'Nothing is too good for you,' he said, kissing her.
'But aren't you going to look at yourself?'

Gently he turned her towards her looking glass. It
was almost a stranger staring back at her, an elegant,
confident lady whose face radiated happiness while
the gems at her throat winked and sparkled in the candlelight.

'They are beautiful,' she murmured.

'*You* are beautiful,' he told her, his eyes glowing
more a warm green than grey as they met hers in the
mirror. 'Do you believe me now?'

They were interrupted by a soft knock on the door.
Hetty peeped in.

'I beg your pardon, my lady, but Mr Stoke says the
first carriage is approaching.'

'Ah, duty calls,' said Ross, walking to the door. 'I shall leave you to fix the other pieces in place and meet you downstairs to greet our guests.'

The ball was a huge success. The rooms were packed, the musicians brought in from Exeter had performed excellently and Ross had heard nothing but praise for his bride all evening. He told her so, when he sought her out just before midnight.

'I intend to take you in to supper myself,' he said, lifting her hand to his lips. 'And I shall fight any man who tries to steal you away from me!'

Carenza looked adorably pleased by this, but before she could reply a soft laugh made them both turn to find Amos Paston had come up.

'An excellent suggestion, Cousin, but first we have a little surprise, do we not, my lady?'

Ross looked from one to the other and Carenza laughed up at him.

'We do indeed, my lord. I hope you will like it!'

She caught his arm and led him to the long windows at the far end of the ballroom, where everyone was spilling out onto the terrace. He grinned as Carenza dragged him outside into the throng.

'Now what have you been plotting?'

Even as he spoke he heard it. The first whoosh of a rocket. Then another.

Get down!

Take cover!

The cries of men long dead echoed in his ears. Shells exploded about them, throwing mud and bodies against him. Somewhere beyond the inferno he could hear Carenza's voice and he tried to block out the rest. It wasn't real, the war was over.

It was no good; Ross knew he had to get away. Flashes of musket fire and glittering jewels dazzled his eyes. He was surrounded, hemmed in by a confusion of bloodied soldiers and colourful ball gowns, and all the time the deafening, painful blasts continued, filling his head until he wanted to scream.

'Ross!'

Too late Carenza realised her mistake. The fireworks were not the colourful, harmless extravaganza she had expected. The rockets zoomed up into the night sky and exploded with a deafening report. Ross was fighting his way back towards the ballroom and she tried to follow him, but everyone was pressing forward, eager to see the display.

She squeezed through the windows and back into the ballroom just as Ross was disappearing into the hall. She ran after him, almost colliding with Amos Paston when she reached the doorway.

'Lady Austerfield!' He caught her arms to steady her. 'Calm yourself, madam, I pray you.'

'Ross is ill,' she cried, trying to shake him off. 'Let me go to him!'

'I assure you it is not necessary. I saw the valet waiting for him at the top of the stairs. He has taken my cousin off to his room. Trust me, my lady, I have seen this before. Brisco is the best person to take care of him now.'

'It was the fireworks, the noise.' Carenza dashed a hand across her eyes. 'I should have known. I should have realised.'

'But how could you, when you had no experience of them?'

Carenza finally shook off Amos Paston's restraining hands but he still blocked her way.

'Ross would not want you to see him like this,' he said earnestly. 'Think of your guests, madam. The display is finished and they are coming back in now, ready for their supper. How will it look if both you and the Viscount have disappeared? He would not want to draw any attention to himself, you know that.'

Carenza hesitated, undecided. Dido came up, declaring it was time supper was announced.

'Ross,' said Carenza in a strangled voice. 'He is… not well.'

'Having another of his turns, is he?' Dido shook her head. 'I had heard he suffered occasionally. Most likely it is the crowded rooms brought it on.'

'His man is looking after him,' explained Amos smoothly. 'I believe Ross would want us to carry on without him.'

'Oh, Lord, yes. He hates fuss,' Dido agreed. She patted Carenza's hand. 'Come along, my dear. Brisco will look after him for now. You can slip upstairs to see him after supper.'

Carenza allowed her sister-in-law to take her back into the ballroom where they rounded up the guests and shepherded them through to the dining room. An extravagant supper was laid out with roast fowls, lamb ribs, hams and raised pies jostling for position with sweetmeat dishes, aspic jellies and platters of sweet biscuits. Carenza had no appetite for any of it, but she knew her duty and tried to hide her anxieties behind a smile.

Ross stumbled into his room, where only a few candles were burning. Where the devil was Brisco? He went across to the washstand and splashed his face with cold water, then stood, bent over the bowl, his hands gripping the washstand.

There was a soft knock at the door. 'Cousin? How are you? Another of your attacks, was it?'

Paston, damn him. Where *was* Brisco?

'Will you not lie down, my lord? Or have some brandy. I brought a bottle up for you.'

Ross sucked in a breath through his rigid jaws, trying to focus his mind. 'Just leave me, Amos.'

'I told my lady I would look in on you. She is too overset to come herself.'

'Those damned fireworks.' His head dropped lower, knowing he had let her down.

'Alas, Her Ladyship was adamant that the guests should be royally entertained.'

Ross barely heard him; his mind was reeling, echoes of the distant battle still ringing in his head. He put his hands to his temples.

'Go away, Amos. You can do no good here.'

'I do not think you should be alone, Cousin.'

Cursing, Ross stumbled over to the window. 'Then find Brisco and send him to me!' He saw nothing save tortuous images of smoke and carnage. 'Or my wife,' he said suddenly. 'Ask Carenza to come to me.'

'Ah. She won't come.' Paston's voice was very close now. Soft, apologetic. 'She is quite distraught, Ross. You have ruined her evening.'

'Be quiet, damn you!' He raked both hands through his hair. 'You think I don't know how little I deserve her?'

'I am sorry to say I have known it since the beginning.' The soft voice continued to pour misery into Ross's ear. 'She is so innocent. It was inevitable she would not be able to resist all you had to offer her. But, alas, she is regretting it now. She is shackled for life to a husband she does not love. One she cannot trust.'

Ross groaned.

'Tonight is further proof of your volatility,' Amos went on. 'She is in constant trepidation, wondering what other horrors and humiliations are in store for her. And she is so very young. How many years will she have to bear with the uncertainty of your temper, wondering when you might lash out at her?' He came closer and the smell of sweet wine on his breath turned Ross's stomach. 'She is afraid of you, Cousin. She knows you can never be a true husband. You will never be able to love her, protect her, as she deserves. I heard her telling your sister she wishes now she had never married you.'

Ross winced and his fingers twisted in his hair, the pain of tearing it from his scalp nothing to the agony inside him.

'Ah, Cousin, you are not well. You are probably thinking that life is not worth living, that she would be better off without you. Get some rest. I will leave the brandy on the table for you. A glass or two might help you to forget.'

The door opened and closed softly. Silence pressed around Ross, mocking him, condemning him. The air was so heavy with taunts and accusations that he swung around, fists clenched ready for battle, but he was alone. There was no one reproaching him but himself.

The bottle Amos had mentioned was on the table along with a glass. A lighted candle stood beside it, the flame glinting off the barrel of one of his duelling pistols. Ross noticed the open case lying on the floor. Brisco must have been cleaning them. Why the devil would he bother, knowing his master was unlikely to fire a weapon again?

Unless it was to put paid to his existence.

Carenza did her duty as hostess, moving between the guests with a word here, a smile there, but all the time she was thinking of Ross, wondering if he would sleep tonight, or if the nightmares would return in force. What a fool she had been! She knew fireworks were made with gunpowder; how could she have not realised they would be noisy?

She felt a touch on her sleeve and looked around to find the maid Ruth beside her. She quickly followed the girl out of the crowded supper room.

'Has Mrs Stoke sent you to find me?'

'No, m'lady.' The girl twisted her hands together. 'It was His Lordship's man.'

'Mr Brisco?'

'Yes, m'lady. I saw him on the stairs with Mr Paston and he bade me tell you the master has gone out. In an awful hurry, they was. They said you are not to worry. His Lordship is on foot and they'll catch up with him and bring him back, safe and sound.'

Carenza's heart stopped. 'Bring him back from where?'

'I don't know, ma'am. Mr Brisco said something about shepherds.'

Shepherd's Leap! She put a hand over her mouth, suddenly feeling sick with worry. 'I must go after them!'

Carenza wasted no more time. Telling Ruth to inform Mrs Burnley what had happened, she went to the front door. A footman was on hand to open it for her, and she paused to speak to him before hurrying out into the night.

Torches flared along the drive and in the gardens and Carenza had an almost full moon to light her way. In her previous explorations of the grounds she remembered seeing a wicket gate in the wall of the shrubbery. That would be the quickest way to the cliffs. When she reached it, the gate was swinging free, confirming her suspicions that others had passed through very recently.

She was too worried about Ross to feel frightened as she ran through the belt of trees beyond the gardens. Brambles snatched at her skirts but she dragged them free, regardless of the damage to the precious silk. Neither did she notice the stony ground beneath her thin-soled dancing slippers. Her mind had a greater, darker worry. Something had been nagging at her throughout supper. She had berated herself for her ignorance over the fireworks, but she had never experienced them. Dido and Amos Paston had. Dido she acquitted of malice; Ross had been careful to hide what he thought was his weakness from everyone. But she remembered that Amos had been at Auster for months with Ross. He would have known what loud, unexpected blasts would do to him.

The idea that Paston was with Brisco, following Ross to the cliff edge, filled her with dread.

Chapter Twenty-Two

Carenza's lungs were bursting by the time she reached the ruined tower. The breeze was making the silk skirts flap around her and she could see nothing, no one. She went closer to the tower, straining her eyes to see if anyone was standing in its inky shadow.

'Ross!'

She shouted his name, but her words were snatched away by the wind. She called again. There was a sound, something like a groan, and it came from the tower. Carenza ran towards what had once been a doorway.

'Ross?'

'Not quite.' Something detached itself from the shadows and she recognised the stout figure of Amos Paston.

'Where is Ross?' she demanded. 'And Brisco?'

'Brisco, I imagine, is still sleeping peacefully. Unless he was disturbed when your husband blew his brains out.'

Carenza pushed a hand against her breast to restrain the hysteria rising inside. 'Ross would not do that.'

'Would he not?' The smile Paston gave her was pure evil. 'If he hasn't yet, then he will do so when he knows you have thrown yourself off Shepherd's Leap!'

Too late she realised what he was about and turned to run. She had not gone far before he grabbed her arm and began to drag her back. She fought wildly, but she was no match for him and her feet could find little purchase on the short grass. She was being pulled inexorably towards the cliff.

They were only yards from the edge when she heard a shout. It was a faint sound, but someone was coming. Paston cursed and redoubled his efforts, tugging Carenza off her feet. She thought he would pull her arm from its socket but at that moment a dark shape cannoned into him and she was free.

Carenza rolled out of the way as the two men wrestled on the ground. At first she thought Paston's attacker was Sam Rigby, but her heart skipped a beat when another look confirmed that it was Ross, pounding his cousin remorselessly with his fists.

'Don't kill him!' Carenza scrambled up and caught his arm as he raised it for another blow.

'Aye, enough, *enough*, damn you!' cried Paston, throwing his arms about his head.

Ross staggered to his feet, his chest heaving.

'Get up,' he snarled. 'Get up and tell me why I should not beat the life out of you!'

Carenza glanced back towards the house. 'Men are coming,' she said. 'It must be your groom. I sent word for him to follow.'

'Not Sam, he was drugged,' Ross told her. 'Brisco, too. How did you manage that, Cousin, a sleeping draught?'

Paston was standing now and dabbing gingerly at his split lip with the back of one hand.

'Aye,' he muttered. 'It was easy enough to slip something into their drinks.'

'And you sent Ruth to me with that false message.' Carenza looked at Ross. 'I wasn't sure I could trust her, which was why I sent the message to Sam.'

Ross grunted. 'She was here to spy upon us. Is that not so, Paston?'

'Of course. I couldn't risk you getting an heir. I thought she might help you sate any lustful desires you might have, but it seems I underestimated the charms of your little bride. Ruth talked her way into the laundry and kept an eye on the sheets from your rooms.' His lip curled into a sneer. 'She saw the signs that you had consummated your marriage and wrote to me immediately. When I learned how close you two were becoming, I knew I would have to do something about it.'

'By persuading me to kill myself.'

'And why not? You mentioned it often enough when you first returned to England.'

'And you kept reminding me of my…imperfections.' Ross gave a hiss of disgust. 'I see it all now. The sly comments, the little hints, all designed to make me hate myself.'

'And the fireworks,' added Carenza. 'They were his idea, Ross. He knew how it would affect you. There was no cancelled order, was there, Mr Paston?'

'Of course not! It was part of my plan, to make him end his miserable life.' He looked at Carenza, and even in the moonlight she could see the venom in his face. 'But you bewitched him! I couldn't be sure you were not already carrying a child, so you had to die, too.'

Carenza was appalled. 'You would have done all that, just for a title?'

'Oh, and the lands, my dear. All those properties. Austerfield is a very rich man, although you would not know it from the miserly way he lives here.' He swung back to Ross. 'It should be mine! When Sebastian died and you were reported missing after the battle, I thought the gods had smiled on me at last. Then, against all the odds, you came back. A broken wreck of a man, not fit to inherit the title.'

Ross's lip curled. 'A better man than you, Cousin.' The servants had come up and Ross nodded to them. 'Take Mr Paston back to the house and lock him up.'

'What do you intend to do with me?'

'In my present mood I'd like to throw you off the cliff,' said Ross savagely. He heard Carenza give a little moan and waved to the men. 'Take him away. I shall decide his fate in the morning.'

He watched his footmen surround Paston and walk him back towards the house, then he turned and reached for Carenza.

'You are shivering,' he said, drawing her into his arms.

With a sob she buried her face in his shoulder and Ross stood for a moment, his cheek against her hair, then he took off his evening coat and wrapped it around her.

'Come, we must get back to the house.'

Silently they began to walk. Beyond the trees the upper floors of Auster could be seen, light shining from many of the windows. The guests would have noticed something was amiss by now but he would deal with that tomorrow. Tonight, it did not matter. Nothing mattered except that Carenza was safe and walking beside him, one arm around his waist, clinging to him.

'He told me you were dead,' she muttered, her voice shaking.

Ross took in a lungful of the cool night air. 'He expected me to kill myself. He followed me upstairs, supposedly to offer me support. In fact, he was dripping poison into my brain, as he has been doing ever since I returned to England, only I was too blind to see it.'

'I had wondered,' she said slowly. 'I thought sometimes he was not very kind towards you.'

'He told me tonight that you would not see me.'

'No!' She stopped and turned towards him. 'No, that is not true! I *tried* to follow you, but your cousin persuaded me I should not leave our guests. He said B-Brisco was with you and you would want no one else.'

'Oh, yes, he was very clever, damn him. He left me alone with my head full of his insinuations and a loaded pistol at hand, to put an end to it all.'

Carenza shuddered, thinking of what might have happened. Ross was staring over her head, his countenance grim in the moonlight.

'What stopped you?' she whispered.

For a moment he did not move and she thought he had not heard her. Then he looked down, the harsh look fading.

'You,' he said softly. 'You showed me I had something to live for.'

'But I have done so little. Mr Brisco and Sam Rigby have been with you for much longer.'

'Yes, they are very good. They understand, you see, and I would be much better now without Paston constantly interfering. They tried to tell me that he was not helping but I would not see it. I felt I owed him something for his care when I first came home. He convinced me no woman could love me for what I am. That I was not worthy of love. It took you to show me he was wrong, my dearest Carenza. I fell in love with you and you gave me hope that one day you might love me.'

'And I do,' she said, gazing up at him, her eyes glistening with tears. 'Never doubt it, Ross. I love you with all my heart.'

His arms tightened. 'I am glad, because I do not think I could live without you now.'

He lowered his head, capturing her lips in a long, lingering kiss. When at last he released her she rested her head against his chest and gave a heartfelt sigh.

'If I have helped you, it is surely no more than you have done for me,' she told him. 'You gave me confidence, showed me I am quite pretty—'

With an angry growl he held her at arm's length and frowned down at her.

'Pretty be damned!' he exclaimed wrathfully. 'You are perfectly beautiful, Carenza!'

'To you, perhaps, but no one is perfect.' She looked up at him and a laugh trembled in her voice. 'Oh, Ross, I believe we might be a good match, after all.'

'We are,' he said, pulling her into his arms for another kiss. 'A perfectly imperfect match!'

Epilogue

July 1821

The elegant travelling carriage was bowling along through the familiar Devon roads and Carenza gave a sigh as she sank back against the luxuriously padded seat. Ross took her hand.

'Not long now, my love. We will be home by four o'clock.'

'Home! How good that sounds, when we have been away almost a full month. I shall be very pleased to be back at Auster.'

Ross lifted her fingers to his lips and kissed them. 'You are not pining for Hampshire?'

'Not at all, although it was quite delightful to visit Morwood again. I was pleased to see Papa looking so well.'

'Aided, no doubt, by the absence of his wife!'

Carenza chuckled. 'She prefers to spend her time visiting Adelaide and Letitia, now she has achieved her aim of finding husbands for them.'

'A mere knight and a baronet,' he murmured. 'Nothing compared to the glittering match achieved by her stepdaughter!'

She tapped his arm and tried to look severe. 'Ross, that is wickedly conceited of you! If they have a fraction of my happiness, then she should be content.'

'I cannot see Lady Bettridge or her daughters ever being content,' he said frankly. 'They are selfish creatures and will always covet what they do not have. I do not see either of your half-sisters setting up a school for the village children or employing wounded soldiers to work for them.'

'Then theirs is the loss and I am very sorry for them.'

'Do not waste your pity. They would spare none for you. I am only glad we did not see them in town. Which reminds me, you have not yet told me what you thought of London? You were not enamoured at our first visit, when I introduced you as my Viscountess.'

'*Then* we had all the ton gawping at us, astonished to see what sort of wife you had found for yourself!'

'Ah yes. And this time your visit was one of unalloyed pleasure.'

His tone was innocent enough, but she turned her head to look at him, her dark eyes brim-full of merriment. 'London this time was…most diverting!'

He laughed aloud at that. 'Admit it, you disliked the pomp and pageantry of Prinny's coronation as much as I.'

'I did, but once you had received the summons to attend, there really was no choice! And I was pleased to see your family again.'

'What, even my terrifying aunt Beatrix?'

'*Especially* Lady Malham,' she said firmly. 'The Countess was very kind to me, even if she is a little forthright in her speech! I am sorry that, with the exception of your sister, your relatives visit us so rarely. They consider Auster far too remote.'

'For which I give thanks, daily!'

Carenza smiled but ignored this, saying instead, 'I was very glad we went to Kilburn to see Mrs Paston. It was a relief to see how well she and the children are faring without your cousin.'

Ross scowled. 'Amos should have hanged for what he tried to do. Or at least he should have been horse-whipped! He has barely suffered at all for his crimes.'

'Surely being banished from the country is punishment enough.'

Ross shrugged. 'He had a choice, go to Boston to look after his business there or be charged with intent to murder. I don't doubt he lives in great comfort. As for the housemaid, Ruth! The cunning little vixen has married his chief clerk—where is the justice in that?'

'But neither of them can return to England,' she pointed out. 'The evidence is recorded and you have sworn witness statements enough to convict them both. Think of the scandal if you had brought your cousin to book for his actions. No, I believe you chose the right course. And Fanny has proved herself very astute at looking after her husband's business concerns in this country.'

'Aye, she appears very content with her lot.'

'She told me, when we were alone, that he had a mistress in Paddington, and another in Bideford. It appears your cousin's visits to Devon were more than merely for business, or to keep a watch on Auster.'

'She is well rid of him, then. The more I hear of the fellow the more I despise him! But enough of that,' he declared, pulling her onto his lap. 'Let us think instead how good it will be to sleep in our own bed again.'

Carenza blushed and laughed up at him and he could not resist the temptation to steal a kiss. She responded immediately, pressing closer, her lips parting beneath his, and he felt the familiar flames of desire burning through his body, so that by the time he raised his head, his heart was pounding hard against his chest.

He gazed down at his wife. Her head was thrown back against his shoulder, the dark eyes glowing in a way that set his pulse jumping.

She sighed. 'I am not sure I can wait until bedtime to have you to myself!'

He stopped her words with another long, languorous kiss, which only came to an end when they were thrown off balance by the sudden turning of the carriage.

Ross cursed gently and looked out of the window.

'Confound it, we are at Auster already.'

Carenza laughed. 'Then we had best behave ourselves!'

She slid off his lap and began to tidy herself, pointing out to him with another giggle that his own clothes were in a state of disarray.

'You are a jezebel,' he muttered, stealing another quick kiss before buttoning his waistcoat and jamming his hat on his head as the carriage came to a halt at the house steps.

A beaming footman opened the door and bade them welcome back.

'Thank you, Henry,' said Ross, jumping out and turning to help his wife alight.

Cries of "Mama, Papa!" caught his attention and he looked up to see a little figure in nankeen pantaloons hurtling towards them, followed closely by his nurse.

'Master Sebastian has had his nose to the window all morning looking out for the carriage,' remarked the footman, grinning broadly.

Carenza dropped down to catch her son as he cannoned into her arms. 'How are you, my darling? Goodness, how you have grown!'

By now a chorus of youthful voices were demanding her attention. Two more nursemaids approaching, each one holding the hand of a small child.

'Oh, my little darlings!' she cried. 'James, Lamorna! Have you missed your mama? I have missed you, most dreadfully.'

Ross grinned as the twins toddled towards Carenza and she gathered all three children close. The birth of Sebastian had been a revelation to him, coming just a year after his marriage. He thought his happiness complete, until the arrival of the twins twelve months later. The peace at Auster was shattered, but he did not mind a bit that during the day the house was filled with childish laughter and sometimes tears. Carenza liked to have the children about her and it was only with the greatest reluctance that she had been persuaded to leave the children with their nursemaids and join him in London for the coronation.

His reverie was interrupted by a small hand tugging at his coat and a little voice saying imperiously, 'Up, Papa. Up!'

Laughing, he lifted little Sebastian into his arms and watched as Carenza gathered up the twins, settling one on each hip.

'Shall we go in, my lord?'

She looked at him with her beautiful smile and Ross marvelled again at his good fortune in finding such a wife.

'Yes, indeed. Lead on, my lady.'

He shifted Sebastian into a more secure grasp and the boy threw his arms around Ross's neck, without any hesitation pressing his soft chubby face against Ross's scarred cheek.

'Papa...'

'My son,' murmured Ross. 'My family.'

And, smiling to himself, he followed Carenza into the house.

* * * * *

If you enjoyed this book, why not check out these other great reads by Sarah Mallory

Beauty and the Brooding Lord
The Highborn Housekeeper
His Countess for a Week
The Mysterious Miss Fairchild
Forbidden to the Highland Laird
Rescued by Her Highland Soldier